The Letters

Fiona Robyn

snowbooks

Proudly Published by Snowbooks in 2009

Snowbooks Ltd.
120 Pentonville Road
London
N1 9JN
Tel: 0790 406 2414
email: info@snowbooks.com
www.snowbooks.com

British Library Cataloguing in Publication Data
A catalogue record for this book is available from the British Library.

Library Hardback edition: 978-1-906727-06-2
Paperback edition: 978-1-906727-07-9

Printed and bound by J. H. Haynes & Co. Ltd., Sparkford

Dedicated to Natalie, Anne, Brenda and Julia,
for keeping me going and for always being there.

"…For there's more enterprise
In walking naked."

W. B. Yeats

Chapter 1

Violet bursts from her lover's house and leaves the door gaping like a mouth. She jogs the two and a half miles back to her own cottage, spitting Catherine-Wheel sparks of fury. The soles of her feet slap the ground as she blows out her breath in short blasts. Rah. Rah. Rah. Her eyes are fixed straight ahead. Houses move past her, trees, parked cars. She doesn't notice the familiar hint of seaweed on the breeze, or that the laces of her left trainer have come undone and are sopping wet and trailing behind her. She turns into her street and doesn't notice her neighbour, Wendy Peters, sweeping crisp frosted leaves from her front path. Wendy gives her a friendly wave and opens her mouth to frame a 'yoohoo' before clocking the look on Violet's face and thinking better of it. Her hand and face remain frozen into a gesture of welcome long after Violet has disappeared down the road. Violet doesn't notice the stars above her, glowing like fading embers in the darkening sky. It's only when she's slammed her cornflower-blue door behind her that the wind drops, and she slumps down onto her doormat like a fallen kite. She's home.

The rage begins to fade like a horrible smell released from a wheelie-bin or from her ex-husband's innards, the molecules dispersing, sinking to the floor or rising to the ceiling. Her lungs start to catch up and her breathing slows. She notices her clock ticking along the hall, tick-TOCK, tick-TOCK, and a threadbare patch of carpet that needs replacing. Thoughts begin to take shape from the mist of red. Most of them are old comrades. How has she got herself into this state? She isn't a hot-blooded hormone-soaked teenager any more – she's fifty-one years old, with grown children of her own. How do her arguments with Tom escalate so quickly and so violently? And why do they go round and round in an endless loop – why can't they move forwards? Now that she's calmer, the content of their argument almost bores her. It's the same old rubbish – Violet doesn't open up enough, Tom doesn't give her enough space, Violet doesn't think about anyone apart from herself, Tom is incapable of making a single simple decision without consulting her at length… blah, blah, blah. They seem so innocuous when they begin – Violet taking offence at an off-hand comment or forgetting that Tom prefers wholemeal bread to granary – and before she knows it she's clattering about in her cupboard of insults, trying to find something that will cut her lover to the bone.

She won't go back there, not this time. She can't afford to. And these thoughts are familiar too – how many times has she planned to cut herself off, move away, never see Tom again? But what else can she do? She can't carry on living like this. It's too tiring – at fifty-one she should be settling down, not riding this unending roller coaster. She's never felt so full to the brim of feelings in her life. Not in her whole life – not when the children were born, not when she got married to Charles, not when she divorced him. She doesn't know where it all comes from – great swathes of rage and joy. Yes, joy too. But there's just too big a price to pay. And as the realisation sinks into her, slowly, she feels sorrow pooling around her ankles. She hasn't felt this sadness before, and she doesn't like it. She brushes it aside like sweeping china from a table. She hears Tom's voice in her mind, saying 'let the feelings come, make friends with them.' What bollocks. How could that possibly do her any good? 'Hello sadness, oh do come in, I just love the feeling of wanting to do myself in. Let's talk about the woes of the world, shall we?'

This brings a little smile, and she becomes slowly aware of her body. She's crouched on the floor like a child, and her thighs and calves are aching. Old bones. She must look ridiculous. She imagines what her mother might say, then quickly tries to un-imagine it. ''Things-her-mother-might-say' frequently pop up uninvited in her head, but they rarely add anything helpful, just like the things her real mother says. She takes a deep breath and says 'come on, you silly moo.' She straightens out her stiff legs, gingerly, and takes off her coat. She has dust on the back of her leggings and rubs it off, thinking 'picking myself up, brushing myself down'. When she kicks off her trainers, the floor feels chilly through her socks and so she wraps her long flapping cardigan around her and goes into the kitchen to fiddle with the thermostat. Now she's here, she may as well put on the kettle.

Her strong milky tea, the colour of satinwood, sloshes in the mug as she climbs the creaking stairs to her tiny bedroom. Blue is sleeping in his usual spot on the landing, curled up with his head tucked under and his bristly chin in the air. He shows her a sliver of one golden eye before closing it again and flexing his legs and paws in a blissful mini-stretch.

'Do you want your mummy, birdy? Who's my middlymuddly-moo, who's my best kitty?' she coos. Her throat feels sore after all the shouting. Blue refuses to play his part, so Violet has to lift him instead. He goes limp, like a gym bag full of tennis balls, and lets out a disgruntled, low-pitched 'Mraow', but seems happy enough to be placed on her rose-pink duvet. He sinks into it, stretching out to his full length with his tail at a right angle to his back, and his spine curved as if flying through the air. 'Supercat!' as her son Guy would say. She has to drag Blue into a different angle to give her the room to push her toes to the bottom of the bed. He half-heartedly swipes at her and catches the back of her wrist with a sharp claw. 'Oi, you bastard!' she says, too loudly and with too much violence, and immediately regrets it. Blue's ears go back and the tip of his tail starts flicking. Why can't she hold her tongue? It was the same with her children – she'd frequently lost her temper with them while they were growing up, as if she were a kettle constantly on the verge of boiling over. She knows that she shouldn't be doing it as soon as she opens her mouth, but it seems hard for her to stop once she's started. Charles was forever raising his eye-brows at her from behind his paper, and occasionally he even dared to stick up for a wronged Megan or a tearful Lucy. This would infuriate Violet further and the argument would usually culminate with her storming from the room, muttering about how nobody was ever on her side.

'Don't mean it, blue-bird. Come on. Mummy's just in her usual rotten mood. I'll tickle your ears, come here. I'll make it up to you, you grouchy old puddy.'

After a time the ear-tickling triggers a deep rolling hum. It emanates from the middle of Blue's being, and she imagines the centre of him as a smooth stone, vibrating. She imagines holding the warmth of it in her hand like an egg.

She gives the fur on Blue's head a final ruffle and leans

back on her headboard. It's plain wood and unforgiving, so she's draped it with a crocheted blanket folded into four to give her back some padding. There isn't much natural padding left on her now. The fat just never came back after her illness, not that there was much there to start with. She wonders where it went – if it's floating around in the ether somewhere, or hiding under the floorboards and waiting to claim her. Those centimetres of soft stuff, insulating her hips, spilling over the waistband of her jeans, hanging from her arms where she could grab it and pull it into wings. What would it look like if she poured it all into a bucket – viscous and heavy like syrup or light and spongy like blancmange? How much would there be? She still pinches it – an old habit. She used to hold onto a fold from her waist or cup a handful of thigh-flesh at night, for security, like Guy's favourite blanket that travelled with him everywhere until he was seven. It's less comfortable now – there isn't anything to get a grip on. It doesn't fill her hand like it used to. She has to tug it from the bones.

She wonders how long she ought to lie there. She never realised it would be so bloody difficult, living on her own. When she decided to move down here a year ago, leaving her career as a Lecturer in Structural Engineering, she only gave serious thought to the advantages. Having the bathroom all to herself. Watching whatever she wanted on television. Getting to know herself again without the distractions of motherhood and wifedom. Soon it'll be a year since she moved in. She tries to work out the date using last week's Committee meeting as a reference point... that was the 26th... wait – isn't it Halloween today? Yes – a year next week. She should have some kind of celebration, that she's survived this far... Her mind makes a move towards thinking about the past year, and she holds it back like a dog on a leash– she doesn't want to go into all that now. Her mind makes another move towards the future, but that's no good either – especially after what happened with Tom this afternoon...

Her eyes criss-cross the room and settle on a trashy detective book on her bedside table. She clicks on her lamp and reaches for it, hoping the simple shape of the story might hold her attention. It's terribly written, really. The characters are riddled with clichés, and the plot holds on tightly to her hand, pointing out the 'important clues' in a loud voice. Just what she needs. She's grown quite fond of the main character, a man called River, who seems to spend most of his time drinking bourbon late into the night and having flashes of inspiration while he listens to the blues. Better than those awful novels the girls read – what are they called, chick flick? She's constantly perplexed by the way her children have turned out. You'd never think they'd come from her and Charles' loins. Eugh, she didn't want to think about Charles' loins. She lets out a snort of disbelief as she remembers a conversation she had with her oldest daughter Lucy on the phone last week, about the rights of illegal immigrants. Where did those ideas of hers come from? Friends, she supposes, the dreaded 'peer group'. She picks up the novel and bends back the spine, aware of her mother tutting at the 'desecration of a book'. Violet gives her mental-mother the finger, smiles sweetly, and bends the paperback even further until it cracks.

The book is slipping out of her fingers when the doorbell goes. The last of the light has gone, and her windows are black. She rubs her eyes and looks over at her clock – it's only 7pm. Who could it be? The realisation hits her when she's halfway down the stairs, almost tripping over Blue, who's (literally) jumped to the erroneous conclusion that she's heading towards the kitchen to get him something good to eat. How do cats get to be so good at putting themselves between you and where you want to go? She shoos him away and promptly stubs her foot on the skirting, letting out a loud 'fuck!' She wonders what the hell she has in her cupboards to give to trick-or-treaters. She opens the front door onto a small ghost, a devil, a snotty-nosed witch, and an unidentifiable ghoul. Violet cranes her neck to look up the road but she can't see a 'responsible adult' anywhere. She imagines their parents lying on their respective sofas and luxuriating in the peace and quiet.

They open their mouths to begin their chorus of 'trick or treat', and Violet nods curtly, holding out her hand with her palm towards them. As she turns her back on them, the littler ones look up at the devil, awaiting further instructions. Violet rummages through her cupboards, cursing under her breath. The closest thing she can find to sweets is a half-opened packet of meringues – she'd bought them for a flying visit from her youngest, Josie, last week. She puts it on the side while she looks for something more promising. There's not much there – would children be interested in dried cranberries? Probably not... and almonds aren't any good either unless they're sugared... When she finally returns to the door with the meringues the children have given up, and she has to call to the smallest ghost, trailing behind. 'Hello, Mr. Ghost?' He looks round and runs back to take the meringues. He looks at the box, then looks up at her and grins. She sees him running to catch up with the witch and showing her what he's got, explaining that 'these are the things that disappear in your mouth'. They both slow down to examine the box, and the devil looks back, bursting with a lifetime's worth of big-sister impatience – 'Petey! Come ON!'

Violet watches them walk down her next-door neighbour's path and then shuts the door, sucking a white crumb from her finger. There – her duty as a kind and responsible adult done for the night.

On her way back upstairs with a glass of wine, the phone rings. She hates the ring of this new phone – it's high pitched and jangly and seems to be shouting 'Pick me up! Pick me up!' She always approaches it saying 'OK, OK…' as if it might stop ringing and wait for her to get there.

'Hello?'

'Hi, Mother?'

'Guy.'

There's a slightly awkward pause here, and she remembers what her middle daughter Megan said to her last week. 'You sound so grumpy when you pick up the phone, Mum. Like we've dragged you away from something much more important.' Well, what is she expected to say? Wonderful to hear from you, my son. What a glorious surprise. She's never been one for those ridiculous social niceties. She can't really see the point. She knows that if she keeps her mouth shut for long enough, the other person will get to the point more quickly. She used this trick a lot on her students at University, especially during that wretched one-to-one stuff they started making her do. All of those weepy girls and sullen, homesick boys – eugh.

'The thing is, I'm in a bit of a… well, you know my…'

She knows instantly what he's going to say.

'Lost your job again, have you?'

'Umm, not lost it exactly, but… well, they said I need to, the occupational health woman said I… It was such a dire place to work, Mum, they're all like robots or something. I just don't know how people can do it.'

'Guy…'

'I was planning on coming down to see you anyway, tomorrow evening, just for a week. A week or so… I know you haven't got much space, but the sofa-bed in the office will be fine, or wherever – I won't get in your way, I just need some time to sort my head out, you know, think about my future, that kind of stuff. I hope you don't mind, I've… well, I've already booked the tickets.'

His voice gets higher pitched and quieter as he goes on. The girls call it his 'poor little me' voice, and it annoys the hell out of them. At least it makes a change from his usual brash arrogance. Mixed in with exasperation about him losing his job again, Violet is secretly pleased at the thought of having some company. Not that she'd admit it to him – the whole family made such a fuss about her not lasting five minutes in Abbotsfield on her own, and it's more than her life's worth to own up to anything faintly resembling loneliness.

'I suppose it'll be fine, Guy, but it doesn't sound like you've given me much choice. Text me when you're on your way, let me know when your train gets in. We'll talk about this job thing when you get here, OK? I haven't the strength right now. Terrible day.'

'What happened? Is it that, well – you know…'

'Whether it is or whether it isn't is none of your business – I'll deal with my dramas, and you can deal with yours. Do you need any money?'

'No, no, I've got the ticket money. I won't have much when I get there, for food and stuff…'

'I can still just about afford to feed my own son. Don't forget to bring your woollies – it's really bloody cold down here. OK, then?'

That's another thing Megan had said, that once Violet has had enough of a conversation she makes it brutally obvious. She remembers this now and so asks Guy what the weather was like up there, but gets bored in the middle of a long rambling story about the damp problem in his flat and cuts him off, saying she's left something in the oven. Megan can keep her 'art of making conversation' – life is too short.

Violet leaves her wine on the table in the hall and goes back into the kitchen. She starts opening and closing cupboard doors again, with great gusto. Blue winds between her legs, getting his hopes up. Does she have any Worcestershire sauce? Guy puts it on everything, even chips. She definitely needs to get some more food in, get some of those disgusting pepperoni things he likes, and some cheesy Wotsits or something… She ought to clear out the office a bit too; the sofa bed is covered in several piles of paper and a flat-pack bookshelf she's been intentionally ignoring. Maybe Guy could help her interpret the instructions and put it up. And they could go to that new film together, the one with Philip Seymour Hoffman – she's always loved him as an actor. She puts her glass of wine in the fridge, fills up the kettle and gets out the posh hot chocolate – she doesn't want a headache in the morning; she has too much to do. Someone is coming into her house – someone who needs her. She knows how to do this. She knows who she is again.

Chapter 2

15th of September, '59

My Darling Bea,

Well here it is – my very first letter to you from this place. I've been simply dying to write to you since the moment I said goodbye at the end of the May dance. I wasn't going to write at all, I wasn't going to say anything until I got back, but I've decided I can't wait until then. I've been going over and over it in my head, trying to work out how I can explain what happened and why I've kept this whole wretched business a secret from you. Oh Bea, I'm in such a dreadful mess. I'm frightened that you'll never forgive me, for creating such a tissue of lies. The thing is... oh, why can't I just say it! I'm tempted to start my letter again, but I've screwed up three pieces of paper already, and it seems like a terrible waste.

I'm going to have a baby, you see. I'm seven and a half months gone now, you can't very well miss it. I'm in a little place not too far from the sea, I won't tell you where just yet. The nuns have a place here where people like me can come and have their babies in peace – 'St. Mary's Convent of Mercy'. 'A mother and baby home', they call it. The other girls here call it a 'hide-away for fallen women' – because that's what I am now, Bea, that's the awful truth.

I'm trying to imagine you reading this letter. You're probably on your bed with your knees drawn up, one arm clasping them towards you like a sweetheart. I'm trying to imagine what your face looks like. Maybe you're running your fingers through your hair, like you do when you get nervous. Maybe your eyes are narrowed, and you're already furious with me, torn between reading on and scrunching this letter into a ball or ripping it into little pieces. You'd be quite right to be angry. But I only didn't tell you because I care so much about you, you know. And because I hope you care about me. All those nice things you keep saying about me – they're all wrong. If you could see me with this lump growing on my front. This stupid lump. When I saw you last we were talking about spending the summer together. You probably thought I dropped off the face of the earth. I've told so many lies. So many wretched lies.

It's Mick's baby, of course. I haven't told him. He'd be thoroughly decent about the whole thing, I know he would. He'd probably even offer to marry me, the silly thing. As if he'd want to end up with a life like that – coming home to me washing nappies, my hair all mussed up and with mashed food on my blouse. It wouldn't be fair on either of us, to pretend to be people we're not. Everyone else'd prefer it, but not us. Have you seen him since the dance? I wish I could ask you to send my love to him, but it's not safe for anyone to know you've got this letter from me. Please, Bea, don't tell. Don't tell anyone, especially mum and dad. I'm glad Mick will be thinking of me settling into my 'new job', he was so pleased for me when I told him about it. I don't miss him at all, what does that say about me? But I miss you, Bea, oh, I miss you like mad.

I'm sure you want to know more, everything. I will tell you everything, I promise, but not just yet. I'll write another letter, soon. I've told you the worst of it. I hope this letter gets to you safely. It's such a relief to get it written down. I know it sounds silly, but the girl I share a room with has auburn hair just like yours. I keep waking up in the middle of the night, and I look over and see her hair and pretend it's you. That's got me back to sleep, knowing you were there. There, I really must go now. We've dinner in twenty minutes. I will write again really soon, and I'm putting a big hug in the envelope with this letter.

Always your best friend,
Elizabeth.

Chapter 3

If it weren't for Bunny Berigan's trumpet, Violet would never have moved to Abbotsfield. It was late summer, and a few bright poppies were still straggling by the roadside. Violet was driving back home after visiting her sister Marta in Exeter. They'd celebrated Violet's Decree Nisi by drinking too much red wine and reminiscing about the olden days, boring Marta's husband silly. Violet was tapping her fingers on the steering wheel to Bunny's music, still enjoying the novelty of being able to play her CDs as loudly as she liked without Charles rolling his eyes or smacking his lip as he did whenever he came across something distasteful. Poor old Bunny – 'The Miracle Man of Swing', born in 1908 and succumbing to alcoholism at only 33. She'd always struggled to reconcile his short, painful life with the sweet notes that spilled from his trumpet. If she hadn't been so immersed in one of his solos on 'Song of India' she would never have missed her turning. And if she hadn't missed her turning she would never have spotted a sign for Abbotsfield, and been piqued by a sudden curiosity. 'Abbotsfield' – it sounded like it might have a neat duck pond, rose-covered flint cottages, and a few kindly old ladies in pale blue hats. There might even be a tea-room with scones and cucumber sandwiches and an elderly Labrador sleeping under one of the tables. It was already afternoon, but her head was still woolly with the residue of alcohol – she could do with a good strong cup of coffee.

She put on her indicators and careened off the main road, narrowly missing an old gentleman in a Mini and giving herself a bit of a shock. In the event it wasn't picturesque in the slightest. A few of the houses were covered in that nasty grey lumpy stuff like porridge, and there weren't any tea-rooms, just a Post Office that was 'closed for lunch'. She pulled up anyway, first eating three pickled onions from her secret stash in the glove compartment and then getting out to stretch her legs. After unsuccessfully trying to make friends with a local ginger tom, she saw no further reason to stay. She almost missed the hand-painted wooden sign pointing down one of the unpromising looking side roads – 'the sea'. She followed the sign down the winding road, her car bumping up and down over the rocks and pot-holes, and parked in the empty car park. And there was the sea – glinting as if the stars had all fallen out of the sky and were bobbing about in the water. It was closer to the village than you would imagine. She was all alone, as far as she could see, and she walked towards the edge of the water, picking up interesting stones as she went. Here was a smooth, pale blue stone with a white slash, here was a shiny grey one in the shape of a half-moon. She crouched near the foamy skirts of the waves, dipped a finger in and licked the salt from it. At that precise moment she decided she was moving to the village.

She'd kept her decision secret to start with, recognising it as impulsive and eccentric and hoping she might come to her senses. Summer faded into winter, and a six-month affair with a friend of a colleague took her mind off leaving home. When the relationship faltered and failed, more from a lack of enthusiasm than anything else, the idea was waiting. It would nag at her when she was in the middle of lecturing her students on the fundamentals of nanomechanics or engineering geology – 'You could be walking along the beach right NOW.' Her dreams cajoled her with oceans full of mermaids and chests of treasure, and helped her to rehearse breaking the news to her mother (although in the dream her mother's head always exploded, which was a bit alarming). She started doing sums on the back of envelopes – how much did she need to live? Could she afford to buy a house outright? How long would her savings last? Charles had surprised them all by becoming successful in his field, and some prudent investment in property had left her with a reasonably substantial divorce settlement. She also had her own money, tucked away over the years like food to save for later. As the weeks went by, she collected reasons to add ballast to her rationale. She'd be closer to her sister, and Guy in London. Her dad had been talking about getting a smaller place. She couldn't walk around her parent's house without tripping over memories in every room. She still hadn't put the weight back on since her illness – maybe the sea air would infuse her with a new ruddy health.

One day she casually broached the subject with her Head of Department, and he surprised her by suggesting a year's unpaid sabbatical from her post on the spot. He also offered her a bit of work she could do from her laptop, 'to stop her grey matter dissolving'. She found herself saying 'yes, please' and after this, things gathered a momentum of their own. She started to research removal companies and took inventories as she walked through the house. What would she take? What would she leave behind? She'd definitely want to keep her battered armchair and her bureau, but her mother might want the huge pine bookshelf – how much would a new one cost? How would her cat, Blue, cope with the change? Who would take over her role as treasurer of the Staff Social Club at University? She'd spent her evenings poring over property online, clicking the 'x' to close the window as soon as anyone came into the room, as though she were looking at porn. Her walk on the beach in Abbotsfield remained central to her scheming, and so when she saw a cottage for sale in the village, almost a year to the day since her first visit, she took it as a sign. Not that she'd ever admit to believing in any of that new age rubbish. She booked a viewing and drove down to see it the very next day.

The estate agent met her at the Post Office and walked her along to the cottage. He could have been half the age of her oldest daughter and spoke in the language of his kind – 'living accommodation comprising of…', 'exceptionally well presented', 'refurbished to the highest standard'. Once she got the knack of nodding whilst completely ignoring him, it was much easier to concentrate. They walked past the lumpy-porridge terraces, turning onto a narrower road edged with semi-detached cottages and backing onto fields, and Violet tried to get her bearings and catch a glimpse of the sea. Where was it? They arrived in front of the cottage, and she paused at the gate, taking it in. It was a plain front – two up two down, with a broken drainpipe and single glazed windows that would let in the cold. It was painted a horrible yellowy grey, but at least it wasn't porridgey. The agent unlocked the door and they went inside. The previous owner had already moved out, and the agent's patter echoed in the bare rooms. She continued to tune him out and tried to imagine herself into the living room, the kitchen. Will this do? Would there be enough space for my children? It didn't have the high ceilings or character she was used to in the rambling Shropshire farmhouse she'd shared with her husband, children and parents for twenty years. There were only five rooms – the hall led into the biggest room, a living room with a real fire and windows that looked out onto the road. Would Blue enjoy sitting on that windowsill? Further down the hall was the kitchen, with a small breakfast bar and horrendous, bright orange walls, and out the back was a small overgrown garden and a tumbledy-down shed. The stairs led up from the living room, and there were two bedrooms and a bathroom with an avocado suite. She stood at the back bedroom's window and drew a circle into the dust on the glass. Trees, a few more houses, a string of pylons off to the right. She stood on her tip-toes. And there it was! Only a sliver of it, cut off just below the horizon, but there it was: a real piece of the ocean. She turned to the agent and cut him off mid-sentence, putting in an offer for the full asking price.

She managed to put it off for another week, but she knew she couldn't just disappear one day when her parents were out playing Bridge. The consensus was that she had lost her mind. Everyone agreed – her colleagues, her children – even her dentist expressed scepticism when she explained her reasoning through an open mouth full of sharp metal instruments. Her mother was especially vocal, as was her fashion. 'You're having a mid-life crisis, dear, we all go through it. I had a fleeting fancy to run off with the butcher at forty-four, and where would that have left your father and you girls? I simply can't see how you can be seriously considering it! Pull yourself TOGETHER dear, for the children's sake. Stop being so terribly selfish.'

Violet charged through most of their protests with her

usual bluster, the way you might get through brambly patches
of forest – by putting your head down and forging onwards,
not stopping to examine the ground for creepy crawlies or
getting twigs caught in your hair. It sometimes felt as if
there were a tangle of hands holding her back, gripping her
ankles, her shoulders, the hem of her cardigan. She'd manage
to shake one of them off and another would take its place –
Josie: 'I won't come and visit you down there.'; Lucy: 'You're
making a complete fool of yourself.'; Megan: 'Please don't,
Mum, we need you up here – if you loved me, you wouldn't
go.' The only one of her family to offer faint encouragement
was Guy, but she was aware that a cottage on the south coast
would offer him a convenient base for his surfing expeditions.
It did matter to her that her girls disapproved, but she didn't
allow herself to think too much about it while making the
arrangements. She didn't usually go in for all that 'be kind to
yourself' rubbish, but there was a part of her that just knew
the move would be good for her, like cod liver oil or a brisk
constitutional when she was feeling low in energy. One by
one, her family realised she wasn't going to budge. Megan
started planning her first visit, and her mother even offered
to help with the move.

On the 7th of November she found herself standing
alone in her new living room amongst piles of boxes. Here
she was – 'Jacquet Cottage' – renamed in honour of her
father's favourite tenor sax player. Her mother had insisted
she pack a separate box with a kettle, a pint of milk, and a
box of PG Tips, so she held a steaming mug in her hand.
She sighed and looked around. She couldn't remember which
box she'd packed her telephone in, so she'd plugged in her
mobile to charge it up. There was an armchair, but her sofa
was missing – she'd got the measurements wrong, and they'd
had to put it in storage in the nearest town. Blue was on the

windowsill as expected, his ears back and tail twitching. The boxes were full of work – plates to unwrap, clothes to sort through, ornaments that needed new homes. She listened to the removal van starting up and accelerating away, and two words looped in her mind like a stuck record. Now what?

Chapter 4

On the drive to the train station to pick up Guy, Violet thinks of the letter which is tucked into the back pocket of her jeans. She doesn't really need to carry it around – the contents have lodged themselves into her brain like a sharp paper plane. It had flopped onto her doormat early this morning, the first of November. The day before Tom's birthday. It had been posted in a plain new envelope, with her name and address printed in small, neat, blue-biro capitals. She can't see any reason why it wouldn't be genuine – the language seems to fit the 50s, and the paper is thin and worn as if someone has folded and refolded it over the years. Who was this girl, Elizabeth? Surely the letter would be valuable to someone – a relative, a historian? Who can she talk to about it? Most importantly, and infuriatingly, what did it have to do with her? She has returned to it obsessively all day, like a small stone denting her heel on a long walk, or a jagged fingernail catching on fabric.

At least it has given her a break from thinking about the ghastly village Committee. The Committee had first entered her life on a visit to her next-door-but-one neighbour Sylvia in January. During her first few weeks in Abbotsfield, Sylvia was one of the three people that Violet had said more than 'hello' to, the other two being Fred the local shopkeeper and a handyman who had un-blocked her sink and re-plastered the office. Once a week or so Sylvia invited Violet over to 'take afternoon tea'. It usually involved Sylvia's fine home-made scones and a good slice of fruit cake or freshly baked shortbread, and so Violet had an incentive not to make her usual excuses. Home baking always reminded her of her father's sister, who had died too early from heart disease. They'd visited her regularly when Violet was young, and whenever they arrived, the aroma of baking hung in the air like a warm fog. She still associates fresh coffee cake or crisp cheese straws with the hugs her aunt folded her into on her arrival and at the slightest provocation during the rest of the visit. They were warm and squishy, and they infused her with energy – the opposite of the business-like clinches she usually received from her mother.

Sylvia and her husband Stan had lived in their little house for longer than Violet had been alive. From outside it looked the same as Violet's cottage, but the interiors were so different that you had to work hard to see the resemblance. Sylvia and Stan had laid down layers over the years – clutches of framed family photos on the walls, patchwork blankets over the furniture, ornaments all sitting on their own crocheted doilies. The paint was stained golden brown with Stan's cigar smoke and this made the rooms look even more cave-like and cosy. Violet watched Sylvia place the squeezed out tea-bag into a small dish set out beforehand for this purpose, and listened to her scold Stan for tearing into his scone with his fingers rather than using the correct knife, and could tell that their routines had settled around them over the years – a slow drip drip drip that had resulted in something as hard as stone. At first Violet had struggled to make conversation, and hated the awkward silences when she could hear Stan slurping away at his tea, but then she'd discovered that if she asked Sylvia for 'news of the village' she could set her off on a series of pockets of gossip that lasted at least until she'd finished her Victoria sponge and could comfortably make her excuses.

That January visit, Sylvia had announced that a local gentleman called Mr. Sykes had fallen at Christmas and broken his hip. She'd heard the news from the Chairperson of the Fête Committee, Margaret – Mr. Sykes had always been treasurer for the Committee and wouldn't be out of hospital for months. With the February Fair fast approaching, Margaret was 'frantic' about finding someone to step in at short notice. Sylvia had already told Violet about the Fête Committee. It was set up twelve years ago by Margaret Meeks, who didn't suit her name in the slightest, and her brother Peter. Peter was a regular in the local pub, The Griffin, and late one night he got involved in an argument that started with an accusation that he couldn't arrange a piss-up in a brewery. By closing time he'd somehow bet £100 that he could organise not only a piss-up but a whole village Fête. He was on the phone to his sister at 7am the next morning, explaining that there was more than money at stake, and that it'd be a wonderful opportunity for her to put her leadership skills to good use (he actually used the words 'good at being bossy', but Margaret read between the lines). By lunchtime the first ever Abbotsfield Grand Fête and Float Parade was already taking shape. Peter collected his £100, but the Fête was a great success and Margaret was showered in something much more precious than money – praise. It was a long time since anyone had approved of anything Margaret had done, and she had resolved to do an even better job of it next year. The Committee (minus Peter) was formed and had gone from strength to strength, gradually taking on new commitments such as a smaller fair in February and a Christmas collection at the local shop. The Committee co-existed harmoniously with the Parish Committee, which dealt with more traditional matters such as the village's sewage problem, and whether or not Abbotsfield would enter 'Best Kept Village'.

Violet had taught herself how to perform the tasks of a Treasurer many years ago at the University. She was recruited to the Staff Social Club by a rather nice looking Maths Lecturer during her first week in the job, and had performed this role for the next quarter of a century. She was well aware that she'd already been in the village for a few months and had struggled to make any friends. She'd never been a natural at developing connections. Other people seemed to find it so easy. She sometimes imagined them as having lots of different coloured strings attached to their bodies, representing the things about themselves that other people would find attractive or interesting. All they had to do was take the end of one of these strings and offer it to a passing stranger, and the stranger seemed to willingly take it and become a friend. It didn't seem to matter what it was – a mutual interest in showing Persians, the perfect recipe for asparagus soufflé, even a common fascination with the weather over the next few days. She saw it happening all around her, half of her scoffing at the inanity of the exchanges and the other half a tiny bit jealous. She wasn't sure if she didn't have any coloured strings, or if she simply didn't have the knack of choosing the right one to offer people. She was going to start an art class next week, but maybe it would do her good to put herself 'out there' a bit more? These thoughts flashed through her head, and she found herself mentioning casually to Sylvia that she might be able to help. Before she knew it, Margaret was knocking on her door and bustling in with a hold-all bulging with papers. There seemed to be an assumption that Violet had already said yes, and so by the time Margaret had explained how things worked and they were on their second cup of tea it seemed a bit pointless to say she'd think about it and get back to her.

Her last job as treasurer had been relatively stress-free – she'd only had to attend the AGMs, and for more than half her time the Chairperson had been an easy-going Chemistry Professor who'd bought her a box of Milk Tray as a thank you every Christmas. The Fête Committee was a different animal altogether. Margaret didn't only require Violet to attend all their meetings, but expected her to come up with ideas, put forward her opinions, and help out with the practical tasks that needed doing. The group seemed to contain more than its fair share of eccentrics, and they never had quite as many members as Margaret would have liked. The meetings often got tangled up in complicated politics and personal differences, and sometimes Violet felt like she was in the middle of a spin-cycle. She cast her mind back to some of the dramas that had unfolded over the past year...

She lets out a sigh as she pulls up at the train station and is immediately distracted by catching sight of Guy. He's balancing on the edge of the curb as if it's a surfboard, with his black woolly hat pulled down low over his forehead. He seems to have enough luggage to last him until Summer. She puts this concern aside, beeps her horn and jerks her head to indicate that he should get into the passenger side.

'Hello, Mama!'

He puts his bags in the boot, slamming it so hard that the car shakes, and gets in. He leans towards her and tries to cover her in blubbery kisses – she shakes him off vigorously, saying 'eugh'. He pretends to look hurt, and their meeting ritual is complete. He puts on his seat-belt and settles back in his seat, content. For a few minutes they drive in silence.

'So – what's news in A-burp-field?'.

Violet often wishes her son would realise how unfunny he is and stop trying to make jokes like that. It's like a thirteen-year-old boy sniggering at the word 'balls'. She usually ignores him, but he doesn't seem to need any encouragement.

'Oh, you know, usual shenanigans. I don't pay much attention to the gossip.'

'You should, Mother. It's vital in a place like this, where you know what colour underpants everyone's wearing. You won't know who to avoid, otherwise. I'll help you out with it – you know, do some snooping around. It can be my little project…' he lapses into silence and stares out of the window, lost in thought. 'I know! I can use it in my – you know, do some pieces around it. Some character studies, or some dialogue – get all the local words in. What was that one you were telling me about the other day? Drummy drone? A bumble bee, isn't it?'

'Drumble drane.'

'Yes, that's it.' He puts on a terrible Somerset accent. '"All these drumble dranes around, it's a wonder a man can find his hat…" Do you still have your laptop? Can I…'

'Oh, GO TO HELL! FUCKING IDIOT!'

A people carrier – Violet hates these vehicles above all others. Their seven empty seats, the way they look down on all the other cars, like they own the road… it makes her blood boil. This one had the cheek to try to cut her up at a roundabout. She'd swerved towards them and made a hand gesture to accompany her outburst. Guy was used to it and carried on as if nothing had happened.

'I'd really appreciate having a bit of time on it, you know, maybe a few hours early in the morning, when the creative juices are really flowing…'

'You know bloody well you're never up before eleven.'

He chose to ignore this with a blank smile, as if humouring her.

'It's all starting to fall into place, now I know I'm a writer. No wonder I haven't been able to stick at any of those ridiculous jobs. It's the universe, it's been trying to tell me. God, what an idiot! I could've got started on it ages ago, but I kept persevering, "find a proper job, like a normal person". That's where I was going wrong…' He's almost talking to himself. 'Well. At least I'm there now. How old was Carlos Williams when he wrote his best stuff? I hope I'm not too late… Ma, how old was Carlos Williams?'

'Have you had any dinner yet?'

Guy sighs and fiddles about in his inside jacket pocket for his mobile phone. He presses a couple of keys and then taps away for five minutes. Her children are forever teasing Violet about her ineptitude with mobile phones. It apparently annoys them that her keys make a little beeping noise when she presses them. They take immediate charge of it whenever they're with her and somehow get rid of the noise, but she does something to it by mistake and the beeps always comes back. They've shown her how to change it a thousand times but she really can't summon up the energy to care about it, and so the knowledge refuses to stick in her brain – it slides out like buttered mushrooms from a non-stick pan. She's only just mastered texting, and her children take delight in her abortive attempts. She'll often press the button that sends them before she's finished, and then loses patience and picks up the phone to call them, or leaves it altogether, so the children text back saying 'what do you mean, "if you want to comb"?' or '"lote" you too.' As far as she can work out, the whole thing is a lot of wasted energy for very little (inconsequential) conversation. It's like when you're sitting comfortably and you want to get your apple from an awkward spot on the table and so you stretch as far as you can and then further and then further and all your muscles are aching... rather than just getting up off your bottom.

As Violet puts the car up onto the curb outside her cottage, Guy stretches and yawns in a way only men can, as if every cell in their bodies is creaking with pleasure.

'I'm stARVing.'

He hops out of the car and bounces to the front door, jiggling about on his heels as he waits for Violet. He's like a puppy waiting to be let out.

She cooks him Spaghetti Bolognese for dinner – a huge mound of it with plenty of garlic in the sauce and cheddar grated onto the top. Blue gets his share of cheese – he has quite a nose for it and can seek it out at twenty yards. The meal does the perfect job of filling Guy up to the brim – he eats enough for several people. It makes him so drowsy, he only manages an hour of television before his eyes start flickering, and he collapses onto his side and curls up to nap. It's only 8pm. Violet sits for a while and watches Blue wash – he's doing that 'face wash' when he licks his paw and drags it across one side of his cheek and over his ear before re-licking his paw, ready for the next sweep. She's a sucker for it – other women get their kicks by watching babies (or men looking after babies), but give her a face-washing cat any day. Blue has never quite got into the rhythm of it and sticks out his long pink tongue at the wrong moments, when his paw has just set off on its journey across his face, or when it's pressing his ear down flat. She laughs out loud at him, causing Guy to murmur in his sleep – 'don't think that's a good idea, Lauren...' She leaves the room to sort out his bedding before she hears something she'd rather not.

That night in bed, with Guy safely ensconced in layers of bedding like a caterpillar getting ready to metamorphosise, her mind returns to the argument with Tom. She's gone to bed and turned off her reading light too early. She's finished her trashy detective novel, and the autobiography she's started is boring her silly – really, who cares what colour this man's pram was or whether he played in the woods with the gypsy children? It's dangerous to lie there looking at the ceiling – uncomfortable thoughts find their way in like ichneumon flies. Ever since she ran out on Tom, their argument has been sitting at the very base of her stomach like a solid blue chunk of poison. Whenever she remembers it, the poisonous lump releases a surge of molecules into her blood, making her throat constrict and her heart speed up. How can her lover have so much power over the way she feels? It had never been that way with Charles. She'd loved him in her own way, of course – she couldn't have spent all those years with him without becoming a bit soft on the old man. And he could certainly get her goat – he'd had a long time to suss her out and knew exactly what to say to piss her off the most – something about her not working very hard, or something mean about her lack of friends. But this... It was as if Tom had squirmed into her very softest part, a pale flat organ with layers of frilled delicate skin, like some kind of sea creature. She didn't even know she had this organ before Tom – it was well-protected, with a hard tortoise-shell carapace and signs around the perimeter – 'go back', 'danger ahead', 'beware of the dogs'.

Bloody ridiculous. She's a fifty-one-year-old woman – she's brought up four children, had a successful career, managed a pretty decent marriage. Her lover is simply skilled at hurting her. Maybe Tom is skilled at hurting people in general – gets something out of it even – aiming the arrows precisely, using tricks that Violet wouldn't have the first clue about, that she wouldn't even recognise. Maybe that explains why her lover wanted to be with her in the first place. She could never really work it out – she'd felt suspicious right from the beginning, six months ago, when they slipped from friendship into a deeper intimacy, when things started getting out of hand. Maybe Tom had seen a vulnerability in Violet that was ready to be exploited – ripe for manipulation. What was it Tom had said to her, at the beginning of the argument? 'You don't let people in, you just stand six feet away and hurl things at them, and then turn away when they try to hurl them back.' Bloody nonsense. Violet feels anger stirring, and it chases the other feelings away. She makes a decision – the best thing for her to do would be to stay away. It's awkward – Tom lives on the outskirts of the village, uses the local shop to buy milk and bread… and she curses the whole situation again, her anger feeding the awake part of her and making it impossible to drop off to sleep. She sits up in bed and turns on her bedside lamp, drawing a deep breath and forcing the dilemma to the back of her mind. She picks up her autobiography again. Maybe she can bore herself to sleep.

Chapter 5

22nd of September, '59

Dearest Bea,

It feels as if I didn't get very far in my last letter. I haven't written for a week as they're keeping me rather busy here – the other girls tell me it'll get easier once I know the ropes, but at the moment I don't have much of a chance to be on my own. My room-mate Dolores (everyone calls her Doll) is an awfully sweet girl, but she can talk the hind legs off a donkey, and the front legs and tail too! She's only fifteen – the same age as little Janie, can you imagine it? I've taken her under my wing a bit, but sometimes I wonder if she ought to take me under hers instead – she seems to know so much about the world. Last night she told me about a couple who lived in their street who take live-in help and then try and tempt them into, well – you can imagine! How would she know about something like that? She's a pretty little thing really, thin as a slip except her bump, with caramel-coloured freckles on her pale skin, a snub nose and silky, dark auburn hair. She's always sucking her thumb, even in front of the Sisters. (Oh, I haven't said anything about the Sisters yet, have I? They've been pretty decent to me, Bea. I didn't think they would be.) Doll makes me feel like I've come through a haystack backwards, with my thick old orangey hair sticking up like a toilet brush, and eyebrows that I simply can't get to look elegant, whatever I do to them... There's something about Doll, though – she has a sad look to her, Bea, somewhere underneath, as if she's covering it all up with layers and layers of 'couldn't care less'. I can't get much out of her, and you know how people usually confide in me.

Well – I've got some more explaining to do. I haven't hardly begun. It was the only time me and Mick did it – just my stinking luck. He'd been on at me for so long, saying he knew what to do, saying he'd take care of it so I'd be safe, and I believed him, like an idiot. Maybe he thought he knew what he was doing – he'd probably been talking dirty with his friends, plotting. It wasn't up to much, I've got to admit, but Mick was so pleased with himself afterwards, like he'd just, oh, I don't know, achieved something marvellous... Poor Mick. I am mean to him sometimes, aren't I?

He said everything would be all right but then I was late, and you know I'm always dead on, to the day, and so I knew straight away that something was wrong. It's odd, it was more than that – it was like I was already certain of it – there was a kind of watery feeling in my stomach, different from the usual way you feel every month. I felt heavy too – a sort of tiredness, but not just my brain – my whole body wanted to make a little nest somewhere and curl up and sleep for weeks.

I think I pretended that it wasn't happening at first. That's probably how I got it past you – you know me so well, it feels like you can predict what I'm going to say before I know myself. Like that time you asked me why I didn't like Mrs. Swithins, and I didn't know what you meant, because I did like her, and it was only when I'd thought about it that I realised you were right! But with my period being late I just thought – well, it'll be one thing or the other, and there's no point getting jittery this early on. Then I pushed it right to the back of my mind, where I put maths and spiders and that horrible thing that happened to us three summers ago. Honestly, Bea, if babies just fitted themselves into your usual body shape, curling up really small and not needing any extra space, I would have just got on with my life for the next nine months and dealt with the baby when it popped out. But my stomach was starting to swell, I could see it through my clothes, and that's when I knew it'd only get worse and I couldn't hide it forever. I couldn't just carry on at work, carry on with Mick. I was in a terrible mess.

I finally went to see a doctor, to make sure everything was all right with the baby. I'd missed for two months and I was starting to feel sick in the mornings, not terribly, but it was as if my body wouldn't let me put it off for any longer. I didn't go to Dr. Stanton, of course – I wouldn't want her knowing my business. I didn't know where to go. I was feeling awfully fed up by then – I felt so alone. Everyone around me seemed to be getting on with their own lives just fine. I almost told you one day, that day we went on a walk around the park after Billy's birthday party, remember? You were studying my face with its stuck-on smile and said 'is everything all right, honey?' and you sounded so concerned. I almost let it crack then, I almost let my face break in two and the tears come out. But if I'd told you it would've been real – big ugly words hanging in the air between us – so I kept it all inside, like rotten meat in a cupboard. That Saturday I was shopping on Regents Street and wandered into a part of the city I didn't know very well. I spotted this sign, very discreet, saying 'Family Health, open clinic on Friday mornings'. It was some kind of a religious place I think – I went to have a look at the door, it said it was supported by the sisters of something or other. I called in sick that Monday, so many lies. It's funny, I spent hours getting ready that morning, as if they were going to make all kinds of decisions and judgements based on what I looked like. I wore my best skirt, you know, the grey one we got from Camden, and I ironed my shirt until the creases were sharp enough to draw blood.

It was horrible, Bea, horrible. As soon as I walked in I got a sinking feeling in my stomach. The paint in the waiting room was dingy, and the light-bulb was too dull. There were quite a few girls there, sat on cheap chairs and they looked drawn, grey. There was a nasty smell too, like antiseptic mixed with damp. I had to wait for an hour and a half. The lady nurse there was quite decent, a little bit patronising perhaps, but the doctor was a brute. He even looked a brute, with his hairy hands and his big squashed nose. He hurt my arm on purpose, I'm sure of it, when he moved me round to a different position. He said some nasty things too, Bea, but I'm not going to write them down because I think it would make me sad. I just about held in the tears until I left the ghastly place but as soon as I stepped out onto the street they just burst out of me. A lovely old lady stopped and asked if everything was all right – she even tried to fetch me a cup of tea. I was glad I didn't have to go back to work – I felt thoroughly exhausted. Everyone on the bus seemed to be in twos, chatting about their children or what they were going to cook for their husbands for tea. I sat right at the back and stared out of the window, without really seeing anything. I've never felt so alone in my whole life.

Well – it's getting late here. I'd better go – once I get started writing I don't seem to be able to stop! I hope I'm not boring you. It doesn't seem fair somehow, that I get to talk as much as I want and you don't get to say anything. I'm just so scared that mum and dad would find out where I was somehow – not that you'd tell them, but that my letter might get muddled up with your parent's letters, or – I don't know, I'm not really thinking straight. Anyway I really must stop now, I think I can hear Doll coming back from her bath. She'll have her hair all wrapped up in her big white towel, and she'll be singing Sinatra's 'High Hopes'. She can't get it out of her mind and is driving us both mad!

Give my love (secretly!) to Janie and Mick and Bill and your parents. Still missing you so much...

Always your best friend,

Elizabeth.

Chapter 6

The story of how Violet's mother met Violet's father was the Ackerman's most important family myth. Later her mother would bemoan the lack of Valentine's cards or flowers, and Violet guessed that he'd burned himself out with that one supremely romantic gesture. It was no wonder that her mother had wanted to save the memory carefully, wrapped in tissue paper, taking it out when she needed to reassure herself that she'd done the right thing by marrying him. At seventeen, Violet's mother Vera was still living with her parents. She had just left school and was studying to be a secretary in a nearby town, hating every minute and making sure nobody forgot it. Between her lessons she was helping her dad out in the family's fruit and veg shop. Bill used to come in most days to fetch groceries for his mother – she had a 'gammy leg' and didn't walk into the village from their farm unless she needed to. He was an ordinary looking boy with a slight chest and neatly combed dark hair, and he walked with a slight limp after having fallen under a tractor when he was a boy. He was four years older than her, so she'd never known him at school. She had no reason to notice him, and served him like she would anyone else. One day he waited until he was the only one left in the shop, went over to the counter and leaned in closer to her. He lowered his voice and said that he wanted to get a gift for a 'special someone'. Could she help him pick out the kind of thing a young lady like herself would be glad to receive? He blushed beetroot and fiddled with his shirt buttons as he talked, and she felt a warm, affectionate pity well up inside her.

These extra purchases became a weekly event. She pointed him towards a good lipstick one day, and a particularly delicious box of chocolates the next, depending on his budget for that week. He always reported back that his special someone had been delighted with her gift. As time went on they widened their net to other topics of conversation. They started safely, with the weather and the gossip in the village, and moved on to talk about their own lives. To his father's horror, Bill had won a scholarship to study accountancy in a local town. He made Vera laugh with stories about how unsuited he was to farming, with his dust allergy, his rat phobia, and his knack for killing anything green and growing. She'd witter on about the complexities of her social life and complain about her tutor at the typing school who'd rap their knuckles with a ruler if they were too slow. As if they were back at school! They started to fantasize about living different lives to the ones they had on offer – Vera would move to a seaside town where nobody knew her and become an actress, and Bill would work in a neat office at the top of a city skyscraper. Vera's father would often appear from the back of the shop without warning, and his stern 'stop nattering and get on with dusting the shelves' looks became more frequent.

A few months passed – just long enough for Vera to date, fall in love with, and subsequently reject four different boys. One week Bill came in just before closing, looking even more flustered than usual, and asked if she'd be able to help him with a special favour. He'd been saving his money and was ready to buy his sweetheart an engagement ring – he was desperate for a second opinion, and Vera had chosen the presents so skilfully... She agreed to meet him in town that Saturday after a class. It was strange to see him outside the shop – he looked taller, and he'd combed his hair differently – it suited him. Together they visited every single jewellery shop in town. Vera chose the perfect ring, and Bill paid for it, and they went to rest their aching feet in a small dingy coffee shop. Vera was in the middle of telling Bill about her upcoming exams when he interrupted her by setting down his coffee cup, sloshing liquid into the saucer. He pushed his chair back clumsily and came round to her side of the table. The other customers started nudging each other and looking over, and so when he knelt down to say 'Vera, will you be my wife?' his words rang out like a peal of bells into a hushed church.

Vera told Violet that it had taken her a full thirty seconds to work out what was happening. She sat there with her mouth open like a goldfish, Bill looking up at her with his serious eyes, and everyone else in the coffee shop holding their breath. All of a sudden she felt a rush of happiness, whoosh! When she told this part of the story she'd demonstrate by moving her hands from her stomach up towards her head, and then she'd tickle Violet who would already be in spasms of pleasure and anticipation. Vera put her hands up to her cheeks and said 'yes', and Bill promptly burst into tears. And then of course he opened up the wicker basket 'full of washing for his mother' that he'd been carrying around all day. There, wrapped in red ribbons, were all the presents that Violet's mother had picked out for herself, unsuspecting, over the previous months.

Their courtship proceeded on a more conventional route after that. Vera's father took a little persuading, as he couldn't help feel that Bill Ackerman was a little 'below' his daughter. He softened when he heard about the accountancy studies, and Bill continued to win him over with his earnest, straightforward manner. Vera's mother had always been a little afraid of her daughter's unpredictability, never knowing where her emotions would fire her off to next, and was visibly relieved to welcome this steady, plodding man into her house. Vera herself found that spending time with Bill was rather comforting after all the turbulence of her previous 'love affairs'. The last of Bill's nerves had disappeared after the proposal, and they chatted easily about anything and everything. They did ordinary things, like going on bike rides and helping their mother with the Sunday roast, and Vera was surprised to find enjoyment in these simple activities. She'd always thought that love affairs consisted of roses and gondoliers and floods of tears, not Scrabble and roast potatoes. She liked the feel of his hot hand around hers when they walked to the butchers to fetch his mother some pork chops. She liked the shape of his nose. And she liked knowing that he liked her too, that she was quite alright as she was. In her spare time she made plans for their wedding with her mother. There seemed so much to do, and she wanted everything to be perfect. Before Vera knew it, she was walking down the aisle to the strains of old Mrs. Vintner's shaky organ, wondering quite who and what it was she was walking towards.

In the Autumn of 1955, nine and a half months after their small-town wedding, Violet was born. Augustine and Marta followed close on her heels. Vera had always been elusive when asked about these early years of their marriage. There seemed to be a ten year jump in the story between

Bill's proposal and the 'unprecedented trauma' of moving three small children to their current house in Shropshire. What happened during this time can only be guessed at, although Marta once overheard her mother refer to them as the 'hellish baby years'. Violet's own memories of her younger years were also blurred and muddled. Except for a few stand out events (her second morning at school, when she realised it hadn't just been a one-off, and being sick all over her favourite aunt) she could only guess at their day-to-day lives. She remembered her father as being rather wonderful but just out of reach, like an expensive doll in a toy-shop window. He always seemed to be on his way out to the office, ruffling her hair and calling her his little pretty, or disappearing into his 'study': a tiny box room dominated by a huge, dark green leather armchair and a desk covered in mysterious stacks of paper which made up his 'work'. At the time she never felt entitled to any more time with him – as a child, her world was simply 'the way things were'. It's only looking back that she wonders how he managed to be quite so absent without her mother complaining. Some of her fondest memories of her father involve jazz. She remembers early mornings in their old house with her sister Augustine, her mother huge with Marta, and her father getting them all up and moving with Ellington or Chick Webb, Billy May's trumpet galloping up the stairs, or Benny Carter's sax seeping under her bedroom door like honey.

Violet's early memories of her mother were even more elusive. Vera was competent at all the practical components of motherhood and negotiated an endless round of dressing, feeding, bathing, and rolling push chairs through the park. She was a very strong presence in the house, barking out orders and making her feelings known. Violet has fond memories of her mother baking her a flower-shaped birthday cake, and giving her a coin or two for passing an exam at school, but she can't remember any physical affection between the two of them. When she fell over, did she cry and run to her mother? If she did, she can't remember it. Did her mother tuck her up in bed? It was as if there was a kind of emotional disconnection between Vera and her daughters. This was very different to the physical distance between her and her father, who she actually felt very close to. She has a strange memory of seeing her mother amongst the crowd of mums at the school gates, and not recognising her as anything to do with herself. It was as if Vera was one of her friend's parents, or someone she recognised from the village. She can't remember where she got the idea, but for a few years Violet was convinced that she was adopted.

When Violet was fourteen she started getting into trouble at school, talking in class and not concentrating during lessons. The final straw had been a fist fight with an older girl who'd called her a 'nincompoop', and because Violet didn't know what that meant, she imagined it must be a terrible insult. Her mother's theory was that all of Violet's problems were a result of her seething jealousy of her two younger sisters. This included when she forgot to brush her hair in the mornings, or said that she didn't feel like going for a walk with the rest of the family. She often commiserated with Violet at length about the woes of being 'the oldest sister', and it took Violet until her mid-twenties to realise that her mother was actually talking about herself. Vera was convinced that sibling rivalry was the reason for her daughter's problems at school, despite Violet's protestations that they were probably more to do with her lack of friends and a fading interest in school-work. As usual there was no stopping her, and she hatched a cunning plan to give Violet a taste of being the only one again. Her parents took her to the seaside at Bognor Regis, while the youngest two were looked after by Vera's sister. They stayed in a modest hotel just up from the front, but to Violet they may as well have been in Venice or Morocco. She spent hours in the long string of shops selling ornaments made from shells, teeth-cracking rock in 60 different flavours, and Bognor Regis branded mugs and T-shirts, or watching gangs of cocky teenage boys take the piss out of each other, or throwing stones into the sea. Best of all, there were donkeys on the beach! Her parents argued constantly about what was going to be 'best' for Violet, which did throw a veil of dampness on the proceedings, but Violet was determined not to have her holiday spoilt. She got permission to walk along the front on her own whenever she could, and concocted elaborate fantasies involving boats and islands and handsome architects (always a handsome architect).

Over the years her parents forgot the uncomfortable atmosphere they'd created during this holiday and saw it instead through a haze of affection. Vera pronounced it 'the turning point' for Violet, and boasted about her parenting skills when people came round for dinner. Violet did start behaving more appropriately when she got back, but this was mainly due to a blossoming interest in insects initiated by a new friendship with a nerdy boy down the road. She had started to make secret plans about becoming an entomologist, and realised for the first time that she'd have to jump through the hoops of exams to do what she wanted with her life. At roughly the same time she took a little step backwards from her mother, as if backing away from the edge of a cliff, and this distance seemed to let in some air. Her mother didn't notice (or didn't comment), and it made their day-to-day relationship less complicated and easier to handle. The distance seemed to grow over the years, and they now related to each other in a superficial way, which suited them both fine.

Her colleagues had thought Violet was mad to move back in with her parents, but it had worked well for many years. Violet and Charles had moved in when she was heavily pregnant with their first child, Lucy, at Vera's insistence. At the time the two of them were renting a grotty bed-sit in Leeds with mould in the bathroom and silvery slug trails on the living room carpet. Charles was struggling to bring in any more money, and Violet had to give up her work at the University. As her mother insisted, it was clearly 'no place to bring a new spark into the world'. They were both reluctant, especially Violet, but her mother had always had a special knack for talking people round. The Ackermans happened to live closer to where Charles was working as a project manager, and the rambling farmhouse did have acres of spare space. In the beginning Violet and Charles took the annex, with a small bathroom of their own and two reasonably sized rooms, but once their third child Josie was born, her mother finally capitulated, and the Ackermans and the Dickinsons swapped round. Vera often made a big fuss about 'the invasion of the Dickinson clan', trying to play the 'poor us' card, but secretly she loved it – drowning in Barbie dolls and muddy shoes and high-pitched chatter, with a never ending list of 'things to do'.

The single thing that had caused more arguments than anything else over the years was the coat cupboard under the stairs. It was a small space, and they'd managed to fit in seven sturdy double coat pegs and racks for a dozen odd pairs of shoes. Vera always said it seemed fair that her and Bill had a double peg each, and that the remaining five were shared by the Dickinson family, as there were a couple of little ones who surely wouldn't need as much space as the bigger ones. The reality was that Violet bought her children far too many jackets and trainers and Wellingtons and hats, and the cupboard was crammed to the brim with various articles of miniature outer clothing before Vera or Bill even got a look in. There was NOTHING more annoying, said Vera to Violet over many a tense evening meal, than coming in to your own house and not having a place to hang your coat. On a couple of occasions she'd even been moved to action, sorting through the cupboard like a whirlwind, pulling the layers and layers of assorted coats from their straining pegs and piling them into a coat soup on the floor. She'd leave her coat alone, luxuriating in the space, and when Violet opened the cupboard door she swore she could see it smirking. Violet didn't give an inch, on principle. Bill and Charles tried to stand as far back from this battle as they could (their usual ploy for self-preservation), but inevitably they would be hooked in by a 'whose side are you actually on, Bill?' ('well, yours of course darling, but…') or a 'Charles feels you make a real fuss about this, don't you Charles' ('well I didn't actually say that you were unreasonable, Vera, but…'). Looking back, Violet is mystified by why her parents didn't just put up pegs in another room.

The years went on, and the children grew. Violet's father, the local family lawyer, slowly rose in his practice until he made partner. His mother wept proud tears – his father had died the year before. He separated his work life from his home life with a sharp knife, and never spoke of the divorces he was handling, or the financial affairs of Guy's teacher, Mrs. Jones. He continued to disappear into his study at every opportunity, but as time went on he'd linger to play with his grandchildren, especially Megan, who he had a special bond with. Vera tried her hand at several jobs – librarian, dental secretary, canteen assistant at the local school. None of these was a great success or lasted very long, mainly due to her inability to follow other people's instructions and her secret belief that she was really better suited to something a little more glamorous. Her real love was the local amateur dramatics group (or am-dram), to which she'd belonged for decades. It was widely known that Vera was a terrible actor, but nobody told her, and she continued to get a great deal from it. The family negotiated the usual dramas and illnesses over the years – Josie's broken leg, Megan's broken hearts, Bill's heart attack scare, and the minor feuds between various family members.

When Violet had last travelled up to see her parents, her father had suddenly looked old. Her mother could still be put into the 'middle-aged' category – her face was wrinkled and sagging, but she still seemed unencumbered by her body – her father had started to stoop and wither. She couldn't take her eyes off him as he moved around the house – his whole body had stiffened up, and he paused before getting out of his chair or lifting a log as if summoning his last reserves of energy. They are both in their eighties now, and as her sisters frequently remind her, she can't expect that they'll go on forever. Their marriage is as fiery as ever, or rather Vera is as fiery as ever and Bill still tries to put water on the flames. When Vera isn't at am-dram, she spends most of her time in the garden or her greenhouse, having developed a taste for gardening late in life. She grows mostly tomatoes with the odd courgette or baby aubergine. Violet and her sisters have spent many a visit sat at her kitchen table doing a blind tasting of her various varieties and giving them marks out of ten for appearance, taste, texture, sweetness, and god knows what else. Her gardening belt seems to have become a permanent fixture, carrying her gloves and plastic name tags and whatever else she happens to have slotted into it that morning. Since retirement, Bill has swapped his legal papers for the daily Telegraph and Sudoku, and he still retreats to his office to listen to his big band records and escape from his wife.

Violet doesn't spend any time worrying about them, as so many of her contemporaries seem to do. They seem to be happy enough in their dotage. They love her, she supposes, but their lives don't intertwine as much as she guessed they would after living in each other's pockets for so many years. She and her mother speak quite often, but they always talk of everyday things – 'Did you manage to get that tap sorted, darling?' or 'Is Dad's cold any better today?' They never had a proper conversation about Tom, and when Violet feels angry or unsettled, her mother is the last person she thinks of speaking to. The relationship she has with her parents still brings her comfort. It's good that someone knows that she's going to the village fish and chip supper on Thursday, and that someone asks how she's getting on with painting the walls in the downstairs toilet. What do other parents talk to their children about? Do they really have deep and meaningfuls about politics or the greenhouse effect or existential angst? What would Freud have to say about her old colleague, who would call her mother twice a day to let her know the precise calibration of her mood? Vera and Bill have their lives, and Violet has hers. Things are just fine the way they are.

Chapter 7

Another bloody letter. This is the phrase on Violet's mind as she strides into the village, towards that evening's Committee meeting. The air is cool and saturated with water – it's not quite rain, more a mist that has become too heavy for the air and is sinking downwards, drenching everything in its path. She pulls her cardigan more tightly around her, wishing she'd worn her coat. She doesn't notice Fred Thompson nodding a greeting from the other side of the road. Another bloody letter. Violet had arrived downstairs before Guy early that morning, the third morning of his invasion, and had spotted it on the doormat. She'd quickly picked it up and put it in her dressing-gown pocket, looking guiltily around her as if someone might be watching through the window. She'd found herself locking herself into the bathroom, running the water for a bath, and sitting on the closed lid of the toilet to rip it open. It was dated three days after the first letter she'd got, written on the same flimsy paper and in the same black ink. Elizabeth's handwriting was so delicate, like rows of tangled spiders. She read it over and over, trying to find a pattern, unlock a code. Maybe the first letter of every other word would make a sentence, or maybe there would be an invisible mark if she held it up to the light at exactly the right angle. Was there anything this girl had written that was out of context – a message for Violet woven into the narrative? She came up with nothing.

This one has left her unsettled. It's as if Elizabeth is sending her letters not only to the wrong address, but to the wrong decade. She could have rationalised the first one – a random mistake by a letters archive, or even one of her colleagues who'd come into possession of it and thought that she might be interested in seeing it. Two letters, on the other hand... Someone was sending these to her as a deliberate act, for a reason. But what reason? What was she expected to think? She supposed she ought to start asking around – to see if anyone knew anything about them. Why did she feel so reluctant to share them? The letters were so private, it was nobody else's business. She needs to protect Elizabeth from anyone else snooping into her affairs. She snorts at herself and her silliness – ridiculous. What would Tom have said about it? She rounds the corner and sees Margaret striding towards her from the other direction and quickly puts the matter to one side.

The Committee are meeting at Peggy's today. They take turns to host it, with Rob getting an amnesty as his flat doesn't have a room which would comfortably contain the six of them. Margaret's house is probably Violet's favourite, even though she's even more insufferable in her own house – her voice a little louder, her opinions a little more steely. She always bakes them something to go with her strong filter coffee – oat biscuits or cheese pastry triangles, and her living room is tasteful and comfortable. She likes Angie's house too – she's a rabid 'crafter' and drapes her house with colourful bits and pieces: patchwork quilts, crocheted cushions, cross-stitched framed pictures… Although the individual pieces leave something to be desired, the overall effect is of an Aladdin's cave, lined with bright parrot colours and soft surfaces. She's never been keen on Sue's because of the smell in the house. It isn't rotten exactly, and her living room looks clean enough, but it sits on the air like a curl of green smoke. She doesn't become habituated to it either, the usual saviour when dealing with eau-de-dog or stale cigarette smoke. It's more a kind of damp smell, maybe, but it reminds her of unwashed skin and she can sometimes hardly swallow her tea.

The most undesirable venue of all, which she's sure is a view the rest of the Committee would share, is Peggy's. As far as the actual Committee work goes, Peggy is dead wood, always coming up with ideas that are completely off the point and making them at leisurely length while Violet looks at her watch and shuffles her papers. She's eighty-seven and the others seem to think this reason enough to let the woman get away with bloody murder. As you'd expect from the random quality of her contributions and her general lack of concentration, her house is in absolute chaos. There are enough seats, but in order to sit down you first have to remove piles of paper, folded blankets, a small dog, or once, to Violet's dismay, a half-eaten doughnut with mould around the edges. Peggy also seems to get a sudden attack of house-pride just as the first Committee members traipse in and will dart around her living room in a parody of clearing up – moving a plant from here to there on the table, straightening a picture that was already straight and leaving it wonky, and then tottering off to the kitchen, oblivious to the teetering pile of roughly folded clothes that have tower-of-Pisa-ed and have shed too-large knickers and flesh-coloured stockings all over the carpet.

Their meetings have stepped up to weekly in preparation for their February Fair, a down-sized version of their Grand Fête minus the Floats. The February Fair was suggested five years ago by a long-time member Julia, who is presently on leave looking after her newborn son. It was intended as something the village could look forward to during the grey anti-climax of January – a burst of colour before the daffodils and crocuses really started blooming in earnest. And here they all are again. Margaret, at the head of the table, is the definition of 'formidable'. She's wiry as a whippet with a sharp chin and an unnatural amount of thick fuzzy black hair. Here's short, plump, flat-haired Angie, eagle-like Rob with his hooked nose and parchment skin, neat, nondescript Sue, and crinkled and harried Peggy. Will, an ex-City man who moved with his wife out to the country for 'rest and recuperation' after a turbulent high-flying career, is having one of his 'off days' which are grudgingly tolerated by Margaret. Violet probably likes Will more than any of the others. He has a quiet, gentle voice, which lulls you into a false sense of security until you realise what he's saying – usually exactly what he feels, regardless of whether his words are easy to swallow or are more likely to stick in your throat. Violet can well imagine him making cutthroat deals and dealing with insubordination.

Violet notices Sue flicking her eyes around the room as she settles herself down into her favoured chair, and can almost see the words forming in her throat, as if the skin has become translucent and the words are dark and lumpy.

'I don't know how you manage in here, Peggy.'

Angie looks daggers at Sue as Peggy jumps up from her chair and looks to her right and to her left, panicky, as if she's seeing the car-crash of her living room for the first time. The expression on her face reminds Violet of the nightmares she sometimes has about being at the front of a lecture hall full of students and looking down to find herself completely naked.

'Each to their own, Sue, each to their own,' says Rob, a little sternly. 'Grandfatherly' is how Violet always thinks of him. 'Sit down, Peggy, everything is just dandy.'

She responds to the authority in his voice and sits down, just as suddenly. Her startled look slowly fades as the meeting commences. Margaret shuffles her stack of papers in her usual imperious way, and looks directly at Rob as he fiddles about in his inside jacket pocket for a pen. When he notices the silence he looks up and meets her eyes.

'All ready!' he says.

'Righty-oh. I declare this meeting open. Angie, do you have a copy of the Minutes from the last meeting?'

Of course she does. She smiles beatifically and hands a neat stack of stapled sheets of A4 around the table.

'Thank you, Angie. So – members present? Apologies?' She speaks the words even though she knows they're not necessary – Angie has already started scribbling in her purple glittery pen. 'Matters arising from the last minutes?'

Violet prays he might not say it this time, but even though she imagines closing up her ears, Rob's words still slip through.

'Some matter arose in my dirty washing up this morning.'

Violet lets out a sharp sigh, and Rob looks a little startled. Violet doesn't catch his eye, and Angie laughs too loudly (brays would be a more accurate description) in an attempt to make him feel better.

'Actually, I do have something,' says Sue. 'It says here…' she finds the place on the second page and holds her place with a well-manicured fingernail. 'It says here that Will was going to do the design for the programmes. Well, I was thinking… I'm just not sure that he's up for the job, you know, with the way things are at the moment. If we want to be sure of it being finished in time, then maybe we should, you know…'

'He did volunteer, Sue,' Angie says quietly, looking at her hands as if she's speaking to herself.

'Yes, but I'm just not convinced that…' She lowers her voice and speaks conspiritially. 'We all know that he's deteriorating.'

'Decorating? Decorating what?'

Peggy is hard of hearing, although she denies it strenuously. According to Angie it causes her family a lot of upset. Last Christmas her daughter even resorted to buying her a hearing aid and wrapping it up with all her other presents, but Peggy insisted the present must have been wrongly labelled, as her hearing was as sharp as ever, and she decided to give it to her neighbour who really could use it. Margaret makes a sweeping motion with her hand, indicating that Sue should sit back from her bent forward position.

'Deteriorating, Peggy.' She mouths the words in an exaggerated fashion and Peggy raises her eye-brows in comprehension. 'I propose we see how Will is progressing with the design at our next meeting and offer him our support if he expresses any misgivings. All in favour?'

Violet, Rob and Angie put their hands up immediately as does Margaret, and so she pronounces a clipped 'carried' and curtly nods towards Angie who nods back and scribbles this down. Peggy turns to Violet.

'Are we voting for Will?'

Violet can't help another loud sigh slipping out of her. She misses Will. She clenches her hand into a fist under the table and wonders if she'll be able to keep her mouth shut for another hour.

That night, Violet crawls up the stairs like one of those big papery moths dragging themselves across concrete. She can hear the TV blaring from behind the closed door of the living room – Guy is watching something dreadful about the war. Why is it that men can't get enough of those programmes? Endlessly discussing different types of tanks and planes and fetishising old canons and uniforms and medals... Surely we should be getting our wars over and done with as soon as we can and moving on to peace? Wasting time examining old battle plans seems a little weird to her, as if men are all swotting up and secretly dying for another war to break out so they can have their chance. Blue is waiting for her on the bed. She gets under her duvet without taking any of her clothes off – soft clothes, leggings, an old jumper, thick socks. She slides a hand up the back of her jumper to unhook her bra and pulls each strap through a sleeve so she can slide the whole thing out. Aaah, relief. It's grey and worn – since Tom, she hasn't been paying much attention to her underwear, it's all big pants and mismatching colours. She pings it across the room and sinks down into her bed, sighing a delicious sigh.

She's had an exhausting afternoon with her son. She'd decided to take him for a walk along the beach to talk some sense into him. She wasn't sure before they set off exactly what she was going to say. She was relying on a vague hope that she could exhort him into mending his ways using a mixture of appealing to his common sense and making him feel guilty. The whole thing began badly when she opened her mouth and he said, 'Am I going to be treated to a little lecture, then, Mummy Dear?' He said it as if he was willing to indulge her, and it reminded her instantly of Charles and annoyed the hell out of her. Why is it that our children have to constantly remind us of our ex-partners? Her 'no!' sounded like someone protesting their innocence too insistently, and then she'd had to talk to him about the bloody problems with the heating for half an hour to get him off the scent. When she finally did bring up his future they were almost back to the car. She asked some clever questions, like 'How are you going to afford your new surfing gear next Summer?' and 'What is it you really want to do with your days?' – questions that should really have got him thinking. But despite her best efforts, she didn't get much out of him at all. He said something vague about finding his way by bumping off the things he didn't want to be doing and some tosh about 'the universe' again, but nothing that actually meant anything. Would the universe pay his rent for him? He wore a fierce cheerfulness when he spoke about his future. She wondered what was behind it.

He'd always been such a difficult child. Maybe she was soft on him – the girls were constantly complaining that she treated him differently. Megan had quite a hang-up about the unfairness of it, and at one point when she was a teenager she hadn't spoken to Violet for a whole fortnight. What exactly was it she'd done again? Something about letting Guy stay at a party overnight, when Megan had been refused despite being desperate to do the same only a year before... Violet had never been able to see their point, but it was true that he had turned out differently from her girls. Maybe she had tried too hard with him? She used to get terrible flashes of 'where-he-might-end-up', when he was ten and failing at school, or when he was fourteen and caught smoking in their pantry (in the pantry! – he couldn't even come up with of a more sensible place to hide). She could picture him older and dirtier and in some squat somewhere, shooting up or whatever it is they do these days, or even worse, sat fat and miserable and watching daytime television, drinking vodka by the tumbler-full and waiting for his disability cheque to come in. So their 'chat', on which she'd pinned quite a few hopes since he turned up three days ago, had come to nothing. What would Tom say?

What would Tom say? Tom isn't here. This thought takes her into even muddier waters. She sits up in bed and fusses with Blue to take her mind off it. One of her favourite cats, Pretty – christened by Lucy – had always been ready to be fussed over. When you came near she'd instantly arch her back up towards you and then roll on the ground, ecstatic. 'Why can't you be more like her, you oaf?' she whispers to Blue, and he opens one eye to look up at her haughtily before rolling over and facing away from her, twitching the tip of his tail. Useless cat. She gives up on Blue. A different kind of feeling settles on her, dispersing the faint prickly annoyance she's carried all day. She recognises this one – it's loneliness. But not just any old loneliness – she is feeling the lack of her lover. She wishes she could just have a hand here to hold, or a neck to snuggle into, or an arm draped around her waist. The anger returns with the loss, and they fight inside her like netted fish. She's wide awake now – cold, hungry again after a disappointing dinner, and lost. She lets out a little whimper, the sound a dog might make to himself when he's given up on being noticed, and curls into a ball. She tries to think of something else, and fails again and again. She takes a pinch of the skin on her side and holds on to it, as if holding on to the side of a cliff with her fingertips. She misses the fat underneath the skin – she feels so empty.

Eventually she remembers a visualisation technique that Tom taught her, where she imagines travelling slowly from her head down to her stomach. When she's there she can open an imaginary door to a calming scene of her choice – a tropical beach, a woodland, a luxury hotel room. She takes her time on the journey down from the crown of her head, relaxing her muscles as she goes. As she focuses on each part of her body she realises how tense she is. Forehead, neck, shoulders, arms… if only there were someone here to dig their hands into the flesh between her shoulder blades. She reaches the door and opens it to her favourite place – her study in her parent's house. There is Blue on the armchair, and also Pretty, and all of her old dead cats. They're curled up on the window-seat, washing their cheeks, perched on her desk, stretched out across the floor. Their purring trembles in the air. She's added a bed to the room in her imagination, and a huge window looking out onto a long garden, not like her parent's garden at all. It's spring, and in the centre of her view a white magnolia tree is in full flower. There's a ring of white and dark purple tulips planted around its trunk, mirroring the sphere of the branches. Squirrels run along the fences and jump into trees, and robins and blackbirds skip across the lawn looking for imaginary worms. A lake stretches out from the bottom of the garden and there are mountains behind it, and a solitary wisp of cloud. She moves three cats to lie on her imaginary bed and looks out at the scene. There is nobody else in the room. She can only hear purring. The leaves on the trees shimmer in the breeze. Sleep drifts slowly over her body and covers her like snow.

Chapter 8

St. Mary's Convent of Mercy
Brighton
Sussex

30th of September, '59

My dear Bea,

So – where had I got to last time? I've started three letters to you this week, but each time something or other has happened. Some of the girls put on a little play last night, and I helped them with their costumes. Everyone swaps their clothes around – it seems silly not to when you keep growing out of them. I've been keeping an eye on Doll too, she's been quiet this week, and seems out of sorts. I wonder what you've been doing since I arrived here. I can imagine you going to work every morning, wearing your smart red dress, and maybe a trip to the cinema with Bill at the weekend. Maybe you've got a new best friend now I'm gone. Maybe you meet with them for coffee and gossip about your idiotic friend Elizabeth stuck in a mother and baby home and getting bigger by the day! I am getting bigger by the day, Bea – when I wake up in the morning I feel like my dinner from the night before has all been transformed into baby over night.

I think I was telling you about that nasty doctor in my last letter. I felt pretty wretched after that. Suddenly it all felt terribly real, and I realised that I wasn't going to be able to close my eyes and wait for it all to go away. I started writing lists late at night in my bedroom, with all my different options, the pros and cons, whether I would make a good mother or not. I even wrote down everything I knew about back-street abortions – Half Moon Street, those black pills. The list I wrote most often was 'telling mum and dad – pros and cons'. The pros were rather short, Bea, and the cons went over the page. Dad's shame at having to tell his colleagues at work, mum trying to force me to give the baby to her to look after – I knew she would. Even having to look them in the eyes, afterwards. I can hear mum calling me a silly little bitch, or worse. I don't know if she'd actually say the words, but I know she'd be thinking them. And dad not thinking about me in the same way every again, and looking at me with... what is it? Disdain – that's it. The kind of look he gave me when I was caught at school showing you my exam paper so you could copy. I couldn't bear that, Bea, really I couldn't. It felt like the only way I could really decide what I wanted to do about the whole thing was to get away from them. Almost that it might be the best chance my baby had of staying with me.

In the end I had the idea of getting in touch with Marjory. Do you remember her? She lived next door to us when I was little, and I called her auntie. She was always so sweet to me. I used to find her so easy to talk to – I told her about getting my period before I even told mum. We've written letters to each other ever since she moved to Brighton – I think I showed you one once, that one when she drew a picture of her garden for me. I looked into mother and baby homes first, and I found one in Brighton – they said they'd accept me for an interview and I booked an appointment for the next week. But I knew I'd be too big by the time they'd accept me – they only took girls 6 weeks before they were due – and so I thought maybe I could stay with Marjory until then. I wanted to offer her some proper rent, using the money that gran left me – I was saving it for my wedding. Maybe I won't need it for that now anyway! I hadn't seen Marjory for five years and we'd only spoken on the phone a couple of times, she called me on my birthday sometimes, so I was ever so nervous writing to her. It felt terrible, asking her such a lot – when I posted the letter I got an attack of the nerves and tried to fish it back out of the post-box. Anyway, she called me, at home, and she just said, 'You poor honey. Just come down, straight away.' After I put the phone down, I had to say something to mum about being desperate for the loo, and I ran upstairs and burst into tears. There wasn't even a tone in her voice, Bea. She talked to me as if I was normal. Why couldn't I have had her as a mum? I shouldn't say that, I know mum loves me and does her best.

She wrote me a letter after that. It was her that came up with the idea of saying her husband Roger had need of a temp in his office, and she'd thought of me. Everyone seemed to buy it all right. Dad even said it might be 'good for my prospects' until mum told him to stop being silly, that I only had a few more years before I settled down with a nice husband and started my 'proper job'. I'm so sorry I had to lie to you, Bea. It probably all makes more sense to you now, why I kept being elusive about the details in all those postcards I sent you. Always remembering to leave off my address, saying I was enjoying my new job, telling you nothing. Marjory was really good to me for all those weeks, and so was her husband. He didn't have much choice in the matter anyway, he joked to us once at breakfast, but he didn't make me feel awkward, not once. He was out at work a lot of the time anyway, working late into the evening, and so me and Marjory had some nice evenings together, preparing dinner for Roger and watching the television, Marjory with her knitting needles clicking away like she was an old woman. I teased her about that, about being old. She teased me about getting bigger, and it was nice – I don't know if I would have liked anyone else to do it. She said it was good for her to have some company.

I often made myself scarce during the day-time, not wanting to be under her feet all the time, and spent hours walking along the beach. It was the end of Spring, getting warmer, but with a chill in the air. I just couldn't get enough of sitting on a bench at the back of the beach and letting the sea talk to me – that sounds silly, but it did. It said the same things to me over and over, 'keep well', and 'you're fine'. I got talking to a young lad one day, he was only 16 and probably had a silly crush on me, but after the first few times he relaxed a bit and we just chatted about rubbish – he'd tell me about his dad, and how wonderful he was, and I'd talk about my job and you and what it was like staying with Marjory. We must have looked a funny pair, but it was good to have someone to talk to, someone who didn't seem to be making his mind up about what kind of a person I was. He was awfully sweet. I really missed you, on those days out in Brighton, wandering about and spending a little bit of money on a cup of tea or a crumpet. I kept seeing all these little things that I wanted to point out to you, or tell you when I got home, and you weren't there. I can't remember any of them now. They can't have been very important after all, I suppose.

I was sorry to leave Marjory's house, although I'm sure they were pleased to get their spare room back again, especially Roger. I still see her – twice a week we meet in the afternoon at a café around the corner and I tell her all the latest gossip from the home. She often brings me a little something – a slice of cake wrapped up in grease-proof paper, or a magazine. Last week she brought me a spider plant to keep in my room. I'm so lucky. It's odd – most of the girls here seem to have no family at all – nobody visits. Apart from Susie, whose mother lives just a few roads away – they seem to get on like a house on fire so I'm not really sure what Susie's doing here. I'd like to tell you more about the girls – maybe I will in my next letter. I hope you're not getting terribly bored by me rambling on like this. I can see you stifling a yawn and shuffling the papers to see how much more you have to read.

Anyway, I've put my address at the top this time, because I can't bear you not knowing where I am. I've had more than my share of secrets, I really am sick of them! I only ask you one thing Bea – PLEASE PLEASE PLEASE don't tell anyone what's going on or where I am, it would ruin everything. I just need some time to think things through, to decide what I'm going to do afterwards. I know it's putting you in an awkward position, if anyone asks after me, and I don't want you to have to make things up. I'll be back before long, and I can sort everything out then.

Lots and lots of love as always, to everyone, but especially to you,

Elizabeth xxx

Chapter 9

After the cycling incident, Violet was forced to admit that there was definitely something wrong with her. She'd been feeling dizzy for a few weeks, mostly first thing in the morning, but had put it down to the stress she'd been soaking up at work for the past few months. Amongst other complications one of her colleagues had left abruptly after a raging row with their Head of Department, and Violet had got the short straw of covering his work. Things weren't going brilliantly at home either – she hadn't spent much time with Charles recently, who'd been busier than ever with his own work, and the house felt empty now that Lucy, Josie and Megan were living with an assortment of boyfriends and friends up and down the country. That morning the dizziness had swept over her again when she got out of the bath, and she had to perch on the edge, with her forehead resting on the sink, and wait for the white sparks to stop dancing in front of her eyes. She'd felt better after a bit of toast and had hopped onto her bike as usual. She had just passed the post box when a rush of faintness came over her again, more suddenly than usual. She had to make an emergency stop and half-stepped, half-fell onto the pavement where she, to her embarrassment, rested her head on one knee as her bicycle fell haphazardly onto the kerb.

Luckily an elderly man rounded the corner a few moments later with his daily newspaper. He stopped and put a hand on her back, saying 'Excuse me, have you taken a fall, young lady?' She heard the 'young lady' part through a haze of nausea and smiled to herself. At fifty she wouldn't be likely to hear herself described in that way many more times. The man insisted on waiting with her until she'd gathered her strength back. He also told her that she shouldn't get back on her bike because she'd be likely to cause an accident. She did as she was told and phoned her mother, feeling like a complete idiot. Her mother was all brisk efficiency, and for once Violet was glad of it. Her father managed to get her bike in the back of their massive Volvo, and they took her home and put her to bed. Her mother brought her hot sweet tea and digestive biscuits on a tray, and then the cordless phone so Violet could call her boss and then the doctor, 'just to get yourself checked out'. She made an appointment for later that afternoon.

Violet hated going to the local Health Centre. Except for cervical smears, she hadn't visited them to talk about her own health for at least ten years, and avoided taking the children whenever she could. It wasn't that she had anything against the doctors – some were alright and some were bloody awful – that was just the way people were. It was the whole antiquated system that got up her nose. There was never anywhere to park, and the building was ugly and depressing. She hated the receptionist's fake smile, and the shabby waiting room full of people coughing their germs at you. Whoever picked up those leaflets? Why would you want to read about 'living with incontinence' in a public place, or admit to needing to diagnose your venereal disease? And then there was the notice board, advertising self-help groups for 'women who loved their dogs too much' or some such rubbish. When she was finally called in to see him, the doctor on duty wasn't very enlightening. Although he did at least try to be genial. He was a keen young man and she could almost imagine his tail thumping behind him on the carpet when she got a bit frustrated at him and he upped his efforts to be liked. He arranged for the nurse to take some bodily fluids from her and told her to take a few days off work, that they'd let her know when the tests came back. Violet went back home to bed and lay there over the next few days as energy seeped from her body and dripped onto the floor like honey.

The test results, as Violet had suspected, weren't conclusive. Her blood did seem to be low in iron, but not enough to 'completely explain her symptoms'. She had a series of nasty tests to rule out horrible sounding things like fibroids and bleeding polyps – all clear. Next she was put onto iron tablets – they were meant to be taken on an empty stomach but this made her feel too queasy. She started popping laxatives alongside the iron pills to correct the common side effect, and was also put onto an iron-rich diet with endless red meat and spinach. When she hadn't improved much after a couple of weeks, there was talk of M.E. Violet had once known a woman with M.E. who seemed unable to lift her head from her pillow some days, but quite able to dance energetically to her favourite band when they passed through town. Violet didn't like to think of herself as in the same category as this woman, and told the doctor that he'd 'just have to come up with something less bloody ridiculous'. In the end what her G.P. mostly did, apart from occasionally sending her to the hospital for unpleasant tests that came to nothing, was to 'keep an eye on her'. Meanwhile Violet lay in her bed and felt completely unable to get up.

Violet didn't do 'being ill' as a rule. Illness was firmly disapproved of by her mother, and she and her sisters had grown up mocking those mere mortals who had time off school because they had a little sniffle, or who let migraines take hold of them rather than setting off on a brisk walk and flushing the pain out with fresh air. Her mother had been blessed with good health, and it was much easier for her father to fight (or conceal) illness than it was to admit to his wife that he wasn't feeling well. Violet remembers walking into his study once and finding him flat out on the carpet with his head under his desk, napping. He'd said he just had a 'little headache' that was already fading, and begged Violet not to tell her mother that she'd found him asleep. In recent years her mother had started getting arthritis in her wrists in the wintertime, and her father was on medication for his low blood pressure, but Violet had no sympathy and dealt with them in the way she'd been taught, by telling them that they were making a fuss, or by leaving them alone with their ailments. The last 'proper' illness Violet could remember was when she got poisoned by the shrimps at the local Chinese, and she spent the day at work disappearing to the toilet every half hour to be sick. One of the secretaries (a kind mumsy type who always got on Violet's nerves) tried to get her to go home several times during the morning, but grew annoyed at Violet's pointless stoicism and withdrew her sympathy by lunchtime.

The illness knocked away all of the structures that usually propped Violet up. Her career had always been central to her, and a small corner of her believed that she was utterly indispensable to the department. If she were to leave, the whole place would crumble through ineptitude and ignorance into a kind of jumbled heap. It was good of her Head of Department to call her every Monday, but she wished he wouldn't keep saying with such conviction that things were running along fine without her. As days became weeks, she grew certain that when she returned they'd say her work had all been easily covered, and that they wanted to know exactly what she HAD been doing for all of these years. It also provoked difficult questions about her marriage. Charles' reaction was a complete shock to her. They had been quite distant from each other for many years, but she had always relied on him being there in the shadows, doing jobs round the house, bringing her tea and generally ministering to her. He seemed to like doing things for her, and so she'd expected him to revel in her illness, feeding her grapes and searching down new detective stories for her to read. Instead it was as if he had become allergic to her. In the beginning he'd hover at her bedroom door (they'd been sleeping in separate rooms for some time because of Charles' snoring) and ask her whether she was feeling any better. When she said not really, he'd disagree and say her cheeks definitely had more colour than they had yesterday, or that her voice sounded more 'lively'. She saw less and less of him, and eventually he'd pass messages to her via her mother – 'Tell her I've managed to book the car in for a service tomorrow,' or 'Say hello.' Say hello? When Violet spoke to her mother about it she said, 'But you know he needs you to be the strong one, darling,' as if she were completely stupid. She lost her independence too – her ability to move herself around, her ability to read and think things through. She couldn't even boss other people around any more – she spoke from her bed with a weak voice and discovered her authority had melted away. Being ill stripped away everything that had kept her safe.

It also sucked away at her flesh. She'd never been overweight exactly, but her mother had once described her as 'beefy'. She had a tall frame and large hands and feet and the fat covered her evenly, giving her a little stomach and folds on her back rather than gathering where it ought to on her breasts, hips and thighs. It was her stomach that she noticed first. She caught a glimpse of herself under the covers and could see new shapes between her hip bones and her navel – a different landscape, with concave dips and hollows where there weren't any before. She'd twist her stomach to one side, lifting her leg, just to watch herself and get to know the new contours of her body. Next she was aware of her legs getting thinner, and her arms, especially above the elbow. One day she looked in the mirror and was shocked by her new face. There were angles where there hadn't been any before, and her eyes seemed a brighter violet, and bigger. It scared her a bit, and she wondered if she had an undiagnosed disease that would carry on wasting her flesh until she was gone. But she liked it too. She couldn't work out if she felt less of a woman or more – there were fewer curves, less flesh in her tits, less to squeeze on her bottom. But there was more of a cinch in her waist now, and those were indubitably a woman's hip bones. She'd stroke herself under the covers at night, especially the area from her belly button down to her pubic hair, noticing the feel of her bones under her skin. She'd lazily touch herself, running her fingers through the tightly-curled hair before pressing one flat finger down on her clitoris. She didn't bring herself to orgasm – she somehow felt too ill for that, too tired, but she aroused herself to a certain safe point and it brought her comfort.

She got to know her body again over those weeks and months, as if getting to know the body of a new lover. There was so little to do, especially in the early days when she couldn't concentrate for long enough to read to the end of a sentence. She'd drift in and out of sleep for most of the day, but when she was awake she'd mostly just look and listen. Her mother had moved her bed so she could see out the window, and she saw birds balancing on the telegraph wire, the tops of buses floating above the hedge, an occasional brush-tailed squirrel. And why hadn't she noticed how many different types of clouds there were before? Different shapes, colours, textures, sizes – and they moved, they changed all the time! Some mornings she felt she could lie there and watch them forever without getting bored. She became intimate with the noises of the house – the low whir of the heating as it warmed up, the exact placing of the creaks on the stairs. She looked forward to hearing blackbirds, and rain. There were small shifts in her mind as well. She often felt slightly heady, feverish – her thoughts were a little more colourful, a little more random, like a dream. She'd see herself rising from her bed like Jesus from the cave when she was cured, and it felt ridiculous to her that she might just go back to work as if nothing had happened. She imagined her colleagues sitting in their little offices and getting on with their jobs – the boring routine, the fierce struggles for small gains in power, the complicated politics. The work that had given her meaning for most of her life began to lose its importance – began to seem, even, a little silly.

In the seventh week of her illness she decided that she had to divorce Charles. The realisation came all at once, like a guillotine. Once this thought arrived, others fell into place around it. Did she want her old life back minus Charles? Did she want to carry on living here alone with her parents? Did she want to go back to the same job? No, no, no. A new beginning was necessary, a rebirth. After that it was just a matter of thinking through the practicalities. She made endless lists in her head – tell the children, ask work whether they would allow her a sabbatical, look for somewhere else to live. The thoughts were exhilarating, and she started to feel frustrated with her body for the first time. She'd need her body if she wanted to get things done. Almost immediately she noticed her energy gradually returning, like drips into an empty cup. Soon she was able to have daily baths, get about the house, and make herself tea and toast. She took her first faltering journey to the local shop, her mother on standby if she needed to be driven home. Her doctor pronounced he'd known she would recover all along. Her appetite returned, and food became a pleasure again rather than a chore. And then one day, a trip to the swimming pool. She'd been craving the feeling of buoyancy for weeks. As she pushed her arms through the cool water she noticed everything. Children's shrieks blurring around the edges. That old woman, lumpy in her black costume, grinning under the hot shower. The thick chlorine smell, the light skipping on the water, the shifting topaz blue of the bottom of the pool. Everywhere she turned there was beauty.

Chapter 10

George Livingstone is Abbotsfield's only famous author, unless you count Florence Mackerby, who knocked out a few Mills and Boon before she married the vicar. Violet was first acquainted with George through her work for the Committee. Margaret sent her to his big house on the coast the past Spring to ask him whether he'd be willing to donate any prizes to the Grand Fête. She came away with a promised huge ham for the produce section, a promised three-wheeler buggy for the most bouncing baby competition, and three month's supply of promised Pedigree Chum for the winner of the dog show. Violet has been back a few times to pick things up or make further arrangements, and is slowly getting to know George and his wife Yevgeniya. Most years George opens the Fête with a little speech. She doubts the villagers who gather to hear him talk are familiar with his oeuvre, but his face occasionally appears on daytime television and that's good enough for them. He writes a strange concoction of sci-fi and murder mystery – not Violet's kind of thing at all, but when she mentioned his name to Guy last week, he went into raptures about Livingstone's 'post-ironic genius' and his 'gift for embodying the consciousness of the decade'. Phrases picked straight from of a poncy review if she'd ever heard them. Ever since then Guy has been pestering her to introduce them, and when they'd bumped into George in the local shop she couldn't avoid it any longer. George had been quick to notice the admiring gleam in Guy's eye and, not being one to pass up the opportunity of an appreciative audience, he invited them both to dinner that weekend.

Violet had decided they'd walk the two miles to the big house – mostly along single-file country lanes. It seems somehow wrong to use her car for such a short distance, especially as it isn't raining. She's come to relish the feeling of her blood pumping through her muscles. She imagines the cold air reaching all her tiny alveoli and feeding her rich, sea-filtered oxygen, and all the dark pollutants being puffed out and carried away and dissolving back into the sea. She listens to Guy as they walk, or rather keeps her mouth shut and allows him to witter on and on. She finds herself drifting away a few times but pulls herself back to what he's saying, like a gentle pull on a horse's reins. Listening properly is such hard work, especially when people seem to say the same thing over and over. Why won't he stop talking, calm down? As he pauses to pick up a stone she's struck by a rare moment of empathy. He's nervous! Tom would congratulate her for that, sounding warmly affectionate or harshly sarcastic depending on how hopeless Violet had been recently. The longer she was with Tom, the more Violet came to realise how completely unaware she was of what was going on in other people's minds. It wasn't that she didn't care, it was just that she never seemed to have learnt the knack of reading faces or body language, and so had come to regard people as generally unpredictable and illogical. They always seemed to be getting angry with her for no reason or dropping shocks into conversations. Was it too late for her to start learning the art of people-reading?

They turn off the narrow lane onto a long driveway and catch the first sight of the moderately grand Victorian house standing alone behind trees, silhouetted against the sky. Who planted those horrible poplars? The last time she visited, George took her to the bottom of the garden and across a field to the sea, but you can't see it from anywhere in the house. As they crunch down the gravel to the front door, Guy links his arm through Violet's. He went through a phase of doing this when he was a spotty sixteen year old, full of himself, showing off his mum to his friends. She'd told Tom about it once – how embarrassed she felt to be displayed like that, like an accessory. Tom had suggested that maybe he actually needed to hang onto her, rather than the other way round. She thinks of this now, and it reaffirms her earlier suspicion that Guy is struggling with his nerves. She's getting good at this! What she is actually expected to do with this information, she doesn't have the faintest idea. She listens as he makes some loud clever-clogs comment about the wind-chime made from shells hanging under the eaves, obviously one of Yevgeniya's additions, and Violet allows herself a knowing smile. Guy notices it instantly.

'What?' he says, too loudly, and he's still waiting for an explanation when the door opens before they've even knocked.

It's George himself. His hair seems particularly rebellious this evening, bristling out of his nose and ears, eyebrows wild. The author picture he uses on his book jackets is of a rather younger him – maybe in his early fifties – and you can see that he'd been a handsome man in a dark, unusual way. You'd need a lot more imagination these days, and Violet wonders if Guy is disappointed with this ordinary-looking man. If he is, he makes a fine job of covering it up.

'Wow, Mr. Livingstone. It's really… You're my… I don't know how to tell you…' He peters off, to finish a few seconds later with a second, quieter 'wow'.

'Well well, that's not the sort of greeting I get from my dinner guests every day. Marvellous to see you Violet, do come in, do come in. Yevgeniya is doing something finicky in the kitchen, but there's a pot of tea waiting for you in the sitting room. Unless you'd prefer something stronger?'

George ushers them through and Guy cranes his neck around him as they go, as if walking through a stately home or a museum. Violet sees the place again through her son's eyes, and unlike the first time she was here she manages to look past the dust and neglect. It's high-ceilinged and every room is packed with furniture of varying quality and age. The wallpaper is mostly floral and fading, the curtains are drab velvet, and there are dark nooks and crannies everywhere. She realises that this place must have been pretty grand in its time – there are some magnificent features; she notices a fanlight brightening the hall, and a grand ironwork fireplace. She wonders how it had looked before George was married. She supposes that at least it's cleaner now, and there are fresh vases of flowers sitting on various tables. In the sitting room there is a tray of tea as promised, and they both sit down on a plush green sofa. George pours their tea and then settles back into a battered, brown leather armchair, looking like a Bond villain.

'So – your mother tells me that you enjoy my books.'

He just couldn't wait, she thinks. And they're off – Guy telling him which books are his favourites, and asking him hesitantly where he got the idea for Pelican-man. Did he ever give himself nightmares about his own characters? How long did it take to write each novel? George is happy to oblige, and prepares to talk at length about his favourite subject – himself. Violet nods politely for a while, but she's aware that she's never been very skilled at faking an interest. She isn't really a part of the conversation anyway, and so waits for George to take a breath and announces she's going to see if Yevgeniya needs any help in the kitchen.

It certainly sent a shockwave through the village when George first turned up at church with his new bride. Various people had gossiped about where he might have found her, and the favourite theories were that she might be a rabid fan of his books who'd written for an autograph and got more than she'd bargained for, or a woman from 'one of these new-fangled foreign bride catalogues', as Rob put it. Yevgeniya is certainly young – at least twenty years younger than George at a guess. She has an interesting face – Violet didn't think you would get away with calling her 'pretty' – her chin is a little too square and her forehead a little too high. She always wears her thin dark hair pulled back hard into a knot at the back of her neck, and this accentuates the odd lines. She doesn't smile very often, but there's a rebellious energy to her, a liveliness, which Violet noticed and liked the first time she met her. She comes from somewhere in Eastern Europe (was it the Ukraine?), and her accent is strong. She likes to be called 'Zhenya' for short, with the first 'zh' like the middle part of pleasure. Violet remembers Angie repeatedly mispronouncing it as 'Shen-yer', managing to make it sound more like she was brought up on a city housing estate with her friends Chantelle and Jade. If George were more famous or more rich, maybe he'd have been able to choose someone more conventionally beautiful. Or maybe Violet underestimates him – maybe he really does love her.

Yevgeniya is standing motionless at the work surface next to the sink, looking out into the dark of the garden. Violet feels like an intruder and considers sloping back to the others, or at least retreating to make another, noisier entrance, when Yevgeniya catches sight of her reflection in the window and spins around.

'Violet! You surprise me!'

Her pronunciation of Violet is closer to Vahl-yet, and Violet loves the sound of it. She's always enjoyed having an unusual name, and Yevgeniya renders it even more exotic than usual.

'Yevgeniya.' She's sure her pronunciation of Yevgeniya is equally as warped to the other woman's ears.

'Please, I said before, Zhenya.'

'Zhenya, then.'

A slightly awkward silence descends between them. Violet is used to it – her presence often seems to usher in some kind of discomfort She's noticed it in her daughters sometimes too – it must be in the female Ackerman gene. Yevgeniya picks up a scrumpled tea-towel from the table and hangs it back on a hook near the sink, and this action seems to give her the time she needs to think of something to say.

'Your son is here?'

'Yes, he's in the sitting room, sharing stories with your husband. He's being a good fan.'

At this Yevgeniya rolls her eyes and flings back her head, making a loud 'tsk' sound. Violet almost jumps.

'We shall be hearing about his new book all evening now. Prepare yourself, Vahl-yet. It might be better if we are hiding in here.'

Violet loves the lack of respect Yevgeniya shows towards her husband's writing. She enjoys listening to her tease her husband about the plots of his novels, which tend to show a passing resemblance to each other, or gently mocking his 'artist temper'. The 'fan' based theories of their strange union must be wrong – she can't imagine this woman writing a fan letter to anyone. It makes her like George a bit more too – he can't be a total egotist if he's chosen to live with this woman. 'She's only interested in those cheap celebrity rags,' he confided in Violet the last time she was here, his tone a mixture of exasperation and fond affection.

'Can I help you with anything?'

This question has often saved Violet at stilted dinner parties or rowdy gatherings. It comes not from a desire to be helpful, but from a preference to stay out of the lime-light, and to avoid those bloody awful clumps of people she doesn't know talking about things she doesn't care about. She hates that awful hover you're expected to do when you approach a new group, while you're waiting to see if there'll be an opening for you. She's noticed that the more submissive women in the group often look over and smile at her encouragingly, insinuating the both of you are really out of your depth with all these men. She hates that more than anything. She's perfectly happy talking to the men, but there are just so many pompous, boring people out there... Yevgeniya gives her the job of setting the table, and she is grateful.

After she's finished arranging the heavy cutlery and the rough cream napkins, they both work at chopping fresh parsley to sprinkle on the soup. They stand side by side in comfortable companionship, and Violet is seized by the urge to tell Yevgeniya about the letters. She has the feeling that she might understand – she has travelled half-way around the world to this strange house in the middle of nowhere, and she might be less surprised by something unusual. Maybe Yevgeniya would have an idea about what to do. Violet follows the train of thought and starts to think about Elizabeth, and whether she'll get more letters. She couldn't bear not to know what happens to her, and to her baby. As her thoughts ramble on, she feels completely unable to tell Yevgeniya again – what changed? Why do those moments of opportunity pass so quickly, and why doesn't she take advantage of them more often? Yevgeniya announces in a loud voice to the other room that they 'must eat'. The men traipse straight through into the dining room, still talking nineteen to the dozen. The secret sits a little higher on Violet's chest all evening, lodged in her, aching.

Dinner goes surprisingly well. Guy and George form quite a double act, and even Yevgeniya laughs at their banter. It's strange for Violet to hear George taking Guy's writing ambitions seriously. She wonders how long it is since she's taken his wild plans seriously herself. Over cheese and biscuits they move on to alien architecture, of all things, and Violet finally feels she's in an area she knows something about. She uses her knowledge to hypothesise about the implications of building in a lighter atmosphere, or of certain gases on various building materials. At one point she glances over at Guy and he's watching her with a look that could only really be described as pride. It flushes her with a feeling of pleasure and she loses her place for a minute, shy. Yevgeniya suggests coffee – everything she says sounds like an announcement, and it reminds Violet a little of Margaret's way of speaking. They retire to a different room, the 'den', and sit comfortably in the misshapen shabby sofas. Yevgeniya circles the room with a lighter to light the candles, which, except for a string of fairy lights strung around the windows, provide the only illumination in the room. The talk turns to the weather, always an easy topic. Violet feels like a cat curled up on a warm pile of clean laundry, until she remembers their long walk home in the dark. There seems to be some kind of a rising tension in the air between Yevgeniya and George – Guy raises his eye-brows at her across the room when

Yevgeniya makes yet another cutting remark. This seems like a good enough excuse for them to be going, to let their hosts have a proper argument in privacy, and so they gather their doggy bag of bread and butter pudding for the next day and wrap themselves up into balls of scarf and hat and click on their torches ready for the walk back.

Back at home, Violet has already said goodnight to Guy and drunk most of her peppermint tea when she notices her answer phone blinking with three messages. A single message is unusual enough, as Mother only calls her at the weekend, and the children will usually wait for her to call them. There isn't anyone else who calls. She has a strange swooping sensation in her stomach immediately. Could it be Tom? Before she listens to the messages she fumbles in her handbag to check her mobile phone and realises that it's been switched off all evening. She switches it on and sees that someone has tried to reach her on her mobile too, four times. She doesn't recognise the number. She shoos Blue away so she can concentrate, and presses the 'play message' button. It's her daughter, Megan.

'Mum, it's me, could you call me when you've got a free minute please? There's something I need to talk to you about. Nothing to worry about. I'll try your mobile now. Thanks, Mum.'

As the machine beeps, Violet reflects that her voice sounds a little thick, as if she's been crying.

'Mum, me again, it's – I don't know if you got my last message. I don't want to be a pain, but I could really do with talking to you tonight. You're not answering your mobile. Are you there? …I guess not – well, I'll… I'll speak to you when you're back. Bye.'

What is it? Why won't she say?

'Mum, look, don't worry, but I really do want to speak to you tonight and I wanted to tell you to call me even if you're back really late – I'll still be up. Love you.'

This last one worries her the most – Megan never tells her that she loves her. Josie went through a phase of doing it, when she was fifteen and all of her school-friends were hugging each other and holding hands all the time. She'd say it in front of everyone, more like a showing off – 'Love you lots, see you later,' or 'Loving you and leaving you, Mother.' When she hit eighteen she was back to 'Mum' and the 'love you's disappeared.

She dials Megan's number too quickly the first time, and the phone rings and rings before being answered by a gruff-sounding old man.

'Hello?'

'Oh, is that – have I got the wrong number?'

'I don't know, love, who are you looking for?'

'My daughter. Umm, Megan.'

'Sorry, love.'

'That's OK, sorry to trouble you.'

He did sound genuinely sorry, and she's hung up and dialled again before she realises she must have woken him up; he must have been worried. She hadn't apologised enough. This time the phone only rings twice before it is picked up. She notices she needs to take a deep breath as her daughter's quiet voice comes onto the line, to get more oxygen into her body.

'Meera?'

'It's Viol– it's your mother, Meg.'

'Oh, Mum.' She sounds disappointed, and despite the circumstances of the call Violet feels a little hurt. 'I thought it was going to be… you got my messages?'

'We were out, our phones were – we've just got in. What is it?'

'Oh, it's mostly OK now, there was… I thought that… it's OK now, I'm sorry for bothering you.'

Violet feels a strong surge of anger rising up in her throat despite herself. It knocks her mouth open and almost takes her breath from her. She isn't surprised when the next words out of her mouth are the kind she'll instantly regret.

'Meg! You stupid… you… I was worried absolutely sick! What do you think you're doing, calling in the middle of the night like that? I thought someone had died!'

On the word died there's a break in her stream of anger and to her surprise her voice almost cracks. Her voice has risen and in the silence that follows she hears a stumbled banging noise coming from the study upstairs. What an idiot she is, what an idiot. She should say sorry now, she really should. Meg still isn't saying anything. And as Guy bursts into the room, with no shirt on and his hair all mussed up and his eyes all squinty and puffy, and looks to her with quizzical concern, she hears a quiet 'click' and the phone goes dead.

Chapter 11

St. Mary's Convent of Mercy
Brighton
Sussex

6th of October, '59

Bea,

Here I am again. No letter from you yet, but I wasn't expecting one, not really. You're quite right not to write. I've betrayed you badly by keeping all of this a secret, and not letting you share it with me. By not trusting you. Sometimes I still try to fool myself that it was all for your benefit, that I didn't want to burden you, put you in a difficult position... I don't know. I was talking to Ruby last night, one of the older girls who's been very kind to me. She said I must have been thinking about you, because it's obvious how much I care about you. But the truth... The truth is that if I didn't tell you, I didn't have to face the full truth myself. The facts. The ones

I'm still not facing. I don't know how you feel about anything yet. I'm quite terrified of you writing and saying 'you must keep the baby', or 'you must give the baby away'. I don't trust myself to go against what you say, you're so often right about these things, but even worse – if I did the opposite of what you thought best then, well maybe our friendship wouldn't survive it. I can't ask you not to tell me what you think, that would be silly. But I'm dreading it, Bea, finding out what you think I should do.

The baby. I haven't talked about it much yet, have I? It's getting more and more difficult to ignore it. The size of it is one thing – I can't pretend I'm just gathering fat around my tummy any more. When I press my stomach I can't avoid the fact that there's a lump of bone and gristle in there, something separate to my own flesh, getting bigger and becoming a person. And there's movement too... I felt it move for the first time a few weeks ago now, a kind of shivering feeling deep inside me. It made me cry. And I'm talking to it now, Bea, I can't help myself. My original plan was to stay separate from it, almost as if it was someone else's, because that's what might happen anyway. I talked about it with Marjory, and she agreed – she said it sounded like a good idea if I was going to keep my options open. But there isn't really anyone here who knows me properly, not really, and I feel so lonely sometimes late at night or doing my polishing or laundry during the long afternoons. At least the baby understands. I know that sounds silly. I just witter on, really – mostly in my head, but when I know that no-one else is around I'll whisper to it. It's making me feel sad, writing this. I don't want to stop writing yet though, when I'm writing to you I can almost imagine that you're here. Do you mind if I change the subject? I said I was going to write about the girls, didn't I? Last time I wrote?

We're a funny old bunch really. I don't know where I got it from, but before I arrived here I had this strange notion that I'd be the oldest one here, the most sensible. I imagined it as a refuge for waifs and strays who'd made terrible decisions and came from deprived, loveless families – what a snob! There are all sorts of different girls. There are about twenty of us altogether, half of us in various stages of pregnancy and half looking after their babies. The oldest girl is Trudie, who's 34 – she's a sweetheart. One of the nuns whispered to me that it's her third visit and that she's desperate to be married and prays for a man every night. She's not really bad looking, except her teeth which point out a bit, and she's got an awfully sweet nature. What is it about people that they can't find someone to love them? It doesn't seem fair. The youngest is Doll, the girl I share a room with. The newest girl is Mary, she turned up last week in the middle of the night, a real palaver. Her mum had said she was going to push Mary down the stairs to get rid of the baby, one of the other girls told me. She was hysterical, they put her in her own room that night and she didn't even come down for any meals the next day, the nuns took them up on a tray. The next morning she turned up at breakfast looking all forlorn and ashamed. Every eye in the place was on her – I felt sorry for her. Then there's a little group we call the 'golden girls' – they're all pretty and most of them are blond. The kind of girls who'd get all the first dances, you know. I'm not one of them, Bea, but you probably would be. They're nice enough but they keep themselves to themselves and I dare say a bit of gossiping goes on. They don't seem to acknowledge that they're in a pickle at all – as if it's the only way to have a child, completely normal, and they have loving husbands waiting for them on the outside and a nice new semi-detached in Hove. Peg is a real character – she's always wanted to be a 'comic actress' and spends her days devising new skits and jokes to try out on us all. Rose, bless her, is what your mum would call 'soft in the head', and I've heard the nuns talking amongst themselves about what they'll do with her baby when it arrives – any day now – she's hardly capable of remembering her own breakfast, so they're not sure how she'll cope. She's decided she's keeping her baby, and getting a job as a home help. She has this great fantasy about finding a lovely family with a small baby the same age as hers and spending all her time looking after them and talking about 'matters of the world' with her employees. We all say 'that'll be lovely, Rose,' when she talks to us about it, we haven't got the heart. Most of us feel faintly guilty around her and have taken to keeping out of her way. I've said about Ruby already, haven't I? You'd love her, Bea, I do hope you get to meet her one day.

And then there's Doll. I think I talked about her a bit last time I wrote? I told you that her eyes were terribly sad all the time? And that I couldn't get her to confide in me? This Tuesday just gone we were playing cards in the main room after tea – me, Peg, Queenie and a couple of the others, and chatting about our families. Queenie was talking about her cousins up in Liverpool, and how when they meet up she feels really comfy and relaxed even though she hardly ever sees them. A couple of the others were all generally agreeing, and suddenly Doll, who'd been quiet, said, 'You're all talking a load of fucking rubbish.' Her voice was loud and shrill and she sort of spat the words at us. I hadn't heard her swear before, not like that. We just gaped at her like stupid goldfish. Eventually Ruby said 'we didn't mean...' but she trailed off, as she didn't really know what Doll was so upset about. The silence was horrid, Bea, it went on for AGES. And then all of a sudden Doll said 'my little sister doesn't feel relaxed with my dad.' Her face was all red and squashed, screwed up as if she'd drunk some bitter lemonade. Ruby took control then, and asked her quietly what she meant. Doll looked stricken at this question, and sort of folded up, she would have folded in two if her stomach hadn't got in the way. She didn't say anything. Then Ruby heaved herself up from her chair and held out a hand and said 'come with me, darling, we've got to speak to Sister Mary.' She got up obediently and Ruby led her out.

It felt like all hell broke loose that night. Two policemen came to the door an hour later, and were led to the office where Doll was waiting with Sister Mary. I was desperate to go in and be with her. They stayed for nearly two hours, those policemen, heaven knows what they were writing down. Soon after that Doll slipped into the bedroom. I hadn't been able to get to sleep. After she'd settled into bed and clicked off her lamp I said 'Doll?' and when she said 'What?' I could hear her voice was all congested, like she'd been crying for hours. She sounded annoyed. I asked her what had happened and she said she'd been asked 'six hundred bloody questions' and that she was going to 'kill that bleeding Ruby' in the morning. I said 'Isn't it better that your sister is safe?' and she didn't answer. And I didn't know if I should say it or not, Bea, but I thought I would, just in case she wanted to talk about it, and so I said 'Your dad, he didn't…' and waited and waited but she didn't say anything. I couldn't hear a peep from her, as if she was holding her breath in the dark. We both lay there frozen for what seemed like hours. And finally I heard the little noises she makes with her throat when she's asleep, and I stayed awake a lot longer, trying not to think about what kind of family Doll had come from, and what she might be going back to.

It's like we've been in a little world of our own, Bea, all these years – everything neat and tidy and our biggest traumas have been when your mum threw you a surprise party that time, or when we went on our first dates... we've been so lucky. I hope you still feel lucky. I'm missing you like mad at the moment. It's only a few weeks until my due date now, the 21st of October. They say most first mothers are a bit late, but I feel so huge. I'm afraid, Bea, I'm really rather afraid. Think of me, if you still care for me, and send me one of your lovely squishy hugs. As fast as you can! All my love to you,

Your Elizabeth x

Chapter 12

Violet was afflicted by a series of painful crushes in her teenage years. They were the kind of infatuations where any possibility of a real relationship had the life squeezed out of it. How could you start an actual relationship with a person after spending a whole weekend replaying his smile to you as you passed him in the corridor, or after deciding that if you could own a single hair from the curl on the nape of his neck that you'd want for nothing more for the rest of your days? She was completely mystified as to how anyone could make the leap from fantasy and start TALKING to the object of their desire. What did one say – 'I've spent several months imagining the palm of your hand in great detail – would you like to go and see a film?' Or maybe 'I've decided I simply can't live without you. Strange weather today, isn't it?' There was a whole series of assorted boys who took her fancy – a skinny Scottish boy whose accent she'd spend hours alone in her room trying to imitate, a languorous older boy who'd flick his long fringe and touch his two fingers to his lips as if he was smoking a cigarette, an arrogant type with bad skin who was always in trouble with the teachers.

Her most violent crush descended upon her when she was almost sixteen. Manny was an older boy who travelled to work on the same bus she caught to school. He fancied himself as a bit of a rebel, although he probably worked at the bank or the local insurance offices like everyone else. He used to smoke roll-ups, and would spend most of the journey building a stock of pre-rolled ones to 'get him through all the monotonous corporate shit'. She'd eavesdrop on the conversations he had with his friends whenever she could. They called themselves, imaginatively, 'the back seat crew'. She knew there'd never be a place for her there, even when she was older – she just didn't have the 'cool' gene. But she'd hover near the back anyway, much to the disapproval of her up-tight school-friend May, who always complained it was bumpier near the back and that it made her stomach 'iffy'. Violet always positioned herself so that when he got off at his stop he had to walk past her line of vision, and one day she dared to smile. To her complete amazement, he smiled back – a wry smile, accompanied by a short wink. She dined off that one for months. During this time she spent her evenings rushing through her homework so she could lie on her bed and stare at the ceiling, meticulously planning casual ways of opening a conversation between them. She wrote the best ideas down in a small note-book she'd hide behind a loose slat under her mattress. She never seemed to tire of certain fantasies about him – her favourite was when the bus crashed and he'd heroically save her life, before keeping vigil at her hospital bed until he brought her out of her coma. She'd travel through it again and again like a child who never tires of a favourite story book.

These excruciating crushes became quite a family joke – fodder for laughs around the dinner table. Her mother, as always, was the ring-leader. She would make a point of asking

Violet about her latest paramour and then draw attention to her fierce blushes with innocent surprise. Once she even made a knowing reference in front of the boy himself, a friend of the family who'd come to dinner with his parents. She thought herself completely hilarious, and would let out peals of laughter and then ruffle Violet's hair in a manner she must have imagined was affectionate. Violet would glare at her mother and beseech her father for help, but he always sat and looked hard at his dinner, apparently fascinated by the shapes the peas were making, or the colour of his chop. She quickly learnt to hide things from her parents, and from her friends too, after confiding in her friend May, who'd been teasing her about it ever since. She could stop other people using it against her, but she couldn't stop the voice inside her own head. She'd take a certain tone with herself, which bore more than a passing resemblance to her mother's – hectoring, condescending. 'For God's sake, Violet, is that really the best you can come up with? You think he's even given you a single thought once he leaves that bus?' or 'Are you going to live in this ridiculous fantasy world for the rest of your lonely life?' She could imagine the look on her own face when she caught herself fantasising about Manny – such a disgusted, disappointed look, that it started to take all the fun out of her day-dreams. Just when she could hardly bear herself any longer he must have got a bike or found a job on a different bus route, because she never saw him again.

After Manny, Violet protected herself by keeping the men she liked a secret even from herself. Slowly she noticed herself 'going off' the whole male species. What was it she'd seen in them again? There were a couple of half-hearted suitors who took her out ice-skating or to the cinema but they didn't leave much of an impression on her. One of them stuck his tongue in her mouth when he was dropping her home, as if he was stabbing at something in the back of her throat. It was such a shock, she stepped backwards and let out a short 'ugh'. He didn't ask her out again. It wasn't until she went to University that she managed proper relationships. There was a fellow tennis player, and a nerdy archaeologist who taught her chess. Although these relationships seemed like the kind of relationships her contemporaries were having, she couldn't help feel that there was something missing. And she never asked any of them home to meet her parents.

As time went on her mother slowly increased the pressure, commenting more and more often that she should 'find herself a nice man to settle down with before it's too late'. Violet was almost giving up hope herself when she met Charles during the final year of her PhD. It was macaroni cheese that brought them together. She was behind him in the queue in the canteen and they both had their eye on the last serving. He noticed her looking at it and offered it to her. He wasn't very much to look at – his glasses were slightly too round to be fashionable, and his shoulders curved forwards apologetically. He did have a kind smile though, and there was something about him that made her feel safe. She said thank you and they carried their trays to separate tables, but she spotted him again that weekend at the Union. He was with a big group of friends, but when she went to the bar he came up behind her and asked her if she'd enjoyed her macaroni. They chatted for five minutes about the food in the canteen before he asked her if she fancied going to a visiting fun-fair the next afternoon. She hesitated for a moment, and was swayed by realising she'd have to miss a dreaded lecture if she said yes. He went back to his friends, looking triumphant, and she went back to hers, who giggled and nudged her and demanded to hear everything.

Their first date got off to a bad start – he was late.

Violet couldn't abide lateness, and had decided not to answer the door if he left her waiting for another five minutes when she heard him knocking. He didn't give her a good enough excuse and so the atmosphere remained frosty until they went on the spinning tea-cups and Charles started to feel rather sick. After the ride stopped he had to sit on the grass with his head between his knees for ten minutes, and he looked so pitiful that Violet softened and started to be nice again. He managed to regain his dignity by winning her a large stuffed donkey at the shooting range, and when they sat down to eat hot salty chips with their fingers, he told her he loved the colour of her eyes. She was also impressed by the chaste kiss he planted on her cheek at the end of the evening, and rewarded him by asking him back to hers for coffee after their second date (to see a dreadful arty film at the University cinema club). The sex was good, if quick, but he made up for it by spending the next half an hour stroking her hair until she thought she might melt into the floor.

Charles was different to Violet's previous boyfriends in that he seemed to think he needed to work to keep her happy (or just to keep her). She wasn't used to being ministered to, and luxuriated in his little presents, self-taught massages and endless cups of tea and slices of toast. Over time Violet seemed to relax into the relationship in a way she'd hadn't managed before, slowly daring to feel safe and wanted. Despite their first date he turned out to be just as anal as she was about being on time, and after repeated testing she started to believe that he'd be where he said he was going to be, when he said he was going to be. They talked about anything and everything, sometimes late into the night. Charles seemed hungry for information about Violet, and she found herself telling him things she'd never told anyone – the time she'd 'stolen' perfume from her mother when she was ten years old, and how she'd once kicked a boy at school, hard, for not asking Violet to his party. He loved it when she told him droll stories about her family, and pestered her about meeting them. He'd lived alone with his father since his mother left when he was only nine, taking with her all contact with her side of the family. From Charles' first 'meet the parents' visit it seemed that the admiration was mutual. He did have a certain charm about him – not greasy or smooth, but eager. He was desperate to get everything right, and was a strange mixture of confident and utterly hopeless. Vera went to town – finding out what he liked to eat, bringing hot chocolate up to Violet's room after dinner, and asking pretend-curious questions about his studies. She couldn't quite help putting Violet down in front of him, but she and Charles would laugh about her later, Violet doing a convincing impression of her plummy vowels and stiff mannerisms, and this brought them closer together. He'd flatter Marta and Augusta to death, and he and her father bonded over their politics. As time went on, it seemed increasingly unfair for Violet to split up with him even if she'd wanted to. The whole family would have been devastated.

It seemed natural that they'd get married and have children together – a fait accompli rather than a conscious choice. Charles was very helpful on a practical level when the children were young, reading endless stories and changing endless nappies, and he loved living with Vera and Bill. Their marriage ticked along nicely for twenty years; they made a good team. Anyone looking in from the outside would have said that Charles was the stable one, who put up with Violet's crazy ideas and frustrated outbursts, and smoothed things over when things got complicated. Violet was good at shouting, but he was the one who disciplined Lucy when she drew all over their bedroom with a chunky red felt-tip, and who spoke calmly with Megan when she announced at fifteen that she was going to leave school immediately and become a florist. Charles would often translate, literally, between the children and their mother – delivering a toned-down version of Violet's feelings to the girls, and then trying to persuade Violet to be reasonable and consider the girls' points of view. He also acted as a buffer between Violet and her parents, especially her mother. The role of piggy-in-the-middle seemed to suit him perfectly.

If you dug a little deeper, you'd find that the workings of their marriage weren't quite so simplistic. Violet became gradually aware that Charles had an extremely low opinion of himself. Once they held a party at her parent's house, and Charles was actually sick before it started as a result of his nerves. He wouldn't tell her what he was so worried about but later, more than slightly drunk, he confided that he was plagued by 'premonitions' playing over and over in his head. These were usually scenes that climaxed in his utter humiliation. This time he couldn't help imagining people arriving at the party one by one, taking a dismissive look around the place and making their excuses five minutes later. They'd be left alone with a table groaning with vol-au-vents and a cupboard full of booze at 9.30pm, and Violet's parents would think it was all Charles' fault. As their marriage continued they grew familiar with each other's Achilles heels, and developed little ways of helping each other out. Violet knew how much Charles worked himself up if he knew they were going out to dinner, and so only ever told him about it half an hour before they were due to leave, pretending she'd forgotten to mention it so he could make a play at getting annoyed at her and huffing about the house while he got ready. And Charles never spoke up to her when she was in one of her moods, but waited patiently until she felt better and then fed her all the saved-up morsels of difficult information bit by bit (Megan got an F for her maths test last week, Vera wants me to talk to you about the mess in the upstairs hallway). People generally assumed that they'd be together forever, and Violet assumed the same.

It was towards the end of her illness that she decided to leave him. It turned out that she was just in time. After she broke the news to him, Charles admitted he'd met someone at work. It was all so clichéd – apparently this woman 'understood him', he was 'desperately sorry about the whole mess', he'd 'made his final decision' and had been working up towards telling her. Violet spent the rest of a week in a kind of daze, trying to wrap her brain around the information he'd given her. When had it happened? Why? Had she really missed all the signs, or had she been fooling herself? She spent long hours imagining this other woman as an Amazonian, with golden hair and a perfect figure. When they finally met she had to put her hand over her mouth to stop herself from laughing. Was this really her? She was plump, tired-eyed, mumsy, and wore an apologetic smile and clothes from Laura Ashley. She'd half imagined giving her rival a good sock in the mouth, but she knew she could never harm this lily-and-roses woman, who was probably on the PTA for her darling boys and made jam for the WI charity raffle. She dreaded what was ahead – the upheaval, the hassle, and she dreaded telling the children. She didn't like the thought of not having someone to come home to at night, the simple fact of loneliness. But it was also the thought of loneliness, of being alone, that made her feel that it would all be worth it. The idea of being alone was a tiny seed in her stomach, planted when she was ill. Now it was really happening, and it started to put out thread-like roots and a tiny pea-green shoot.

Chapter 13

Violet shuffles around in her still dark kitchen, stopping several times to shake her head like a dog shaking water from its coat. She spoons an extra mound of dark fragrant coffee into the cafetière, hoping the caffeine will do the trick. Guy must have cooked for himself after she'd gone to bed last night – he's left a snail trail of dirty pots and kitchen implements. He can sort it out himself when he gets up – she'll use the tunnel vision she developed when the girls hit teenagerdom. She's pouring on the boiling water when a shard of last night's dream returns to her. She's been dreaming about Elizabeth. She and Violet have ended up in various anxiety-producing scenarios over the past few nights. Violet's subconscious has conjured Elizabeth as a short and rather thick set girl with straw coloured hair (did she get that from a letter?) and big blue eyes, always wide open as if she's just heard something terrible. Last night Elizabeth was Violet's protégée at the University and was leading her first ever lecture, with Violet sitting at the back to give her support. The students all trooped in and were clattering about with their folders and gossiping about who had snogged whom at the Union over the weekend. Violet couldn't take her eyes off Elizabeth waiting at the front, rigid and pale, with one hand fastened onto the lectern and bright spots of white at her knuckles. Violet was desperate to go up and stand beside her, but when she tried to get up her legs were completely useless, and she couldn't make a sound. The whole auditorium slowly quietened down and the students started looking at Elizabeth one by one and nudging their friends. They mocked her, laughing at her clothes and miming her stiff posture. Then they all suddenly froze to the spot, their faces twisted into a hideous piece of modern art. Elizabeth's fear held them in a kind of spell, her fingers still grasping the lectern, her frightened eyes flicking from side to side. Violet knew it was all her fault, and when she woke up she was overwhelmed by a terrible guilt, a crushing sense of failure.

Elizabeth's story hangs around her like the taste of yesterday's garlic. Violet still doesn't know what is going to happen to her or her baby, or who the hell these people even are. Maybe they're completely fictional – the product of someone's sick imagination. The worst thing is that she still doesn't have anyone to talk to about it. This in itself seems a little worrying. Is there really nobody she can discuss things like this with any more? It used to be Charles, although she seemed to feel less and less of a need to share things towards the end of their marriage. There simply wasn't time for deep and meaningfuls when the children were growing up. Don't women talk to their girlfriends about this kind of thing? Violet has never quite mastered the art of girlfriends. She's never understood the appeal of days spent trawling cities for yet another blouse or handbag, or minute-by-minute reconstructions of conversations with spouses. 'When he said that, maybe you should have said this instead,' and

'What do you think he really MEANT when he said he was bored with me?'

She remembers being trapped in a conversation like this once, when she stayed with a colleague before they attended a conference the next day. He had the stupid notion that she'd prefer to spend the evening with his wife and her cronies rather than in the pub with him and his friends, and he abandoned her. They were nice enough women, and they tried to include her, but after two hours of neurotic tentative twittering she wanted to stand up and shout, 'You – LEAVE the bastard! You – get a different fucking job! And you – if you mention the size of your thighs ONE MORE TIME I'll get a knife myself and cut them down to size for you! Have you really got NOTHING BETTER to DO WITH YOUR TIME?' Of course she was far too house-trained to set off an explosion like that, but she thinks little puffs of disapproval must have escaped her anyway, because a couple of the ladies looked at her askance a few times, and towards the end of the evening they stopped giving her the background to people she didn't know and situations she wasn't familiar with. How does one go about finding girlfriends? She doesn't want them. She wants someone else instead. She needs Tom now, more than ever.

She drags out a stool and sits with her coffee cup, enjoying the feel of the steam wetting her face. She's wearing the fixed, hazy gaze she uses when it feels too much of an effort to focus or flick her eyes around the room. She's not expecting Guy to emerge until at least eleven, and enjoys these quiet hours alone in her own house. He visited George and Yevgeniya without her last night. George had invited him when they'd bumped into each other in Amberly a few days ago. She hopes that the old man didn't fill his head with too much rubbish, about 'suffering for your art' or keeping yourself pure by not having a day job – that's all very well for writers but what about the writer's mothers? Are they just expected to support their off-spring's artistic tendencies with no questions asked, ad infinitum? She doesn't know what is to be done about him. He's made absolutely no movements towards looking for another job, or even thinking about looking for another job. He's also taken to scribbling away at the kitchen table during the afternoon, and is carrying a new small black leather notebook around with him everywhere. When she was in the butchers with him last week she saw him scrawl something down in it – she tried to see what he'd written but he bent away from her and then stalked out of the shop. She imagines it was something scathing about mothers and shopkeepers.

She returns to the girls' theory that he was spoiled. She recalls making him a packed lunch for him to take on his walk a couple of days ago. Is that spoiling? Is she still doing it? And if she did spoil him, is it too late to undo it all now? Spoiled. Such a horrible word, redolent of rotting meat or curdled milk. Maybe she'll speak to Charles about him, see if he can knock any sense into him. She lets out a sigh. It's too early in the morning for all this worrying. At least the house feels a little warmer than it did yesterday morning. She's only had to wear one jumper this morning, and one pair of socks. Whenever she complains about the cold to any of her daughters, or even mentions it in passing, they make some comment about her loss of insulation or her poor bones being too close to the air – she imagines they must have plotted together to form a co-ordinated attack. She doesn't understand why they feel so strongly about her losing weight, or rather not putting it back on again after her illness. Could they be jealous? None of them is what she'd call overweight, although Megan has been getting a little rounded recently.

Her thoughts arrow back to the middle-of-the-night phone-call with her daughter last week. She's handled Megan's anger in the way that she usually handles conflict, by ignoring it until Megan calms down and makes the first move. Preferably, when the other person does get back in touch, they pretend that nothing has happened, and things continue as normal. If they do hold a grudge, Violet puts up with it for as long as she feels ashamed of her part in the argument. When this shame runs out she simply lets the other person know that she's had enough. This method seems to have worked fine in her dealings with everyone in her family and most of her colleagues over the years. The odd friend who had wanted to 'have a conversation' about what had happened like some dreadful talk show had tended to drop by the wayside. There was a particular colleague at work who Violet had snapped at one day, and their relationship had never quite recovered – not, the colleague had said, because of the snap, but because of the 'apparent total lack of respect for him' when she didn't apologise. Apologise, shmapologise. That's what her mother always said to her, and Violet agreed. What good was an apology when the deed was already done?

She certainly never expects an apology from anyone who takes their anger out on her. She sees it as something that just happens when she inadvertently presses someone's 'button' rather than a personal attack – she's just the person who happens to get in the way. It had been a big bone of contention between her and Tom. Tom thought Violet 'unbelievably arrogant' to find her own twisted ethical argument for not apologising, rather than actually thinking about what the other person might need. They had had long, heated discussions about the issue, both arguing their case using examples of various situations involving conflict, and how they felt they should be handled. The main thing they discovered was that Violet's usual methods didn't work for their own disagreements. These were painful and protracted, and as their relationship developed, the length of time between them fighting and 'making up' grew longer and longer. Violet even said 'sorry' once as a last resort, thinking it would shorten their separation, but Tom didn't believe her, 'couldn't see it in her eyes', and so that didn't seem to work either. How did other people get past arguments like that, arguments that spiral round and round?

It has been concerning Violet that Megan hasn't yet called her back. There – she's admitted it to herself. She tried her yesterday afternoon, left a short message on her answerphone, and she still hasn't heard from her. She tried her other daughters afterwards and got through to Lucy, and when she asked her if Megan was OK her reaction was a little strange. First she said 'have you talked to her yet?', and when Violet said no she sort of mumbled that she didn't want to get in the middle. 'In the middle of what?' Violet asked, but her daughter would say no more, except reassuring Violet that 'the crisis has passed for now' and that she was 'safe'. Violet didn't like the sound of this – what crisis? Had she been unsafe? There is still a slow fizz of anger underneath Violet's worry, that her daughter had scared her like this and then not got back to her – really, how inconsiderate. This thought helps her to keep the worry at bay. She knows where she is with anger. She drains her coffee and looks down into the gritty remains in the bottom of the cup. No answers there.

Her morning proceeds in the usual fashion, looking at her mail and then flicking through *the Guardian*, tutting at anything that strikes her as ridiculous. She finds more and more to tut at these days. Do we really care if the Minister of Funny Walks got caught with his pants down? Why bother writing an article about how skinny models should be (literally) fed up if you fill your weekend magazines with photospreads of the same bony women? She tuts at adverts too, and it used to drive Tom mad. She couldn't help expressing her outrage at yet another airhead joyfully removing stains from her husband's shirts, or another barely-disguised attempt to induce guilt in mothers to sell them something pointless. Next she moves on to tackling her domestic chores – washing, tidying (especially now Guy is staying), and this morning tackling the pantry, which she thinks might be growing its own variety of mushrooms near the back. Today she pays extra attention to tidying her living room – the Committee are meeting at her house later and she doesn't want Sue turning her nose up at the dust on the mantelpiece. It prompts her to finally sort through and tidy away a pile of jazz records her dad had left her on their last visit, 'modern rubbish', as he'd said; he didn't know if she'd want any of them. She'd put at least two dozen of them straight into the 'charity shop' pile after being horrified by the song titles: '*Walking the Moon on a Leash*', '*The Ineluctable Green of Grass*' and other pretentious codswallop. Anyone who resorts to including the word 'ineluctable' in their titles surely can't be very confident about their music-writing ability. There were six she thought might be worth a tentative listen, and she put these underneath her record player with the rest.

She'd half-planned to bake something impressive, maybe from her River Café cookbook, something dense and dark-chocolatey to out-do Margaret's usual standard WI offerings. In the end she'd left it too late, and bought the poshest biscuits she could find in the local shop instead. She sometimes wonders how she had time to do anything at all when she was working full-time. Her days pass so quickly now, and there are always things on the 'waiting to be done' list, like putting up new curtains in the lounge, and driving half an hour down the road to visit an ex-colleague. She's been meaning to go for months. She supposes she'd squeeze these jobs into an early Saturday morning in the olden days, while the children were watching their bright noisy TV shows or involved in one of their projects. It's one o'clock before she knows it. She shares a lunch/breakfast of bacon sandwiches with Guy and then presses a fiver and her car keys into his hand, bundling him out of the door to 'amuse himself' for a couple of hours.

He's out the door just in the nick of time, as she spots Margaret marching down the lane like a sergeant major. By the time Violet gets to her front door, Will has joined her. Violet greets him warmly and only realises once she's moved through to the living room that she practically ignored Margaret. Never mind, she'll survive. She's hardly sat them down with their cups of tea when the door goes and Sue, Angie and Rob are there waiting. Once they've taken their places Angie announces that Peggy had rung to let them know she has a 'chest cold', and a couple of the Committee members can't quite help letting relief show along with their concern. Violet hopes she never ends up like Peggy, drawing only annoyance or impatience from other people wherever she goes. She'll ask her daughters to shoot her before she gets to that stage – they'd probably enjoy it, anyway. She sits on the edge of her seat and fidgets with her silver bracelet. She isn't keen on being host in any situation. She can't bear the expectation that everyone's comfort and well-being are in her hands, and is convinced for most of the time that she's getting it wrong without quite knowing why or how she could do it better. Sometimes flickers of fantasy slip through afterwards, of her guests sharing their horror at the grime at the corner of her carpets, or the weak tea, before she manages to give herself a stern talking to. As she looks around the room she notices that Angie is wringing her hands and has red spots on her cheeks. Maybe she has a fever.

'Are you ill, Angie?' she asks, cutting off an interminable story Rob had been telling about his neighbour's gout, and everyone in the room looks at Angie.

This seems to make matters worse, and she starts pinching skin from her arms as if she's trying to pull bits of flesh off. She smiles a stuck-on smile and says, 'Yes, I'm fine thanks, Violet,' in a strained voice. In the silence that follows, Violet wonders if something had been wrong with her question. She had imagined she was being thoughtful. Margaret clears her throat.

'Righty-oh. I declare this meeting open. Angie, have you got a copy of the Minutes from the last meeting?'

Angie looks relieved at having something to do, and makes a great play of shuffling them into a neat stack before she hands them to Will on her right. And they're off. Rob is on top form and makes a few comments that could almost be described as witty, and Violet enjoys exchanging knowing glances with Will when Sue makes a particularly Sue-ish comment, or when Margaret starts tapping her fingers on the table, which is her way of letting someone know that they've gone off on a tangent. Sue seems to be being especially nice to Will for some reason, and an aura of discomfort lingers around Angie, who occasionally slips her fingers inside her collar as if the room is too hot for her. Violet wonders what might be going on that she's missed. She wishes that Lucy were here; she's always had a real knack for working out 'group dynamics', as she puts it. Tom always seemed pretty good at judging situations like this too. She only realises how far she's drifted from the meat of the conversation when Margaret clears her throat again and she notices everyone's eyes on her. She feels like she's been caught out talking to her neighbour at school.

'What?' she says. She sounds defensive – it's not the 'pardon' tone she'd intended at all.

'I can't wait until AOB!' Angie says suddenly, staring ahead and flushing redder by the second.

'Do you have something you want to share with us, Angie?' asks Margaret.

She nods quickly, managing to keep whatever it is pushed down inside her for a few more seconds as she lowers her eyes and waits for permission to speak.

Violet wonders what it would take for her to just say whatever she wants to say without waiting for the go-ahead from Margaret. She can see Margaret struggling to decide – a contribution out of the usual order! If she says yes to this, who knows what will it lead to… After only a few seconds Will interrupts, very uncharacteristically, with, 'Oh for God sakes, Margaret, let her speak.'

Angie looks gratefully at him. Margaret blusters 'of course, of course', as if no-one should have doubted she was about to come to that decision herself.

Now she's been given permission, Angie seems to sway a little under the weight of their gazes. Violet wonders for a second if she's going to faint, and tenses her muscles in case she has to lurch forward to stop her from crashing all over the nice tea-cups she got in Bath. Instead Angie takes a very deep breath, screws her eyes tight shut, and says in a loud voice:

'Sue has been stealing money from the collection box in the shop.'

Three things happen all at once. Sue gasps audibly and draws herself up in her seat as if she's about to run off or hit somebody. Blue knocks something from a shelf upstairs and bolts into the room, where he's met by a room-full of strangers, causing him to freeze in a parody of shock before hissing and skittering back upstairs at top speed. Margaret chokes on a half-swallowed gulp of tea and starts a coughing fit which results in her tea being spilt, Violet running to get a cloth from the kitchen, Rob standing up and ineffectually banging her on the back, and Will following Violet to fetch a glass of water and not finding any glasses and banging frenetically around in the cupboards.

Violet is the last to take her seat again. Margaret has caught her breath and they are all looking at Angie, except Sue, who's staring straight ahead furiously. As usual Margaret takes the lead, and for once Violet is glad of it.

'Righty-oh, then. Angela, before you continue I want you to know quite how serious this accusation is. You do understand?'

Angie nods mutely, the gravity of the situation made very clear through Margaret's use of her full name.

'Can you start by telling us what you think you saw?'

Sue interrupts. 'This is ridiculous. We all know she's been gunning for me since I didn't choose her stupid picture in the crafts section in 2003. Honestly, are you really going to...'

Margaret turns to her and holds a finger up straight. She turns back to Angie.

'Go on, Angie.'

Angie's hands are trembling, and she's twisting about in her seat.

'I... I... when I...'

Her face screws up and looks sideways at Sue, and Violet feels a stab of impatience. She really is quite a child. Violet has never been any good with these weepy types.

Some people seem able to be patient with them, indulge their inflated, over-dramatised feelings. Violet has a switch inside her which goes from 'tolerant' to 'intolerant' in a second. Sometimes she thinks she uses up most of her energy simply keeping what she'd like to say back, or saying it anyway and then having to put up with the consequences. It was happening now. Right now the outburst she's keeping inside her would go something like this:

'For fuck's sake, Angie – you're a grown woman, you can't live your whole life feeling intimidated by little worms like Sue, what do you think she's going to do to you? We don't have high levels of gun crime here in Abbotsfield, you know. What the fuck would you have done if you really did live somewhere dangerous, somewhere where things like this actually mattered?'

Etc. etc. She knows it isn't very dignified.

'It's alright, Angie. Take your time.'

There's a new softness in Margaret's voice which Violet has rarely heard before. Maybe this is the voice she uses to talk to her beloved Shih-Tzus. She has four of them and walks them twice a day, whatever the weather. They get shut into her bedroom when she holds meetings at her house. Violet has seen her in the village bending down to them, her mouth moving, and she's always wanted to know what Margaret's saying. Maybe she stays in her seargent major mode and she's telling them to hurry along, or berating them for making a mess, but Violet suspects there's a soft squishy part somewhere inside Margaret Meeks. She supposes that might be true for everyone, however prickly they are on the outside. She briefly considers her own soft squishy bit and finds herself bristling internally, and changes the subject in her own mind. Angie is slowly gathering her crumbs of courage together and takes a sharp breath.

'I saw her in the village, a month ago. She was talking to Fred behind the counter and pouring all the money into a little red bag, like a kind of pocketbook, and I thought it was a bit odd at the time because Will was on rota to do the weekly collections. It was only a Tuesday too, and we usually go in on a Friday, don't we? I wanted to be sure, so I checked with Will, was he doing the collections, had he been able to do them all himself this week, with his illness and all, didn't I?'

She's looking at Will for confirmation, and he nods.

'I didn't want to think it was true, it seemed… So, so…'

She breaks off again, and they all hold their breaths.

'Go on, Angie.'

Violet notices that Margaret is taking notes. Angie turns her head towards what Margaret has written so far, her eyes glazed, and then continues.

'So I talked to Fred, said to him we were doing a check to make sure our Committee members were doing their collections on time. I asked him when Will had come in that week first, and he said, every Friday, just about, and that he'd missed a week or two – sorry, Will.' She hangs her head as if she's exposing something terrible about him, but he flicks a hand dismissively. 'And then I asked about Sue, and he said, he said "She's regular as clockwork, that woman, every Tuesday at 3pm, you could set your watch to her." That's what he said, Margaret, that's what he said!'

She's looking at Margaret now and beseeching her. Sue makes a loud noise, letting out air from her pursed lips in a burst, and folds her arms, and then unfolds them and looks around for her handbag. She's on the verge of walking out, and Violet has a vivid mental image of Margaret letting out a war cry and tackling her on her way past, gripping her

slightly hairy ankles in a vice and sitting on her until the
police arrive. But instead something extraordinary happens.
There's a noise in Sue's throat, as if she's struggling to get
enough air, and her eyes shut tight and she starts shaking
with sobs. It's very ugly, and Violet watches her with a kind
of sick fascination, like craning to see inside the cars after a
crash on the other side of the motorway. Angie is looking at
her in horror, and Rob is saying 'oh dear, oh dear', over and
over under his breath. They all look to Margaret, but to their
surprise she's sitting with her eyes widened in shock and,
maybe for the first time since she learnt to speak, lost for
words. Violet shifts her eyes to Will and sees him stand up.
He puts his hands up, palms forward, in front of him.

'OK. This is what we're going to do. Angie – into the
kitchen with Violet and make Sue a cup of tea. Rob – fetch
Sue some tissues, or toilet paper or something. Margaret. Up
to Violet's office with me for a quick word. Sue – you just sit
tight. OK? OK.'

Everyone scuttles off to their various tasks with visible
relief. By the time Margaret emerges from the office with
Will she looks calm again. The only evidence of Sue's tears
is a faint pink tide-mark around each eye – she's sitting with
her back perfectly straight and is sipping her tea. Margaret
looks around the room to get everyone's attention.

'Alright everyone. We can handle this in a civilised
manner. What I'd like you to do, Angie, is to put what you've
said today in writing and bring it round to me by the end of
the week. Sue, I'd like you to put something in writing too
– Will and myself will then arrange a meeting to discuss our
next steps, depending on the contents of the statements and
our own enquiries. If any further action is necessary we will
propose a course of recommendations and ratify this with
the Committee. Is that quite clear?'

Everyone nods, except Sue, until Margaret looks at her directly and she says 'yes' in a quiet voice.

'Is there any other business?'

They have the rest of the unfinished agenda to cover, but everyone shakes their heads.

'This concludes our meeting for today. Thank you to everyone for attending.'

Sue gets up immediately and picks up her things, draping her coat over one arm as she moves towards the door. She turns and searches their faces blindly for a second, and settles on Will and says 'thank you for the tea'. She's shut the front door behind her before anyone else has got up from their seat, and there's an awkward silence as they all separately consider bringing the matter up, knowing how inappropriate it would feel, but desperate to start the post mortem. Rob finally says 'Angie, would you like to be escorted home?' She agrees gratefully, and they say their goodbyes. Margaret gathers her papers together and leaves. Violet doesn't want to be left alone and asks Will if he might have time for another cup of tea. He says he'd love one, and she leaves him in the suddenly quiet room to go and brew another pot.

By the time she comes back into the room Will has coaxed Blue into his lap and is tickling his chin. She's pleased – she likes it when her guests make an effort with him. She notices that Will's eaten four of the fancy biscuits, and he takes another one to have with his tea. She sits across from him and draws her legs up underneath her.

'Well, Will. What a bloody business. How on earth did you keep your head?'

He smiles and stares out of the window for a few seconds as he finishes munching his mouthful of biscuit.

'I surprised myself a little, to be honest, Violet. The 'old me' would have dealt with a situation like that in a jiffy. The emotional pitch at work was always pretty... well, you had to be rather good at remaining calm. Not letting other people see behind the façade, being in control of every conceivable situation – it becomes a bit of a habit after a while I suppose. A bad habit. I sort of lost touch with what I was really thinking, just kept it all in the back. You really were out on your ear if you showed weakness, if you let it get to you. I don't know how anyone can go on doing that forever, without something cracking. Ha! I certainly cracked!' He takes another bite and chews thoughtfully while Violet waits for him to continue. 'I don't really talk about it much. Even to Helen. She's been hugely supportive, I don't deny, but she gives off a sort of air, as if she doesn't really want to hear too much. She says she wants to listen but... I think it gave her a bit of a scare, to be honest. Her and me both. I've always been the one to depend on, and when your rock starts to crumble away...'

He fades off. Violet is surprised to note how comfortable she feels in this conversation – it's the kind of thing that would usually have her running for the door. She doesn't feel she has to do anything, or even say anything. And so she decides she will say something.

'Will?'

He looks up from Blue, who has just yawned a gigantic yawn.

'Me and Tom had another, you know. We haven't talked for weeks. I'm not sure whether I should... whether I ought to...'

He says 'hmm', and rubs his chin with his forefinger. Violet feels silly, a school-girl waiting for the teacher to tell her what to do next. She feels mildly annoyed too, but isn't sure why.

'What is it you want from the whole thing?'

She sighs. 'I wish I knew. That would make it simpler, wouldn't it? There are just so many bloody complications… what with… well, you know, and the arguments have been murder – I've never really argued like that before, with anyone. It can't be good, can it?'

'I suppose it depends if the arguments are taking you through something, however slowly or torturously, or holding you in the same place. Difficult to tell sometimes, I suppose. I've no qualifications to be giving you advice on your relationship. What do your children think?'

'I haven't really said anything to them. And they don't seem to ask. Guy knows we've not been talking, but he's a bloody man. No offence. I suppose it would suit them all if we didn't get back together – make things much simpler for them. Oh, I don't know, Will. Sometimes I feel like I'm banging my head against a wall, a really thick wall, and other times… well, it's just that I can't stop thinking about it.'

He smiles and nods, and she can see in his eyes that he understands. And to her horror she feels the prick of tears behind her eyes, and has to jump up and start clearing away the empty cups and saucers to cover it up. In a moment the feelings have gone. In a cheery voice she says 'do you think she did it, then?'

'I don't know, do you? The stupid woman. Really, it's a terrible breach of trust. All those pensioners with their 20ps.'

'But why? It doesn't make any sense.'

'We all have our secrets, I suppose. Who knows what's going on in that head of hers? Can you imagine?'

They both laugh, the thought of being Sue somehow ridiculous and terrible and funny all at once.

Before Will leaves, Violet asks him to wait, and walks

around her kitchen opening and shutting cupboards. She finds a jar of mango chutney, posh home-made stuff from one of her daughters, and hands it to him without really knowing what she's doing. He says thank you. They kiss cheeks at the door, and Violet is grateful for the press of his cheek on hers, warm and solid like a crust of freshly baked bread.

Chapter 14

15th of October '59

Dearest lovely Bea,

Thank you, thank you, a million trillion thank yous! I've kept your letter under my pillow ever since it arrived, smoothed out so it doesn't get too crinkled, and in the middle of the night when I wake up and feel frightened or alone, I slip one of my hands underneath and touch the edge of it with my fingertips. It gives me such comfort, you wouldn't know. I never really believed you'd speak to me again, that's the honest truth. I've been writing the letters and pretending – that you were getting them and reading them, that you cared about what I was telling you. But another part of me kept thinking 'don't be ridiculous – why would she want to be your friend after the lies you've told her? After the mistakes you've made?' It's a horrid voice, really quite scornful and bitter. I thought it was right. And now you've written, and you've said you forgive me for lying – you've said you forgive me! The girls thought I'd gone mad the morning it arrived. I've been feeling so heavy this last week, I can hardly bear the effort of dragging myself out of bed and standing upright, and I've been walking around with a face like a slapped fish. Even Doll asked me if I was all right. And then I got your letter. I read it over breakfast, and when I finished I jumped up out of my seat with a strange sort of shriek. It was like I had a few drinks inside me. And I ran around the table – did laps – or as close to running as I can these days. The others all started clapping and cheering and that just egged me on even more and I did a funny little dance at the head of the table – I must have looked like a complete idiot!

I understand the things that you put in your letter. Of course I don't mind that you wanted to think about things. And I feel terrible about what you said about not knowing what was going on, and how it reminded you of your brother. I hadn't even thought of it, Bea, I'm so sorry. I get so angry when I think about your parents not letting you know what was happening, then not even letting you go to his funeral... It was wrong of them, to not give you a chance to say goodbye to the poor little chap. I simply adore your parents, but they weren't thinking straight, they really weren't. I haven't told you how I felt about that before, but now I have. I never imagined you thought I might be ill all this time, getting some sea air as things got worse and worse. How you must have fretted! And how angry you must be with me. You didn't say you were but I know you must be furious, and it's quite right that you are. I'll give you a chance to hit me over the head with an oven glove on your fist when I get back, that might let some of it out! Or you can stick pins in my letters! I'm just so happy to have your letter, and so glad – more than anything – that you'll be on my side whatever I decide to do. I know you must have an opinion one way or the other, and I think

I know what that is, but giving me the choice is the nicest, most wonderful thing you've ever done, that's how I see it, anyway. Shall I stop pothering on about that now? You're probably wondering if I'm going to talk about anything else!

Poor sweet Doll isn't doing too well, I'm afraid. She seems to have gone downhill since the business with the police. She hardly says a word to me now, or to anyone else. Even when we try and jolly her along, ask her to play cards with us, or ask her in to the nursery to coo over Queenie's baby. Even worse, she's started doing this odd thing in the night, Bea, like she's talking to herself under her breath, but I don't think she can hear me. When I say 'Doll?' she seems to stop straight away, as if she is awake, but when I said to her yesterday 'What have you been nattering about in the middle of the night?' she didn't know what I was talking about. I can't catch all of it, but the things she's saying aren't very nice, Bea. She says 'don't', lots of little ones all in a row, and also 'I'm a bad girl,' in a voice that gives me the chills, like she's still a child. And then last night she said, 'It hurts, please stop, it hurts.' I'm not sure what to do, Bea – what do you think I should do? I so miss being able to talk to you properly. I would have talked to Marjory about it but she's been on holiday for a week. And what would I say, anyway? I can't really say what I'm afraid of, but it feels like something is going to happen. I'm probably getting worked up over nothing.

So... what else has been going on in the sin bin, as we like to call it! More games of cards, more lovely chocolate pudding and nasty corned beef, more chores, more laughter, more hormone-induced tears. Peg decided to go for adoption a couple of days ago and it seems to have knocked her for six, she keeps wandering in and picking something up like a glass or a biscuit and looking at it as if she's never seen it before, and then putting it down and wandering away again. I haven't got much further thinking about my baby. I get a strange feeling when I even start thinking about it – or writing about it – a sort of gripped feeling, in the pit of my stomach. I'm sure the baby knows what I'm feeling, and if I felt too sad it wouldn't be healthy for it. Does that sound silly? Maybe I'm just using it as an excuse to not think too hard about what to do next. I've been looking in The Lady, every week, for domestic positions that take a baby, and there are a few here and there... But I'm not completely stupid, Bea. I know I'd be dooming my child to a lifetime of, well, of being not-quite-normal, of having a mother with loose morals, and I'd never get a husband, and so the baby would never have a father. Do I have enough love in me to compensate for all of that? Do I? I know I have plenty of love, I try not to feel it too closely, hold it back, because I know it'd make the decision more difficult. But is it enough? I have other feelings too, it's hard to admit to them, but sometimes I just want this thing out of me – this thing that has ruined everything for me. I didn't ask it to turn up, to start growing inside me. Oh, I sound awful. It's been a bad day, Bea, please forgive me. There are things you still don't know.

All this doom and gloom. Maybe I should finish with the story Ruby told me last night, about her little brother – it made me laugh anyway. Just to stop you wanting to kill yourself! When he was about three years old, he was pestering his mother for some cake while she was trying to get some juicy gossip from her friend. The cake was in a tin was on the coffee table, and he couldn't quite open it. He was pulling on his mother's skirt, making a thorough nuisance of himself, and in the end she turned to him and snapped, 'Oh, use your head!' So he goes back to the coffee table and dips his little head and uses it to push the tin across the table! She's a good friend to me, Bea, I hope you can meet her. She'd love you. She knows all about you, I never shut up about you.

Have the loveliest of days today and I may be a little smaller when I next write to you – my due date is only in a couple of weeks now!

All my love, your Elizabeth xxx

Chapter 15

At the end of a long, drizzly week at the seaside, seven year old Violet and five year old Augustine constructed the most magnificent sandcastle of all time. They'd had dummy runs for three days in a row, and had spent the previous evening plotting at the dinner table and then in whispers under the duvet until their mother had finally lost her temper and reduced them both to muffled tears. Their father had started it off after breakfast by creating a humungous mound of sand, before retreating gladly to a paperback war novel. They spent the first hour wetting the pile of dry sand with buckets of water, and adding wet sand of their own. Violet can remember how surprisingly heavy the stuff was, and how she could only fill her bucket up to the halfway mark if she wanted to carry it all the way from the sea's edge without stopping. Stopping to rest would be wasting time! Next they moved onto molding – inventing new kinds of turrets and walkways and courtyards, using their fingers shaped into scoops or the flats of their hands. Next on the plan (Violet consulted her mental notes) was decoration. They used all kinds of flotsam and jetsam; pieces of bright sea-battered plastic, seaweed, discarded chip forks, their own shoes, and whatever else they could find. The best job they left until last – digging and filling the moat. They roped in their reluctant father again as hired muscle, and the pile of sand from the moat grew and grew. It disturbed Violet – she felt they really ought to make it into another sandcastle, but then what would they do with the sand from the second sandcastle's moat?

As they worked their mother was kept busy by toddler Marta, who was feeling a bit peaky. She seemed to be feeling a bit peaky for most of Violet's childhood. Violet was convinced that she came out of the womb pale and limp, noticed immediately how effectively it brought her attention (even if it was physical rather than sympathetic), and was ill on purpose from then on. With their mother preoccupied with Marta, and their father already a shadowy figure in the background, Violet and Augustine had become pretty good at keeping themselves amused. The fly in the ointment had always been Violet's bossy streak. As an adult Augustine was often heard to say that her childhood was 'hell on earth', although Violet easily dismissed this as one of her wild exaggerations. She described it as an endless series of small tasks carried out for Violet, and she got every single one wrong without quite knowing why. Augustine would 'tell on her' when her sister became particularly bossy or something struck her as especially unfair, but her harried mother's standard reply was 'sort it out between yourselves'. After a while she gave up asking and hit upon a different method of protest. When Augustine had had enough of being treated like a servant, she went on strike. She'd sit as tight as a stone with her little arms folded and her eyes facing straight ahead, and she wouldn't say a word for love nor ice cream. Once her father managed to pull her out of her sulk when it was time to go home by tickling her almost to the point of weeing herself, but whatever Violet tried had no effect – saying horrible things to her, sprinkling dirt in her hair, cajoling her with compliments. She even tried her killer move – lifting up her own skirt and showing Augustine her knickers – this usually had her in peals of giggles. Eventually Violet was forced to acknowledge this power that Augustine had over her – playing on her own just wasn't any fun. She treated her sister with a little more respect, and Augustine felt better too, knowing that she had the sitting-still weapon at her disposal.

During their sandcastle building, their working relationship unfolded as usual. Augustine put up with a fair amount of strict instruction and criticism before she finally rebelled. The final straw was when Violet told her she was filling her bucket up with sand in the wrong way. Couldn't she even be trusted to do this properly? She put her bucket down carefully and took her cross-legged position, looking out to the sea like a miniature Zen master. This was a terrible delay to the schedule, and so after Augustine had emerged from her protest Violet managed to behave herself for the rest of the morning. They were so engaged with their task they didn't realise how hungry they'd become until their mother called them back to the towels and striped wind-break. The paste sandwiches, sandy apples, warm blackcurrant juice and melted chocolate biscuits they ate for lunch were the best they'd ever tasted. Violet even allowed them twenty minutes rest-time stretched out on sandy towels before they got back to work.

Of course, the tide came in. When Violet looks back on it now, the whole event feels like a cliché – two little girls having their sand castle ruined – but at the time she was the only one it had ever happened to. She wasn't really used to hearing 'no' – her mother would rage at them but was too distracted to follow through with consistent punishment, and her father was always a little soft. This was the biggest no she'd ever heard. So you've worked hard all day on this – so what? I'm going to ruin your sandcastle anyway – and there's nothing you can do about it! She could hardly contain her fury. She can't remember this part, but years later her father told her that she'd stood at the edge of the sea with her hand on her hip, pointing at the foaming edge of the water and shouting 'Go back! Go back, you stupid sea!' And of course the grown-ups laughed, and told Mr. and Mrs. Scutt at dinner, and the owner of the hotel, and so Violet was doubly betrayed. On the way home she told Augustine that she hated the sea, and vowed that she never wanted to see it ever again.

Violet's next encounter with the sea was when she was nearly thirteen and growing more inwardly self-conscious and outwardly cocky by the day. Marta had been experiencing a rare period of full health and so Augustine was luxuriating in some extra attention from her mother, but the appeal for Violet seemed to have passed. She preferred to do things on her own anyway – other people never got it quite right, and her mother especially was always full of helpful suggestions – 'do it like this' or 'don't do that' – it was utterly infuriating. That year they had gone on holiday with another family. Violet can't remember ever doing it before or since, and she supposes that the adults had driven each other mad by the end of the week. The other couple had two children – a thirteen year old boy with painful looking spots, and a freckled younger girl who was friends with Augustine at school. On top of all the usual things she could complain about, Violet resented all the extra complications – having to find bigger tables in restaurants, and waiting while the grown-ups negotiated when they'd go down to the beach or come back for tea.

As the week went on she started to develop a grudging respect for the boy, Stewart, who seemed to disagree with everything his mother said – sometimes even in front of her. He called her a silly old woman one night in a loud whisper, which Violet thought very daring. He was obsessed with The Kinks and The Small Faces, and wore nothing but T-shirts emblazoned with Ray Davies' face. She hadn't known anyone her own age before who was passionate about something their parents didn't approve of, and this added to his appeal. He seemed completely unaware of her for most of the holiday, but on the last night they were 'watching' the younger children while their parents went out for a meal and he muttered under his breath that he was going for a walk along the sea. Was she coming? They swore the littler ones to secrecy and sneaked off, her sandaled feet slapping the pavement along the front, and then filling with sand as they walked across the beach towards the sea. To start with he was his usual reticent self, but as they walked along something child-like rose up in him and he stopped and took off his socks and shoes so he could splash and paddle in the water. He dared her to do the same, and the cold pulled shrieks out of both of them. She can clearly remember standing still with Stewart behind her and looking out over the water. The man-made noises coming from the shore receded, and the whooshing of the waves came into the foreground. Her legs had goose-pimples up to the knees. The sea was everywhere – she could have been the only one on the planet. There was a sprinkling of lights near the horizon – an oil rig? ships? – and the sea was black and glistening. It was beautiful and terrifying – what was it hiding? Deep sea creatures with strange bulging eyes and thousands of suckers? Mermaids?

Drowned sailors? She felt like a child, and at the same time she felt older than she'd ever felt before. This is it, she thought to herself. This is my life.

The sea became just the sea again, until she found out she was pregnant with her first child. She'd visited the doctor without telling Charles or anyone else, and the news had a strangely unsettling effect on her. She decided she needed some time to think (although she wasn't sure exactly what she needed to think about), and arranged a few days at the seaside on the pretence of visiting an old school-friend. The owners at the small guesthouse she'd found left her pretty much alone, which was exactly what she wanted. She rose late each morning, giving her body as much sleep as it wanted, and packed her knapsack with a novel, a book of crosswords, a jumper, and a towel to lie on the beach. She'd walk to the front and have tea and scrambled egg on toast in the same café each morning, exchanging a few impersonal words with the kind elderly owner. Next she'd step down the concrete steps to the beach and lie herself down on the sand – whatever the weather – and think of nothing. She ran her fingers through the sand, digging down to the cooler damp stuff, or rolling a few grains between her finger and thumb. She counted seagulls. She drifted in and out of sleep, sometimes waking with a start and wondering where she was. The novel stayed in her knapsack unread, the crosswords didn't get started. Occasionally she'd wonder what was wrong with her – what exactly was she achieving? When would she know when she was 'finished' and ready to go home? On the third day she started to feel bored around tea-time, and went straight to the station to catch an earlier train home. She read her novel on the train and then told Charles about the pregnancy as soon as he was within earshot on the platform. There wasn't time to think any further about what had happened. Charles coped badly during all of Violet's pregnancies, helplessly prophesising deformed babies or Violet's death in childbirth, and she had to manage his anxieties as well as keeping any of her own hidden. When she wasn't doing this, she was swept up into her mother's plotting, receiving a portion of her advice gratefully, and trying not to lose her patience with the rest.

She next felt the same strange, animal urge to be alone in the latter stages of recovery from her illness. The first time it appeared she was lying on the sofa downstairs under her duvet, as she seemed to do for most of every day. She was watching a programme about a man who'd got bowel cancer. It certainly wasn't the kind of thing she usually watched, but the alternatives at the time were a snooker match, yet another repeat of a dreadful war film, or Jackanory. This man had had the standard variety of epiphany that TV programmes insist upon, and had retired from his terribly unfulfilling job, started voluntary work at a refuge for stray dogs, and was now spending 'quality time' with his children, his wife, his hamster... the usual hackneyed stuff. It was a scene near the end of the film that snagged Violet's attention. He was walking through some woods, leaning heavily on his cane and looking a little ungraceful. There was no music, just the faint sound of bird-song and the crunch of autumn leaves under his feet. He was gazing up at the trees and the camera kept lingering on his eyes – there was a certain look there, was it wistful? Peaceful? Whatever it was, it wasn't something Violet could ever remember feeling, and she wanted to feel it. She really wanted to feel it. And she somehow realised that she'd need to be alone to track it down, and started planning another trip to the seaside. She realised later that he wouldn't have been on his own at all – that there would have been a camera crew following him on their tiptoes and trying not to get leaves in their equipment. Nonetheless the image caught hold of her imagination and slipped its way into her dreams, with her taking the place of the cancer man and wandering through the forest like a nymph. Shortly afterwards, she came to what she thought at the time was a completely unrelated decision to divorce Charles.

She went to the seaside for a fortnight as soon as her illness allowed her to. She didn't know it at the time, but it was her trial run for her new life in Abbotsfield. Preparations for the divorce were already underway. She returned to the same seaside village she'd visited when she was newly pregnant – the old guesthouse she'd used was no longer there, but she found one nearby. Her days mostly took the same pattern as before, but this time she spent the bulk of her time with her nose in a book. Her illness hadn't allowed her the concentration to read, and now she was going through novels like wildfire. The books she'd chosen to take with her all had a connection with the sea – Woolf's *To the Lighthouse*, Murdoch's *The Sea, The Sea*... Most of them seemed to have a sinister air which she relished – she couldn't buy in to this hippy, eco-warrior view of the sea as a calming benevolent presence that healed like a balm. The sea was fierce, the sea was relentless, the sea didn't care for people. People were too small for it to consider, too meaningless. After lunch she'd walk along the beach for as long as she had the strength, and then a little bit further. She'd rest, read, eat, drink, walk a little more, and sometimes have a sneaky nap in the back seat of her car.

It wasn't an easy two weeks. The boredom kicked in again after a few days. She barely spoke to anyone from one day to the next, and most nights she woke up feeling terribly homesick at least once. It was mostly pride that kept her there for the whole fortnight, and a dread of her mother saying 'I told you so.' There was only so much reading one person could do. Once she lay on her bed and stared at a crack in the ceiling for an entire afternoon, and the next morning she packed her case and unpacked it again twice, just for something to do. But there were moments, rare moments, when she felt something quite new to her. On one of her after-lunch walks along the beach she glanced down and spotted the perfect oval grey-blue stone nestled amongst all the ordinary others. Another time she was exchanging pleasantries with the man behind the counter at the local shop when she spotted an old lady struggling with the door. After Violet had helped her through with her shopping bags, the old lady gripped Violet's hand and looked into her eyes to say thank you, and Violet felt tears well up. It was difficult to explain – somehow the world was getting inside her in a way it never really had before. It was as if she was becoming more porous – maybe she'd slowed down enough for the first time in her life to let things touch her, or grab onto her with their suckers. It was a vertiginous feeling, and she didn't want too much of it at once. But during the evenings her mind would roam again over the details of the day, and these moments stuck out as if they were lit up from within. It was like discovering orgasms all over again. It seemed too ridiculous to try and explain it to anyone else, and there was a small part of her that was a little afraid that she was going mad, but she knew one thing about these moments – she wanted more of them.

She had one of them as she neared Abbotsfield and Jacquet House for the first time. She was alone in the car, unless you counted Blue, who had finally tired himself out after an hour of plaintive miaowing and curled up in a ball on the back seat. She could see the furry mound of him in the mirror. When the signs said Abbotsfield was five miles away, she started to feel nervous. She found herself straining to see the strip of water on the horizon, as she and Augustine had done from the back seat as children. She became aware of a feeling in her that grew the closer she got to the water. It was something like being anchored, but the thing anchoring her was so vast, so chaotic, that she could easily be sucked into it, swept away, pulled under. What about around this corner? Or could it be behind those hills? All of a sudden, there it was! The light skipped on the water, Charlie Parker filled her car with his own variety of sunshine, and Violet dissolved like a sugar lump dropped into coffee.

Chapter 16

It's a Friday morning, and Violet wakes up to an empty house. Guy stayed at George's big house last night after drinking too much red wine and not trusting himself not to fall into a hedge on the walk home. After an indulgent breakfast of kippers and brown bread and butter (cat and cat owner) Violet thinks she'll try Megan once more before going into town. It's been a week and a half since her late night phone-call and she hasn't responded to any of Violet's messages. Her daughter picks up after a single ring.

'Hello, Megan speaking?'

'Megan – thank heavens. Where have you been?' Violet is surprised at the sudden sense of relief in her chest, even though Lucy had told that her sister wasn't in any trouble.

'I've been here.'

Her daughter's voice is clipped, angry. Violet isn't sure of the best approach to take and so hesitates, leaving a pause that stretches on and on. Eventually she capitulates and breaks it.

'I've been worried, Gannie.'

Violet uses the nickname from her daughter's childhood, the name the whole family called her by until she got self-conscious at twelve and demanded they all start using her proper name. Violet hasn't spoken it out loud for years. It has an alarming affect on Megan – she starts to cry. Violet can hear her little snuffles down the phone, and pictures her forehead furrowed, her face all screwed up.

'Megan! What on earth is wrong?'

She's never mastered the art of sounding calm and reassuring in a crisis. That used to be Charles' job, to quietly go and fetch the First Aid box, or to envelop the children in a big hug, whilst Violet flapped around ineffectually barking orders that no-one paid any attention to. Megan just manages to speak through her tears.

'I... wanted to... tell you. I was... worried... you'd... that you... wouldn't...' She sighs. 'That you wouldn't understand.'

'That I wouldn't understand what?'

'It's... it's silly I suppose, I don't know why I'm...' She makes a 'hwaagh' sound in her throat, frustrated at herself. 'I've been talking to Tom.'

'What? When?'

'Quite a lot, really, over the phone.'

'Why?'

'Tom's helped me with this thing, this thing I want to...'

'Are you gay?'

'Mum! No!' She laughs and Violet is relieved that the tension between them is broken.

'Well, what then?'

'I think I'd like to come down, talk to you properly. Don't worry Mum, it's not a bad thing, but I just want you to understand. I want to explain it all properly. Would that be OK?'

'Of course, darling, but...'

'I can't do this weekend, what about next Friday? I could borrow Lucy's car and drive down, she might want to come too. Is that alright?'

Violet's imagination is going wild. Pregnant with triplets? About to emigrate to the Caymen Islands? She supposes at least she'll have a couple of weeks to prepare herself, to make sure all her anger and impulsive reactions are squashed down far enough to give her daughter a chance when she makes her announcement. They make their arrangements and say their goodbyes. As Violet leaves for Amberly she makes a mental note to visit the deli and buy some of that fudge her daughter enjoyed so much last time she came.

When Violet returns later that day she can see Guy through the kitchen window with his back to her. He's making bizarre movements with his shoulders. It's only when she opens the front door that the movements make sense – a blast of music meets her like a wall of smoke, and she pushes her way through it with heavy bunches of bags banging against her shins. Blue jumps down from his spot on the windowsill to greet her, butting her ankles with the side of his head.

'Hello, birdy birdy, good cat.'

She dumps the bags onto the table and without looking at Guy goes straight to the stereo and turns the music down. It's a variety of dance music, something she's never understood. Artificial drums playing the same rhythm over and over and over… how can that be called music? Her father gets quite worked up about the music his grandson plays. He's suggested to Violet that he might put some headphones on him when he's sleeping and intravenously feed Guy some good old big band – something classic like Benny Goodman or Count Basie – to ensure that his music-responding brain cells don't die away completely. Now Guy's music is clattering around in the background rather than bashing her across the face. She looks over at him – he's still jigging about and moving his bent, taut arms up and down in a kind of engine motion. She thinks of the Thomas the Tank Engine videos he used to watch. Can do it, can do it, will do it, will do it. He closes his eyes every so often and opens his mouth, 'baaa ba baaa', in time with the beats. Now he's moving towards her and she flinches, knowing what's coming – he sweeps her into his arms and waltzes her around the kitchen. His 'dear little mother', as she's heard him refer to her on the phone to his friends. She wriggles a little at first but relents and relaxes into his grip. She notices a kiss-curl in his hair and is struck by a bolt of affection. Wasn't it only yesterday when she'd lift him from his bath and swaddle him in his favourite red towel, his eye-lids drooping with sleepiness? How did he get so big? He leaves her for a second and she stands in the middle of the kitchen floor, stranded, feeling the loss of him, until she hears the music booming more loudly again and he's back, making his movements even more exaggerated, lifting her off her feet at the end of every four bars when a kind of whistle goes off.

After a few minutes she finds herself starting to understand a little. The beats are so simple, there's no distraction from the simple business of moving your body in rhythm. It reminds her of tribal drumming, when you see dark-skinned, sinewy men smeared in paint and making flapping movements with their arms while they stamp a heartbeat onto the soil, their faces glistening with sweat and a kind of ecstasy. Not the same kind of ecstasy she found in her son's bedside table drawer one day, when she was searching for the spare corkscrew, but probably a similar kind of feeling.

She starts improvising and making little movements of her own, fluttering her hands as she's seen her daughters do at family parties. She imagines leaving trails of light as if each finger is a sparkler. Something starts to resonate in her belly, to accumulate, as if the repetitive beats are lifting her up. When the track ends she's a little disappointed. She catches her breath while her son goes to turn the music down again before the next song starts. Although she supposes they're probably not called songs – don't songs have to have singing in them? Guy comes back over and lightly punches her arm, his usual affectionate gesture, and as usual it sets off a little spark of annoyance in Violet. Her feelings of affection are leaving her a little vulnerable for her liking, and she latches onto the annoyance and coaxes it into a mild anger, bringing her back to earth.

'Have you just got back, then, lazy?'

'Mother, how could you?!' He always calls her mother when he's in these playful, teasing moods. 'I've been back since… when did you go out?'

'Twelvish.'

'Just after twelve – in fact I got up at eight. I was applying for jobs all morning at George's place, couldn't you hear my pen scratching across the paper from here? Scratch, scratch, scratch…'

'Hmm.'

She turns away from his attempt to convince her through the medium of mime, and starts to unpack her spoils from town. A few books from the small library that opens three times a week, some pork pies and slices of quiche to pack up for a walk she's planned with Will tomorrow morning, the fudge for Megan, a few groceries for their evening meal, and a necklace, a birthday present for Lucy. It isn't her birthday for a few more weeks but she'd spotted it in a shop window and thought she could give it to her if when she comes down with Megan. She's not entirely sure if its Lucy's taste or not – it hangs low on the chest and dangles with lots of individually crafted spear-like shapes made out of coloured metal, all blues and greens and aquamarines. It makes a pretty jangling noise when you move it. She can see her daughter looking beautiful in it. She can see it matching her eyes – Lucy is the only one to have inherited anything remotely like her own eye-colour, but they're more blue than hers, a gorgeous piercing blue. She makes a squealing noise as Guy gooses her from behind, but she's had enough of playing and pulls away, passing him tins of tomatoes to stack in the cupboards. He seems relaxed. She wonders if it might be a good time to try and tackle him with what's been brewing inside her for a few days.

'Guy?'

'Oh no, I recognise that tone. That's "the lecture tone". Shall I make us both a cup of tea first? If we're going to be here a while?'

She scowls at him, and then softens. 'Am I that predictable?'

He moves over to the kettle. ''Fraid so, Mother. That's OK. It's what I love about you best.'

Where did he get this talent for schmoozing? Certainly not from her. Maybe from her mother. Vera can be quite charming, flirtatious even, Violet supposes. When her mother was younger, the few school friends Violet invited home all loved her. She was never quite sure if they were coming to play with her or coming to spend time with her marvellous mother. Maybe there's something in the genes that misses a generation, and Guy got the lot. It was always impossible to stay annoyed at him for very long, and she doesn't think that is always a good thing. She gathers resolve to push through the charm, not to get distracted. She finishes putting the things away as he dunks the teabags and stirs in three sugars for himself. He holds the mugs in front of him and motions towards the living room with a question on his face, but she shakes her head and holds her hand out, sitting at one of the two kitchen chairs. If they sit on the sofas she won't be able to stay focussed, she'll settle back into the comfy squishiness and Blue will jump up and she'll feel all sleepy and forgiving. The kitchen table is for business. He sets the mugs down on the kitchen table with a loud noise, tea slopping from one of them onto an electricity bill that arrived that morning. She tuts and after the mess is mopped up they sit across from each other like they're about to conduct an interview. Which she supposes they are.

'So, Mother, would you allow me to begin by guessing how the general gist of this will be going?'

'If you feel you must, Guy.'

'You'll start by asking me some pointed questions about how I am, how I'm managing the boredom, that kind of thing. You'll have your concerned face on, when you wrinkle up your forehead, but actually it looks more like you've forgotten your glasses and can't quite see me. Then you'll move on to something a little more threatening – when might I be leaving you in peace, what am I actually going to do about my credit card debt. You'll start getting frustrated with me and you'll try to hide it to begin with, but it'll start leaking out of you anyway and you might even storm out of the room. If you get past that stage then you'll move into what I like to call 'resignation', and you'll sigh gently and generally feel sad for me and despair of me ever making anything of my life. Oh, and you might not be able to resist one final spiky comment, involving me and the cold rainy streets of London or an empty syringe. Then we'll both eat a biscuit and go in and read our books in the living room until it's time to make dinner.'

He's been looking out of the window as he talks, glancing over at her, and now he's finished he rests his chin on his hands, elbows on the table, and gazes over at her, smiling smugly. She looks at him for a few moments and then widens her eyes, putting her hands face up in a gesture of resignation. Playing right into his hands. She sighs and sits drinking her tea for a few minutes without looking at him. And then she does start to think about where he'll end up, not on the cold and rainy streets of London, but in some dank sour bedsit somewhere, where he never invites his friends because he's ashamed of the smell. She imagines him coming to visit her at forty and asking in a round-about way if she has any spare money as he really needs to get a new bicycle. She imagines his disappointment when a future girlfriend, one he really loves, leaves him as she runs out of patience and money and energy. Here he is sitting on a park bench, alone, with the tears rolling down his face. And this reminds her of a time when he was ten or eleven. All of his friends had suddenly taken against him for no reason she could understand. They'd arranged to go on a trip to some theme park – one brave (or stupid) mother had volunteered to be responsible for the five boys. When she'd dropped him off she'd seen him approach the other boys and then walk away again, as if repelled by an opposite magnetic force, and she'd watched him scuffing the stones in the car park on his own as if that's what he really wanted to be doing anyway. What she really wanted to do was to jump out of the car and run towards him and sweep him up into her arms, shouting something horrible at the other boys, but she knew this would only make things worse. Instead she drove off in a cloud of fury, and took it out on Charles when she got home. Useless, she was useless to him.

It's not anger that comes to her now, as she sits at the kitchen table with her grown-up son, trying to discuss his future. It's grief. It rises in her quite unexpectedly, like a physical thing, up from the pit of her stomach and through her throat and pushing behind her eyes. Her diaphragm cramps. She blinks and each of her eyes release a large tear which roll down her cheeks without a sound. She prays that Guy will carry on looking out of the window, but he doesn't, he turns to her, and his face splits open with astonishment. He pulls back in his seat as if he's about to leap up and run out of the room.

'Mum, are you ill? What's wrong?'

She doesn't speak, as she fears her voice will crack. She sits there helpless, frozen. Useless. Completely at sea. She hopes more than anything that he doesn't touch her – she couldn't bear it if he touched her, she might crumble into dust. After a short silence Guy speaks again.

'Do you want me to get you anything? Some more tea? A biscuit?'

She's sickened by the thought of tea but nods dumbly. While he's clattering about she squeezes out another two tears and then manages to start composing herself. She tells herself off for being such an idiot, and the disparaging voice in her head reminds her of her mother. There's a mean edge to it, a disgust.

'I'm fine, darling,' she tries, and her voice is clear. 'I was just thinking about something silly from when you were little. When I wasn't much good to you. And I suppose it's the same thing now.' The sadness threatens to rise up again, so she decides to stop talking about it and change the subject. She looks at her watch.

'I don't want tea at all, Guy, would you fetch me a small glass of that Rioja in the fridge instead? Help yourself to some if you want it. Shall we go and watch Countdown, like we used to – you know, make it a competition? It's just starting.'

She wonders if he'll let her get away with it, backing away from her tears without comment. She can't remember ever crying in front of him, or in front of any of the children – not since they were tiny. He seems grateful to leave the subject alone, however, and his only concession is to pat her briskly on the arm after he gives her the glass of wine. Like a man back-slapping another man – expressing a deep affection, but each keeping the other at bay. They take their drinks into the living room and Violet fetches a notebook and felt tip pens.

Will picks her up in his shiny Mercedes CLK late the next morning. She still hasn't got an exact fix on what he did for a living before he got ill, but it must have been something pretty important. Something to do with sales, she thinks. He doesn't seem to like to talk about it very much. Come to think of it, what will they talk about for the next hour? It's the first time they've seen each other outside of the Committee meetings. It was Will who suggested it, under the pretext of discussing a minor financial matter with her, and she was flattered – she knew they got on well, but she would never have presumed he'd want to spend extra time with her outside of the meetings. But maybe he does have a reason for wanting to see her. Maybe he's planning on telling her all kinds of uncomfortable, embarrassing things on their walk and she'll be expected to come up with some sensible answers as an older, wiser woman… fuck, she hopes not. An awkward feeling hangs in the car between them for a few minutes but Will manages to disperse it by putting on a CD she'd recommended he get, Red Norvo and his Orchestra. The track is 'Too Marvellous for Words', originally released in the mid 1940s. Helen Ward's vocal is slow and sweet, and bumps up gently against the shuffling saxophone solo. The lyrics are delicious – languorous words like glamorous, amorous, glorious... 'it's all too wonderful'... 'you're just too marvellous for words'... Violet remembers that it's Dale Pearce on trumpet, and tells Will to turn it up louder and louder. They start getting looks from pedestrians, their heads swivelling with slight disapproval and looking slightly perplexed that the music isn't the usual hip hop or disco rubbish. Will does a silly dance by moving his head forwards rhythmically and jerking his shoulders about. This makes Violet laugh and eases them into a much more comfortable silence.

They mostly gossip about the other Committee members as they walk towards the old boat they've chosen as their turning point. Will has been supporting Margaret in dealing with the whole Sue business, and tells Violet what's happening in the strictest of confidence. They looked at the figures, and there definitely seemed to be a substantial sum of money missing. Apparently Sue wrote a long letter to Margaret, accusing Angie of all sorts of things, bringing up all kinds of dirt, and throwing in a couple of barbed comments about Rob and Will for good luck. Violet is surprised that she came off unscathed, unless Will is being kind by leaving that bit out. Sue also completely denied taking any of the money. Margaret has already written back and politely informed Sue of a date when they would hold a formal meeting to discuss what, if any, action would be taken. Neither of them knows what to make of it. It's only after demolishing their lunch and sitting and saying practically nothing for half an hour that they start walking back to the car and get onto more serious matters. First they talk a little about Will's wife, Helen, and how suspicious she gets of him seeing other women. She even gets jealous of the close relationship he has with his sister. Will makes it funny, and they laugh about what an honour it is for Violet to be allowed some time with her husband without her waiting up in the car with a long-range pair of binoculars. Will says she sometimes writes him letters as she finds it difficult to speak about how she feels. The mention of letters brings Elizabeth into mind, and Violet realises she's actually with someone she wants to talk to about them.

'Actually, I wanted to run something by you Will.'

'Fire away.' There's a silence as he waits for her to continue speaking.

'Well, not really run it by you, I suppose, just – I've been getting these bloody letters. For a few weeks now – every few days. The silly thing is... well – they're from 1959.'

'What do you mean?'

'The letters were written in 1959. By a girl called Elizabeth. She's in one of those mother and baby homes, you know, like the Magdalene Laundries, that kind of thing, and – well, I'm pretty sure they're the genuine article.'

'What, someone's sending them to you by mistake?'

'Well, I don't see why they should be sending them to anyone – they're fifty years out of time. The whole thing is pretty weird. I've been keeping it from Guy, from everyone...'

'Why?'

'...oh, I don't know really. I didn't want to worry them, I suppose. I wondered if someone might be out to get me, well – not in a malicious way, but...'

Again Will waits for her to order her thoughts. She stops to pick up a round stone and absentmindedly throws it into the edge of the sea. She sighs.

'I'm not making much sense, am I? It's like there's some kind of message I'm meant to be getting, and I'm just too stupid to understand it. She's really got under my skin, this girl.'

And she tells him about Elizabeth, all she can remember – her lack of faith in her family, her brisk dismissal of the poor father of the baby, Doll and Ruby, how she was terrified by what her friend Bea would think… It feels good for Violet to be saying it all out loud, in daylight. These things really happened – there's no reason to assume that they're an elaborate hoax. As she talks she feels a growing sense of relief, like she's been carrying a bag of heavy sand around with her all week and somebody has made a small slit in the bottom and it's all trickling away. When she gets to the end of the story she's also a little surprised at how she feels as she waits for Will to respond. It's important to her that Will understands Elizabeth, that he doesn't judge her. She feels protective towards her.

'So there's no-one to look after the poor thing.'

He sounds sad as he says this, and then lapses into a ruminative silence. A few hundred metres down the beach he continues.

'I haven't really talked to anyone properly about what went on, you know. Before I came here. Except my idiotic psychiatrist.'

'Not even Helen?'

'I tried, but…' He kicks a mound of seaweed as they pass by. 'Well, no, I probably didn't try very hard. I told you she found it difficult to hear?' Violet nods. 'Well, I'm sure if I… she's a pretty determined woman, you know, despite her little insecurities, and if it would be good for me to talk to her then she'd, well, brace herself to listen. Sometimes I think she'd do anything I needed her to. No, I didn't try too hard…' He's thinking out loud. 'I don't know. I suppose maybe it was a risk.'

'What kind of a risk?'

'Oh, I don't know really. It's all terribly confusing, this whole business. Have you ever…?'

'What, been… in the same sort of position?'

He nods.

'I don't think so. Me and Charles had our ups and downs over the years, especially with the children, but I don't think I've… well – I don't expect I know what it was like for you.'

He takes this as a question, and stops walking so he can think more clearly.

'If you could imagine me as a building, I don't know, say a nice old castle, on a little green hill,' he says, smiling. 'I suppose the things that have happened to me before in life have resulted in a bit of a change around of the furniture, maybe the turret has been damaged, maybe the entire wall fell down when my mother died ten years ago. But it's all been pretty fixable – I've still been a castle, I've still known where I was, you know?'

Violet nods, sticking out her bottom lip.

'But when I started losing it at work… It was a stupid thing that started it all off, you know, I'd forgotten to send an email to my Director and he was in a vile mood and he came in and bawled me out. Called me a twit – of all the insults in the world it's probably not up there with … I don't know… motherfucker, or cunt-breath, or…' He continues to search for some worse curses, encouraged by Violet's laughter, but after a few seconds concentration he gives up. 'Well, anyway. I couldn't forget it. The word rang through my head like a bloody bell, every few minutes. I could hardly carry out a conversation at one stage. That was the first crack. But this crack, Violet, it wasn't in the south facing wall or on one of the windows. It was deep deep down, right down in the foundations. Right underground. And it was all pretty raw down there, I think – it actually hurt, as if a shaft of light was getting into it for the first time and showing it up, and it was horrible to look at. Am I making any sense?'

Again Violet frowns and nods.

'And the crack grew and grew, and I couldn't do anything to stop it, as if that first 'twit' had set off some chain of events that I was utterly helpless to prevent. Even if my boss had said 'look, I was an idiot, we all think you're a valuable member of the team', whatever he'd said, it was too late. And the crack meant that the whole thing shifted, the whole bloody thing. Like an earthquake. The walls started curving, and one wing was totally reduced to rubble. I didn't know where the hell I was any more. Didn't know who the hell I was.'

He becomes quiet, and they continue walking. The sun moves out from behind a cloud. Violet tries to imagine what it might be like to have this kind of crack appear. It scares her, to think of people as having foundations like that, that go down so deep, in the dark. Shouldn't they be protected if they're underground? She's managed to protect hers pretty well, over the years. That's a good thing, isn't it? Will sighs explosively and pulls her away from her own thoughts. She looks over at him. He looks shattered, he looks like a shattered man. She feels an urge to soothe him somehow. What can she do? She settles for putting a hand on his back and patting him, as her son had patted her the day before. He turns to her and smiles a tired smile.

'Good old Violet.'

There's a moment of real affection underneath all the gruff awkwardness, and it tastes sweet.

When Violet gets in, the house is quiet. Before she takes off her coat she moves to the phone and impulsively dials Tom's number. She reaches the answer phone. She almost hangs up as the message plays but makes herself wait, forces some words out. 'It's me, I was just calling because I – well I just am. I'm not sure what to say.' And she hangs up. Not brilliant – she couldn't quite manage 'I'm missing you' or 'I hope you're OK' like any normal person, but at least she's done something. She can't remember making the first move after any of their previous arguments. It was always Tom who turned up on her doorstep, Tom who sent a text or a postcard to re-open the lines of communication. Was it a good thing, that she called? Or would it be better to put the relationship out of its misery once and for all, like a sick cat?

Chapter 17

29th of October '59

Sweet Bea –

Thank you so much for your two letters – I received both of them before I even had time to put my pen to paper. It's wonderful to hear all of your news – I can almost imagine that I'm safe at home. I read them over and over, sometimes in the middle of the night, with my bedside lamp on and quietly rustling the paper so I don't wake up Doll. Doll... I'm still not sure what to do about her, Bea, or if I should be doing anything at all. She's distant, as though there's a part of her that's split off and gone I don't know where. I wish she'd let me in.

Anyway, marvellous news about your pay rise – I wish I could go out and celebrate with you! Maybe we can when I come back. And I'm sorry to hear about Janey's horrid flu, and glad that you've escaped it so far. I can't remember what it's like to feel properly healthy, what with all the weird little things that happen to our bodies while we're here – it's remarkable what becomes normal after a while. Not being able to lie in the position you want to in bed, a constant ache in my back... I'm not complaining, Bea, I'm really rather shocked at how well I've coped. I suppose I've had it a bit easier than some of the girls in here – poor Ruby has suffered quite dreadfully with her piles – I know, not very glamorous! – and Peg is still being sick three times a day, like clockwork, even though she's almost due. I could hardly bear that. Although I suppose you just have to bear it – we've made our beds, as we've been told often enough. It's Sister Agatha's favourite phrase – along with 'DO get a move on' and 'if you MUST...' We make fun of her when she's out of the room – Queenie is much more wicked than me – and I don't feel guilty at all, Bea, she really is quite a battle-axe. I've been as nice as pie to her but she doesn't seem to have a heart. If she does it's buried so deep under proper behaviour and hospital corners that the poor thing only has enough energy to pump blood around her body rather than performing any of its other functions. I feel a little sad for her sometimes, when I'm not busy hating her.

Oh, Bea – if you could only see how huge I am! My due date is tomorrow but it feels like this pregnancy lark might go on forever! I wish I could just open up a flap in my forehead and show you how I'm feeling at the moment. I'm desperate for someone to understand, but I'm afraid I hardly understand things myself. I feel a bit like a little boat in a storm sometimes, getting blown about by all the minor things that happen to me during the day. This morning Sister Edith was a little sharp with me at breakfast about a duster I'd left on the floor where anyone could fall over it, and to my embarrassment I burst into tears, right in front of everyone else. I had to run out – or rather waddle out as quickly as I could, and if I didn't have this huge lump stuck onto the front of me I would have thrown myself face down onto my bed and wept for hours. As it was I had a good cry for ten minutes and the tears all ran out, and I felt suddenly famished and so went down and finished off my breakfast.

Now that my friends have been to the labour ward before me, I've been spending more time with the babies. Ruby had hers a few days ago, a bonny little boy she's called Malcolm, and he's such a darling! I suppose I've never really had much experience with babies before, if you don't count that girl at the Exchange, Doris, was it? When she kept going out and leaving us with her baby for hours on end – we didn't have a clue, did we Bea? I can remember lifting him up as if he was a delicate ornament, terrified of snapping one his legs off or his head rolling forward and just falling onto the floor! They're really rather resilient after all, you know, you'd only have to watch sweet Rose with her Patrick to know that it takes quite a lot of rough handling to damage a baby! I know I still haven't talked to you much about the baby, have I? Mine, I mean. I've been avoiding it, I suppose. It was only when you asked me in your last letter how I was feeling about it all, very tactfully, that I started to realise how much I haven't been telling you.

I call it 'nubbin'. My baby, that is. I don't know how it started, I was thinking of how I could refer to it in my head when I talk to it, it felt rude to just call it 'baby' all the time. I've already told you I think, that I've been talking to nubbin for months. I want to tell nubbin everything about me, just in case. Everything about me, and you, and my family, and my job, and what kind of person I think I am, and what other people think about me, and – oh, I don't know, I've spoken enough words into my stomach to fill up an entire football pitch and I still have thousands left to say. Millions. I haven't said enough for a lifetime yet. Not yet.

Am I going to keep nubbin? That's the big question, isn't it? And another question is important too – do I want to? If you asked me the second question, I wouldn't know the answer, because I've not looked – I've not asked myself. I've refused to think about it. It would confuse the first question too much. The first question is about nubbin, and the second question is about me and my selfish needs. I got nubbin into this mess in the first place, it's entirely my fault. A lifetime of being looked at in the street, people whispering, and that word – that awful word, that I've heard other people use all of my life. I've even said it myself, God forgive me. Those things I said about Judith at work when she became 'a fallen woman'... how awful of me, how despicable. I've done that to nubbin. I've given my baby the worst possible start in life, however clever she is, however pretty or handsome, however kind. The first question – am I going to keep it? – contains other questions too – how would I put food on our table? What would I tell people about the father? What would I say to my child when it was old enough to ask why it didn't have a daddy like all the other boys and girls? How will I cope when it comes home from school with that word lodged in its ear like an angry bee? How will I make it all better? How, Bea, how? I need to concentrate on the first question. I'm trying to find answers for all of those questions, but they keep multiplying, they breed like rabbits, wherever I turn a new one is taunting me. And they taunt me in the voice of Sister Agatha, because I know what she thinks. The others, especially Sister Mary, seem to have open minds – despite what society says, they say it should be the mother's decision. But Sister Agatha thinks the others are all in cloud-cuckoo land. You can see it in her face when they say something encouraging to a girl who's having last minute doubts. It's a kind of disgust. How COULD you do this to your child, her face says. How could you sentence your own child to this kind of a life? What kind of a mother are you? What kind of a mother are you?

Sorry, Bea. I got myself a little upset. I'm back now. It's not a rare sight in here for someone to be wandering about with red eyes, and I fetched myself a nice cup of cocoa, which usually does the trick. Now Ruby's with her baby she hasn't got the time to watch over me the way she did before. She still cares about me, I know that, but – well, life changes, doesn't it? Priorities... On a happier note, I had a visit from Marjory yesterday. I spend a lot of my time waiting for people to give themselves away, to show their true feelings about what I've done. It just doesn't seem to be there with Marjory. It makes more sense to me after what she told me yesterday. I don't know why she chose yesterday, maybe she could tell I was feeling pretty low. We were taking in some air, walking about under the trees in the garden, me with a blanket wrapped around me as it was bitterly cold. We'd been walking for a few minutes without saying anything – we'd been talking about her husband Roger and their next holiday. And then Marjory told me about some friends of theirs, a younger couple, who'd just had their first baby – and how much her husband was enjoying bathing him, despite protesting at first that it was 'woman's work'. We both looked at the trees for a while – I don't know what they are, their leaves were mostly gone but some scraps of dark yellow remained, such a lovely colour. It seemed like the colour that a crown ought to be, or maybe a hot toasted crumpet dripping with butter...

And then out of the blue she told me that when she was younger, she'd got pregnant. It wasn't with Roger, it was a boy she'd been dating for a year, a boy who lived just down the road from her and wanted to be a butcher like his father. She was devastated – she was careful to say it might not have been the same for me, but for her it was like her entire life had fallen apart. This was 15 years ago, so the way it was seen, she said, it was even worse. She thought she only had one option – to marry this boy – but she really didn't want to – she had never imagined spending the whole of her life with him. She didn't tell him. She didn't tell anyone. And she found an advert, in a phone-box, for back street abortions. She said that as soon as she saw the advert she knew what she had to do, she needed to save her own life by killing a life that was growing inside her. She used just those words, Bea – killing a life inside her – it was brutal. It made me wonder what it was like for her to do that to herself. She didn't tell me. She didn't tell me anything about the procedure either, but she went pale when she mentioned it. Her and Roger have been trying to start a family for years now, she said, and the doctor said there isn't much hope left. The doctor wouldn't tell her if it was because of what she'd done. She'd had to tell the doctor, in the end, privately, and I could tell it had been perfectly awful for her, Bea, to tell this to 'a man she respected' and who had respected her, thought she was 'an upstanding citizen'. 'No woman deserves to be seen like that,' she said to me, and she'd forgotten all about me by then, she was talking to herself. After she told me we had a little picnic in the back room – Marjory had brought some food for me as she thought I might be tired of 'nursery food', and she'd brought some lovely things – a tin of pineapple, some good ham... She'd made a cake from Elizabeth David's cookery book too, she's crazy about her. I ate a huge slice of it and made Marjory laugh. I felt closer to her, both of us looking out into the garden. She trusted me enough to tell me. Like I trust you enough to tell you... well. I was going to say anything, but that wouldn't be quite truthful. And I – oh, Bea, I can't do it just yet. I'm sorry.

Well – I've gnawed your ear off again. This might be it this time – the last time you hear from me with a baby in my belly. I'm feeling a little more frightened with every day that comes. I can't really avoid it now, can I? Nubbin has got too big, and is coming out of me one way or another. And I'll tell you something else I haven't told you before. I think it's going to be a girl, Bea. I can just feel it in my bones. All the nuns say that's rubbish and that girls who are sure of the sex of their baby are just setting themselves up to be disappointed, but I don't care, I know it's a girl. And it if is, I'm going to call her Beatrice. If you don't mind, that is. I'll wait for a letter from you, just in case. Maybe you're saving it for your own daughter, who I'm sure you'll have one day, and a son too, and you'll be a wonderful mother. A proper mother. I had better go now, there's someone making a noise in the hall and I ought to go and see what's happening. All my love, until the next letter...

Your Elizabeth.

Chapter 18

Violet was thirteen when she first saw her body as anything other than a machine to get her around. She was left alone in the house where Augustine's friend lived. Her sister and her friend had got top marks for their science project at school, and the punishment for Violet's 'ungracious response' had been to stay in whilst everyone else went out for a celebration meal. It didn't seem like much of a punishment to Violet. She relished the thought of a few hours on her own to explore this strange house, imagining what kind of people might read books about astronauts, and why they would need so many hats. The best type of alone – safely bordered by someone returning at a fixed point. By the end of the first hour she had exhausted looking into all of the drawers, and she'd made and consumed a cold beef sandwich with extra mustard. She'd also tried unsuccessfully to get the unfamiliar record player to work, although their record collection was completely embarrassing – Des O'Connor, some country and western, no jazz at all. She wandered from room to room and found herself lingering in the master bedroom. It was a study in pastel pinks – the bedspread, the curtains, and the carpet

– even the ornaments on the window sill (a knitted ballerina doll and a ceramic poodle). The friend's father was a hulk of a man, employed as some kind of construction worker, and Violet raised her eye-brows at the inner workings of marriages – how did he lie down in this room with a straight face? How had the wife got away with this monstrosity of interior design?

As she read the spines of the books on the shelf above the bed (Nevil Shute, Agatha Christie) the full-length mirror next to the dressing table caught her eye. They didn't have any full-length mirrors at home, her mother calling them 'an unnecessary vanity'. Violet stood in front of it and studied her reflection. Her eye-brows seemed thick and straggly, and her lips were chapped. Her eyes were all right, though, with their piercing colour, and she quite liked the look of her cheekbones when she turned to the left side. She'd been growing out her hair, and it had finally started to lie down flat at the crown. Her body was another thing entirely. She was suddenly disgusted with her clothes – a shapeless T-shirt with a mustard stain, cord flares the colour of cat sick... She wasn't quite brave enough to pull any clothes out from the friend's mother's desk of drawers. They were all neatly folded and she doubted she could achieve the same when she replaced them. Over by the big window was a whole wall of white fitted cupboards. She opened them all up – she couldn't find any of the father's clothes at all – instead there was rack after rack of slacks, cardigans and blouses. Not owning any herself, she was drawn to the dresses. She pulled out a few and laid them on the bed – a red jersey one with sequins around the neck, a long cotton flowered one, a dusky pink one with a full skirt and a pinched in waist. She might just see what they looked like... They looked ridiculous on her – she looked like a boy in drag. She started to feel annoyed and grimaced at herself in the mirror, making body-building postures with her arms.

She was starting to think about going to watch some television when she found one last dress tucked away at the back of the cupboard. It was made from a beautiful heavy silk – aquamarine-grey, the colour of a stormy sea. It looked narrow and she doubted that the friend's mother would have been able to get into it any more. Did she keep it for old time's sake? Did she smooth the silk up against her cheeks and remember? Violet undressed down to her knickers, discarding even her vest, and pulled it carefully over her head. The silk licked at her skin. When she let go of the bunched up fabric the dress fell over her body into shape all at once, like a woman shaking out her hair. She touched her hips through the silk. Even before she looked in the mirror she knew that this was the one. The colour seemed to set off her eyes, which glowed a brighter violet than she'd seen them before. The dress had clever darts in it, and emphasised her barely budding breasts and the slight jut of her hips. The skirt narrowed before kicking out into swirls around her ankles, which gave her something to flounce about with. The neck and the material below the waist were embroidered with tiny silvery-blue beads and they glittered as she spun and swished in front of the mirror. She looked like a woman in this dress. She touched her thighs through the silk and juddered at her first frisson of sexual pleasure.

Once she became aware of the possibility of her own body as a sexual object, she started to look at her peers in a different way. A girl at school, Suzie, was lucky enough to own (in Violet's estimation) the perfect body. Her plump breasts jiggled in her shirt like crème caramels, and her round bottom balanced them out with same the pleasing symmetry as the hourglass in her mother's kitchen. She found herself magnetised to Suzie's body, watching her move across the games field in her too-tight hockey top, and wind between the desks like a cat. Violet wasn't the only one to notice her. The male half of the class would talk about her in whispers. Once a whole gang of them dared a particularly brave boy to go over and sink his finger into her breast through the material of her blouse, to the poorly hidden delight of Suzie. Violet would go home and joylessly examine herself, taking the small mirror from her wall and balancing it on the bed, contorting herself into different positions so she could see her own body in profile or from behind. There wasn't anything to see. She watched the other girls in her class continue to blossom, and their bodies had all the promise of fat peony buds. Violet could almost imagine that her own fleshy bits were shrivelling up. She even started to wonder if she'd been born into the wrong body. She'd regularly examine herself under the blankets to make sure she didn't have any unusual lumps or bumps that could be unformed penises or retracted testicles. She wasn't sure what she should be looking for, or what a normal vagina was meant to feel like anyway, and so these frantic exploratory sessions only added to her anxiety. It was only when her period started when she was nearly fourteen that she could properly relax.

Throughout this time her only consolation was a brief alliance with Suzie. Violet helped her out in class one day by dragging the focus of a particularly nasty teacher away from Suzie's unfinished homework towards Violet's 'bloody cheek'. Suzie casually offered her a 'ciggie' in the corridor after the lesson. It became a little ritual that Suzie and Violet would go for a smoke in the woods beyond the playground after Science every week, crammed into a small space between a broad tree-trunk and the wire fence. Their main preoccupation seemed to be to practise blowing smoke sexily, and they gave each other marks out of ten for 'artistic merit' and 'sex appeal', giggling into their hands. They also practised their 'suggestive looks' on each other – Suzie was a real pro and Violet sometimes felt her cheeks burn or her knees wobble. After the first time Violet tried to greet Suzie in the corridor and drew a blank from her, she realised that they were only going to be a certain kind of friends. She took what she could get. Their smoking sessions lasted for several more months before Suzie got a serious boyfriend and abandoned Violet altogether. A week before they stopped meeting, Suzie gave Violet's smoke-blowing a perfect ten.

Violet's series of intense teenage crushes led to lots of action in her imagination, but apart from a bodged kiss with a boy at a Christmas party she didn't get a chance to seriously practise her suggestive look again until University. It all started on the tennis courts. An arrogant boy from her structural engineering classes was one of the top players in the University, and she spent long hours imagining him taking her under his wing and standing behind her to show her how to swing the racquet. She especially liked to imagine the sensation of his hot breath on her neck. When she joined the tennis club it turned out that he already had a perfectly formed tennis-girlfriend, with bleached blond hair and a brilliant white tennis skirt that barely covered her bottom, but Violet surprised herself by actually enjoying the game. She enjoyed the power in her legs as she dove towards the net, the sound of her racket-strings dicing the air, the moment of bouncing contact with the ball. She never excelled at the game, but she found a partner who was interested in playing as often as her – a pale girl who, Violet suspected, had some kind of eating disorder. The more Violet played, the more the muscles in her arms and legs took on density and shape. Sinewy was her favourite word at the time – she wanted to be sinewy. If she could never have Suzie's tactile, cushiony curves then at least she could be slender, elegant, muscled. Her shapely calves attracted a series of socially awkward fellow players, who asked her for a game to get the metaphorical ball rolling. She'd ask them back to her room afterwards and snog the faces off them until she was covered in stubble rash. She was determined to make up for lost time.

She lost her virginity when her body was at its absolute peak. She gave it to an on-off boyfriend of hers – another tennis player who preferred to run, and who coveted the look of muscle swelling beneath skin. He spurned the various running clubs and went out on his own in all weathers, pushing himself to better his previous times. He had a slightly frosty side that Violet was a little wary of, but he could also be tender and loving, and once he talked to her about his mother and cried in her lap. The first couple of times were predictably clumsy for both of them, but they managed to give each other a reasonable amount of pleasure. He loved to lie propped up on one of his elbows and gaze at her body, the covers stripped to the bottom of the bed; her flat stomach, her boyish breasts, the sinews in her neck. She had mixed feelings about his gaze – it felt good to have his attention, to be appreciated, but the look was also covetous, as if he were a housewife deciding which cut of meat to buy. Or as if he were making a decision about how long he wanted to keep her. Which, as it turned out, was not very long.

Violet's pale tennis partner fell out with her and so Violet also turned to running as a more reliable way of keeping fit. She enjoyed the long solo journeys around the edge of campus, not really noticing anything around her but going into a kind of trance where she didn't have to think about anything except where her legs were and when to breathe. Her body stayed lean, but no-one was seeing her naked any more, and so she didn't see any reason to pay much attention to it herself. She still had a sexual appetite – after getting a taste of honey with the runner she masturbated more regularly, snaking her hand down under the sheets when she was safely shut in her room, but she never touched any other parts of her body – her breasts, her thighs. It was straight to business and quick relief. After a while she started to think that maybe it was easier this way anyway. She couldn't quite remember what was better about sex with someone else. Surely when she could move her fingers where she wanted, the whole process was more efficient, more satisfying? She didn't have to think about what the other person wanted, or have that horrible anxiety about getting it wrong, she didn't have to lie there feeling frustrated as he touched her just to the left of where she really wanted him to concentrate, or panic that he'd get his fill before she had a chance to get what she needed. And then, after a chance encounter on an out-of-campus training course that lasted the full three nights of the course (involving a total of 6 hours sleep), she remembered. Sex with another person was better because it involved frustration – frustration built desire. It was also better because it involved false starts and butterfingers, and with mistakes came laughter and an easy affection. It was better because there was another person there, to give to, and this was such a novelty to Violet that she wondered if she'd somehow previously missed out on it altogether. And it was better because she was given to – she could lie there and do nothing and put herself entirely in someone else's hands. She could trust them to get it right, eventually, and this careful boy certainly did.

In the first year of her PhD she started to notice her body again. The food in the canteen at her small Scottish University was in a class of its own. The kitchen prided itself on cooking 'home made meals' rather than the plastic packaged flapjacks and frozen chips she was used to. Now she could gorge herself for very little money on steak and kidney pie with thick buttery pastry, creamy mashed potato, and nursery school puddings with custard or cream. She was further away from home than she'd ever been, and although she'd never admit that she missed her family, she was lonely. She had never really mastered the art of making friends, and this made matters worse. The kind ladies in the canteen sniffed out her desperate isolation and started being extra nice to her, giving her an extra spoonful of shepherds pie or sprinkling some cheese on her Bolognese before she asked. She gratefully accepted the food in lieu of love, and after a couple of months she started to notice her blouses gaping at her chest, and her stomach bulging softly over the top of her jeans. She found it disgusting, this extra fat, but had never had to diet before and so wasn't sure how go about it. She restricted herself from everything that tasted good for a whole week, feeling miserable as hell, saying no to the concerned canteen staff, and at the end of the week she bought an entire cream sponge from the local bakery and ate every crumb, bathed in a heady mixture of guilt and pleasure. For most of the first year she'd put on ten pounds and then lose it, then put on a stone more... Eventually she made friends with a Spanish girl on her course and her need for rich food subsided. She just didn't fancy it any more. Apart from a brief obsession with her weight after each of the children were born, food receded into the background once more.

Her sex life with Charles had always been 'comfortable', right from the beginning. They first had sex on the night of their second date, on Violet's narrow bed with the lights on. Both of them climaxed without any fuss. They took things a little more slowly the next morning, and afterwards Violet held his softening penis in her hand until they fell asleep. This became a habit which persisted throughout their marriage. Charles had a thing about nakedness being 'the most natural thing on earth', and insisted that they go away frequently for 'dirty weekends'. They didn't seem to have any more sex than usual on these weekends, which were really an excuse for him to spend time with her in a hotel room with both of them starkers. Violet would sit and do some marking, he would have a bath and then read the papers, or maybe use the trouser press... If they hadn't ended up living with her parents he would have been one of those people who hardly ever wore clothes around the house – maybe a dressing gown loosely hanging open if it were cold – meeting shocked postmen and mother-in-laws at the door. She humoured him with these naked weekends, teasing him about having Scandinavian blood, but she wouldn't go so far as to visit a nudist colony, however persuasively he presented his arguments. The opportunities to escape became fewer as their children were born, and their last attempt at a naked weekend was rudely interrupted by Lucy's measles.

He was always very fond of her body, and this helped her to come to an easier relationship with it herself. He especially liked the way her hip bones protruded when she lay on her back, and he used to put a cupped hand on one of them to help him go to sleep. It's the one thing she regularly misses about him, even now. Charles also made a great fuss of her small, boy-like bottom, which he was constantly referring to as 'two-peaches-in-a-string-bag' or 'the girls'. It was a joke that passed between them – he'd think of a new slang name every year or two and use it until she was utterly sick of it and him. She'd hung on to the view of her bottom as one of her best features after the divorce – it seemed to have remained pretty pert. A little sagging is to be expected, she is fifty-one after all, but she looks into the mirror behind her most mornings after her shower, just to make sure its still there. Charles' new wife has a rather large bottom – a classic English pear shape – and this is something that gives Violet secret pleasure. He'll never be able to call her Sweetcheeks. He must miss her bottom a little bit, whenever he looks at his new wife's – she can't see how he wouldn't.

Age started to affect Violet's body much later than it left its mark on her face. When she was thirty she became perturbed by a series of lines on her forehead that stayed visible even when she relaxed her face. She knew it was too late to un-make these lines, to develop the habit of different expressions which would give her crows-feet instead – she'd even prefer creased eye-lids or a smoker's mouth, that puckered dogs-arse look. The lines on her forehead were angry lines. They became deep and black when she practised her 'keeping-the-anger-back' face in the mirror, a sort of concentration. Guy called it her 'bulldog look' once, after he'd left home and felt brave enough. She didn't want her face to give this away about her, and for several years she tried to calm the muscles whenever she caught herself screwing them up, thinking that must have been what her mother meant when she said 'don't make that face, the wind might change'. She was slow to admit that the wind had already changed.

Her body's metamorphosis was relatively easy to handle in comparison. As she grew older she felt more and more blessed to have the kind of body she did – the body she hated when she was at school and the other girls were blooming all over the place. Her classmate's firm pockets of flesh will be moving towards the ground now, succumbing to gravity, softening like overripe fruit. Their skin will be developing puckers and waves and lumps. Her body, in comparison, stayed mostly where it was. It was her turn to look half decent, and her turn for other women to be jealous of her. There had been changes, of course – even the skin above her small breasts was tiring, and her upper arms had become crêpey and loose, but once she was dressed those things weren't important. She loved her body anew after her illness, at Abbotsfield. Once more it would take her confidently along the beach as far as she wanted to go, it would carry in firewood, open stubborn pickle jars, even move that heavy wardrobe from her bedroom into the office. She owned her own body again. And then there was Tom.

Chapter 19

Violet scoops up dollops of white bubbles and presses them between her palms like dough. They resist half-heartedly before letting go of their air. The bath is getting a little cold, and the light from the small window is fading. She should have lit a candle or two. As she looks closely at a white blob of the stuff on her finger she remembers a time in the ancient bath in her old house, when the bubbles turned pink. She couldn't understand it until she noticed the string of her tampon snaking in the water between her legs. She isn't capable of turning them pink any more. She gushes the hot tap for twenty seconds and then sinks back down so her earlobes are submerged and the bubbles pop gently against her chin. Mmm, the smell of fresh lemons. She's enjoying her own space. She heard herself saying this to Will earlier on the phone and noticed how rarely she's said this before and really meant it. Guy was in London yesterday – he went to a gig on 'a kind of date' with a friend's sister. It's not his usual thing, he told her, calling the music 'zombiecore' and saying something about the band dressing up in bandages and fake blood... Her mind boggles. He'd popped in earlier that evening to change his clothes and then went straight out to the big house for another dinner date with George. She's not expecting him back until late, and is making the most of his absence. She was able to tidy the kitchen earlier without bumping into his knees as she moved from cupboard to cupboard, and without having to listen to him read out various hilarious headlines from the local paper with a straight face – 'local man found with trousers down' or 'cat with bad breath needs a loving home'. When she did the washing she didn't have to fish his dark blue tie-dye T-shirt from the linen basket full of her pale knickers and vests to stop it from infecting the entire load. She didn't need to think about him when she considered her evening meal – did he say he didn't like sardines? Will that piece of pork be big enough for both of us?

It seems that she's starting to crave time alone. Maybe the long lonely first months in the house did her some good after all – kick-started an emotional self-reliance she's never managed to cultivate before. It's certainly forced her into thinking about herself – not the children, not Charles. What do I want for breakfast? What shall I do with those three hours before my haircut appointment? She's never had the opportunity to ask herself those questions before, certainly not since Lucy was born. Or could these new hermit-like urges be a bad thing? Maybe she'll turn into a finicky old spinster who needs everything in its right place, and who heaves a sigh of relief whenever a visitor finally leaves so she can put everything back where it should be. No – she doesn't think she's quite there yet. When Guy moves out she'll probably feel elated for a full half hour before Countdown comes on and she hasn't got anyone to play with. Or she'll remember the fresh trout in the fridge, and realise it's far too big for her to manage alone.

She turns a hand around and makes a mental note to cut her fingernails. She examines the creases at her knuckles, and then her belly-button through a window in the film of white bubbles. Looking at her stomach reminds her of something Tom had told her. Tom imagined everyone as having a beam of light shining from their stomachs – you could tell who was who by the colour of their light. Some people had a strong, bright light and other people's you could hardly see, depending on how well they knew themselves, and how authentic they managed to be. Violet imagined hers as a pale purply-blue. She started catching sight of it when she was walking alone on the beach, or making breakfast for herself, or even lying in bed and feeling angry or alone. It felt good to imagine it radiating out from her belly – it was like catching sight of herself in the mirror and being reassured that her nose was still in the right place. A sort of 'there I am!' feeling. She noticed that her light seemed to get weaker when she was with other people – maybe the light coming from them got all mixed up with hers, or maybe she was too busy looking at theirs to notice her own. Although that never seemed to happen when she was with Tom. Which doesn't really make sense, because Tom's colour was pretty strong. A brilliant green, like fresh spikes of grass. Maybe she can learn to hold on to her own colour when she's with other people – but how?

She steps out of the bath and wraps herself in a huge towel. She brushes the tangled thoughts from her mind as she combs her short hair back from her face. Lights, colours – what bollocks. She'll be chanting 'ohmmm' and harnessing the magical energy of crystals next. She's settling down on the sofa with a book when the doorbell rings. She considers ignoring it for a few rebellious seconds, but an image of a police-officer announcing that her son has been found washed up on the beach suddenly inserts itself into her brain. She laughs at the ridiculousness of being a mother as she heaves herself up off the sofa. The laughter dissolves away the anger, and by the time she opens the door she's ready for anyone.

'Angie!'

'Violet.'

There's a pause and Angie begins to fidget about on the doorstep, looking behind her as if someone might be watching her.

Violet remembers herself. 'Oh, do come in,' she says, stepping aside. 'Would you like a mug of something? I've just made myself some tea, the kettle's hot.'

'Oh, a glass of water would be fine, thank you, Violet.'

Violet shows Angie into the living room and when she returns with the water Angie is sitting on the edge of one of Violet's armchairs with her back straight. She accepts the water, takes a sharp sip, then places it on the coffee table. She doesn't touch it again.

'I won't keep you long, Violet, it's just that I'm visiting all the Committee members and, well, you're the last on my list. Except… anyway, it's about this business with Sue.'

Violet nods, taking a sip of her Rooibos tea. It tastes so rosy and comforting. Lucy made her a cup at her flat last month and Violet's had a box of her own in her kitchen ever since. She's tried to convert various guests to the stuff with mixed results. It just tastes so pink! She makes a mental note to thank her daughter for introducing it to her, and her train of thought jumps to considering where she's going to put all of her children when they come for dinner in a week's time. Could she fit Guy in the upstairs hallway? Would Josie mind sleeping on the sofa? She has to drag herself back to Angie as she continues speaking.

'Well, I haven't been sleeping very well, since it happened, and I've had this constant feeling of butterflies in my stomach. I've seen the doctor but all he can do is give me some sleeping pills, and something else, but they don't seem to be doing me much good, and well I'd much rather...' She catches the look on Violet's face and changes tack. 'Well, the thing is... I came here to talk to you about whether I can count on your support, Violet.'

'My support?'

'Yes, you know, whether you'll back me up, be on my side.'

Angie has flushed pink and seems unable to look Violet in the eye. Violet feels under a palpable pressure. This doesn't fit with what she can see – Angie is squirming on the sofa with her eyes cast down, doing a brilliant impression of a school child caught throwing stones at the gym windows. But the feeling is there, nonetheless. Would it be a problem for Violet to say she was on Angie's side? Surely there oughtn't to be sides in this kind of thing – it's about the facts, isn't it? What is that uncomfortable feeling in her stomach? When she looks back at Angie she seems to be in an even worse state – Violet can see one of her hands trembling as she fiddles with the pendant around her neck.

'I'm not sure what you mean. Do you want me to vouch for you in front of the others, or is there going to be some kind of vote... you see, I don't know anything about what happened and I don't know you or Sue very well...'

In response to this, Angie picks up her handbag.

'No, no, I see, if you feel that... you've made your position clear.'

Violet has never felt daunted by other people's anger. She's noticed that some people will go to extraordinary lengths to prevent other people from becoming angry with them. She'd watched one of her ex-husband's colleagues repeatedly ridicule him over the years, and when Violet questioned him about why he didn't retaliate he'd just say – 'I don't want him to get annoyed with me.' Violet used to say 'so WHAT if he gets angry with you?', feeling the red mist rise in her own body, but there was no budging him – it was a perfectly reasonable deal as far as he was concerned, let the man call him an idiot every so often, and have no anger directed towards him as a result. Violence – now that was a different thing. Physical violence could leave actual damage – bruised flesh, broken bones – she could understand people wanting to avoid that. But even bodies healed, mostly – and surely murder wasn't that common? Especially by the kind of ordinary small-time bullies who use the threat of anger to get their own way.

People like Angie who hardly ever get angry are another thing altogether. Violet has come across several in her career – the worst of them a man called Trevor who worked in her department for a while. He couldn't bear for anyone else in the room to be less than completely happy, as if their negative emotions would leak out and infect him like mustard gas. He spent his entire time asking people if they wanted anything, or making complete U-turns on his views when challenged, or apologising for imagined slights. Whenever Violet spent time with him she felt frustration rise in her like mercury – filling her up – and before too long she'd want to bang him on the head with a book – for fuck's sake, Trevor, if you want the window open then just fucking open it! I don't give a shit if you disagree with me, don't try and pretend you're on my side! It always left her feeling guilty, as everyone else thought he was a lovely, sweet man, and when she tried to explain what was quite so infuriating about him she always got a bit stuck. 'Well, he never thinks of himself,' she'd start, then a little more uncertainly, 'He's always trying to make everyone else happy.' And then they'd ask, 'Yes, and why does that make you angry?' and she'd admit defeat, and vow to start seeing him as a sweet man like everyone else did. But where was his anger? That's what Violet wanted to know. Is it possible for a person to never feel slighted by someone else, to never rear up in defence? Surely that's what anger is − a sign that we need to protect ourselves when someone crosses an invisible boundary? Would we always be aware of these violations if it wasn't for the pumping of adrenaline, the urge to push the other person onto the floor? She couldn't see that there was anything wrong with it, really. So Violet is completely unperturbed by Angie's small show of displeasure, and simply raises her eyebrows without saying a word.

This seems to have quite an effect on Angie. She turns her head as if she's been burnt, and then rolls her eyes to the left and back to the middle several times. After a moment's silence she launches into a stream of sorries − 'Sorry to have bothered you at home,' 'Sorry to ask you,' 'Sorry for being like that, I don't know what came over me, what with all the stress,' and then, 'Will you let me wash up this cup for you?' and, 'No, don't get up, I'm fine, really,' and, 'Could I make you another cup of tea while I'm in there?' It's all very convincing, and she becomes Angie again, sweet Angie with her low self-esteem, Angie who's always thinking of other people. That is, if it weren't for the nugget of anger still lodged in her centre like a glowing hunk of steel.

After Angie has gone, Violet spends a long time fussing Blue on the sofa beside her. He flops off her lap when it gets too hot, but he keeps one of his paws pushed up against her leg, like a lover placing a flat hand on the other's thigh, reluctant to completely separate after making love. He grows tired of receiving her affection before she's tired of giving it, so she calls him a grumpy bastard a few times and turns to the television guide, wanting to make the most of the rest of her evening alone. There's so much sensationalist crap on these days; 'It's Me Or Your Motorbike' or 'Fat Pets on Drugs'... she can't quite believe that these programmes really represent the average intelligence of UK citizens. She manages to find something to watch that doesn't make her groan – a film, quite mainstream, but with a streak of quirkiness running through it. Thank heavens they occasionally manage to slip that kind of thing through Hollywood – maybe they do their pitch when the producer isn't really concentrating. Some of the actors actually look like normal people, and act like them too. It follows a pair of old men as they go on a kind of pilgrimage to a small wood near their childhood home town, after the death of the third of their 'gang'. They bump into all kinds of interesting characters along the way – a woman with a beehive hairstyle who collects the mini-windmills you stick in your front garden, a young man with a limp and a predilection for sex with women twice his age. Violet likes films like this, films that admit that exciting things still happen to people when they're over the age of thirty-five – and that it's never too late for epiphanies. Maybe there's hope for her yet.

She blows her nose as the credits roll, glad that no-one was there to witness her little over-sentimental weep. A political debate comes on after the adverts and she can't be bothered to change the channel. Her eyes-lids feel more tired than the rest of her, and she lets them fall; they feel as if they've been straining to stay open for hours. Aaah, delicious. As she listens to some minister ramble on about grants, she thinks about the letters. She has an overwhelming urge to get in touch with Elizabeth and help her out – it feels unbearable to be fifty years too late. The girl can't be fictional – she refuses to believe that. She thinks a new thought – maybe Elizabeth herself is sending them to her, an older Elizabeth – how old would she be now, about seventy? She does a quick inventory of all the women she's ever known who'd be this age, especially her new acquaintances in the village, but nobody fits. Why would Elizabeth send the letters to Violet anyway? What is she expected to do with them? She feels again that she's failing somehow, that there are clues she's failing to see. She'll get them all out tomorrow, the ones she's received so far, and see if she can make any sense of them – maybe the dates have some significance, or the location…

She wakes up to a huge crash. She freezes for several seconds, imagining burglars and desperately flicking her eyes around in the half-dark to see what blunt instruments she has within reach, before she remembers that she has a noisy, clumsy son.

'Guy?' Her voice is more of a croak.

'Oh, Mother! What are you doing in there!'

He pops his head around the corner of the door. He's drunk. He's delighted to see her, and she's hit by an unexpected wave of affection towards him. She doesn't want to be on her own after watching that film, thinking about Elizabeth – she could do with some easy company before she goes to bed. She looks over at the clock on the television. 03.18. Guy bounds in and bends over to kiss her on the forehead, a wet sloppy smacker, before disappearing back into the kitchen. He leaves a cloud of alcohol behind him, mixed with his sweat. It's not an unpleasant smell – there's no stale tobacco mixed in, and there's still a faint whiff of his deodorant underneath. She gets up from the sofa, gently shifting and stretching her stiff legs and hips, careful not to disturb Blue, who's curled up in deepest sleep at her feet. She gives his fur a quick ruffle and enjoys the noise he makes, a sleepy sort of chirrup, alongside a stretch of his own – his feet pushing forward and his claws flexing before he settles back into exactly the same position to go on dreaming of wide windowsills and creamy milk. She takes the crocheted rug from the back of the sofa to wrap around herself like a huge shawl. There's a nip in the air – she could do with a hot drink. She shuffles into the kitchen like an old lady.

Guy is waltzing around the kitchen as if he's in a world of his own. He seems to be making a sandwich for himself, although from the miscellaneous array of jars and foodstuffs on the kitchen table she daren't imagine his plans. He seems very happy.

'Turn the kettle on for your old woman, will you?'

'Certainly, mother. La la laaaa, la la la la… that's been running though my bloody head all night. Can you remember it? La la laaaa, you know, la la la la… sung by some shrieking woman, I think.'

She shakes her head, smiling a little. He looks suddenly self-conscious.

'What are you smirking at, Mother? Am I a little the worse for wear? God-damned Georgie, the way he plies me with drinks, first fine wines, then an after-dinner sherry. We want the finest wines available to humanity! And then he brought out that bloody brandy.' He's frowning, then suddenly breaks out into a wide grin. 'Tasted fucking amazing, though. Oops, sorry, Mummy. Mustn't use the f-word.'

'And why the fuck not?' she says, feigning annoyance.

She used to protect the children from the worst of her language – it was something Charles felt very strongly about. It often seemed ridiculous to her, that once the children were of a certain age they'd go off behind their backs with their friends and swear until the air was blue, whilst Violet did exactly the same. Guy looks confused and turns back to his sandwich, saying 'Why the fuck not, indeed?' under his breath. By the time he looks up again his mood has changed again, back to brash happiness.

They sit at the kitchen table together. Violet has hot chocolate with cream on top and is dipping her finger into it between sips. Guy holds his enormous sandwich with both hands and begins to demolish it with great relish, making 'mmm' and 'mrow, mrow, mrow' sounds as he eats.

'Good evening, darling?'

'Oh, yes, very cool. That George, he's really a top geezer, you know.'

He lapses into a rumination and stares into space for several seconds, the sandwich hovering centimetres from his mouth, before he gives his head a little shake and takes another huge bite.

'The bloody walk back was bit of a nightmare though. He told me to stay, but…' Again he drifts off. Violet feels a small stirring of impatience and thinks this might be a good time to end her evening.

'Well, I'm going to be off up to bed, then,' she says, pushing her chair back and taking the mug to the sink to wash it out. She's always been quite anal about needing to come down to a clean kitchen in the morning, even if the crockery gets dirty at 3.30am. Such a horrible way to start the day, faced with last night's crusting lasagne and the milk curdling in yesterday's coffee dregs.

As she turns to Guy she sees he's got up out of his seat and is standing in front of her with both his hands up, as if he's stopping traffic.

'Mother. I came home because,' he chokes on a piece of sandwich and tries again. 'I came home because I need to tell you something.'

She lets out a sigh and sits back down at the table. When Guy was a teenager, she was subjected to a few of these late night confessionals. They were usually about something pretty insignificant that had become magnified in his head, and he used to take so long to get to the point. Once he felt compelled to tell her that he'd called her a 'bore' when talking to one of his friends. Was it a bore or tedious? She can't even remember now. What a fuss over nothing.

'OK, Guy, but you'll have to be quick, I'm really beat.'

He holds one hand up to pause her as he finishes the last mouthful of his sandwich, swallowing hard, and then sits back down, looking doleful. She can see him swaying gently in his seat and it gives her the impression that they are both in a ship's galley. She imagines the water outside under the stars, navy blue and rippling, with the moonlight glinting on the little crests of the waves, and maybe a dolphin or two frolicking... did dolphins frolic at night?

'I made you cry, didn't I?'

Violet moves her head backwards and frowns, but Guy holds his hand up to her again and speaks over her imagined protest.

'No, no, no, don't say anything, I did, I did, I know I did. You've had it up to here with me, I know it.' He slashes at the top of his forehead with a flat hand on the 'here', savagely. As he continues, he grows more angry. 'You've raised me, you and dad, you've raised me well and look how I'm repaying you. I can't even stick at a job, at twenty-three. Twenty-three! What am I doing? Where am I going? Where am I going?'

He repeats this question in a quieter voice, a sad voice, as if he's talking to himself. Violet is waiting to interject, but she knows better than to cut him off in mid-flow. She pulls the blanket around her more tightly and takes a deep breath.

She's so tired, all she wants to do is to crawl under her duvet and let sleep take her.

'Well – I've got an announcement! I'm going to be a writer!'

He looks like a triumphant small boy, his cheeks red, his eyes shining.

'But you've already told me that, darling.' She tries to make her voice gentle.

'No – but I'm really going to be a writer! George is taking me on – a six month contract, then more if it works out… I'll do typing for him in the morning, replying to all his correspondence, you know, that sort of thing, then I'll be free to write in the afternoon. He's giving me the annex, I'll have my own tiny kitchen – you've seen it, haven't you? He's seen my stuff, mother, he likes it. Honestly. He said I had 'a fine eye for observation' and 'an acid wit'. He said that about my stuff!'

Violet is surprised. She wasn't aware that her son had actually written anything yet. She couldn't imagine him actually sitting down and concentrating for long enough to put down a sufficient number of words in a row to fill a page. He's looking at her with intense anticipation – and she realises that he wants her to be pleased more than anything else in the world. He really cares about what she thinks, and she accepts it as a gift. God knows that children spend most of their lives trying to pretend how little they care about their parents.

'That's wonderful, darling.'

They can talk about it properly tomorrow, she thinks. She gets up and goes round to him and gives him a brisk hug. He grabs her and buries his head into her, puts his arms round the back of her and holds on, past the time she would have naturally pulled away, and she hopes desperately that he isn't going to start crying. One tearful mother-son chat is enough for one week. She looks down on his scruffy hair and absentmindedly touches it with her fingers. It's softer than it looks, it always was. Eventually he pulls away and his face is all crumpled where it's been pressed against the folds of material on her stomach.

'I will be a success, Mum, I promise you,' he says. 'Just you wait.'

Chapter 20

3rd of November '59

Well Bea – nubbin is out! And she is a she after all! She finished her grand entrance into the world eight hours ago. It's seven o'clock in the morning, and I have had a little sleep. I woke up with a start an hour ago and asked Sister Mary if she'd bring my baby through to me. My baby! She's lying fast asleep right next to me at this very moment. A few minutes ago I had a sudden urge to write to you. You've said how you wanted to know immediately. I'm sorry I haven't phoned. Oh, I missed my mother yesterday. I re-read all the letters she's sent me while I've been away, in between the pains. I know I've hardly mentioned her – I think it's been the only way I could cope. I remind myself of all of her faults as often as I can, to help with the homesickness, and there's a long list as you know! But I missed her yesterday. I missed you too, Bea, I really did.

Maybe you want to know the gory details? For when your time comes? Well – Lucy was right, it does hurt! It hurts stupidly. It's difficult to even compare it to common old garden hurts, and I went into a sort of world of my own, as if I wasn't quite there for all of it. I was concentrating so hard on the pains when they came, and on getting her out. It's a kind of work, almost, that takes a certain kind of focussing. I managed most of it, but there was a dreadful part where I was getting really tired and I knew with absolute certainty that it was going to be completely impossible to get her out. I thought I was going to split in two, and that she'd be an orphan. Either that or she'd get stuck inside me and we'd both die. Sister Mary was marvellous, I was so glad she was there. She stayed the whole time and held my hand for most of it – she has such a cool, white hand. She radiated calm into me! It almost made me want to become a nun and spend the rest of my life holding young girls' hands, smoothing the hair from their foreheads.

I don't know what else to say, really. The giving birth bit feels like weeks ago already. You'll have to ask me questions if you have any when I see you. It's odd – I was worried before I had nubbin that I'd be lonely when I had her, desperate to have my friends and family around me so I could share her, show her off, but that's not how I'm feeling at all. I feel like all I need is her, and that all she needs is me. If only the second part of that were true. But I don't want to talk about that, not today. Oh – it was lovely to hear about Janie's party, it sounded like you all had a grand time. How sweet of Bill to buy you a new dress – it sounds lovely, you must have felt beautiful! I can just picture you. And lovely that so many people asked you how I was. Thank you for keeping my secret, darling. I don't deserve to expect it, but I'm so grateful.

The Letters

I could write more, but I can't keep my eyes off my little honey. I keep stopping my pen and glancing over at her – she's like a magnet – her tiny crumpled face, her delicate red skin, her fingernails. Oh Bea, if only you could see her fingernails! They are the most perfect and tiny things you've ever seen. What a shame she has to grow, she's perfect exactly the way she is. I think I'm going to just lie here and drool over her, the way sweethearts gaze into each others eyes. I think I've fallen in love with her already. I don't want to think about what that means, not today. The other girls, the ones who have, you know, have told me to enjoy every single minute of the next six weeks, whatever happens. They said I should fix her into my memory forever, exactly how she looks right now, exactly how she smells, all the little folds of her body, all her little quirks. It seems like an awfully big project for six weeks. Doesn't that usually take at least a life-time? At least I have the next six weeks. Oh – she's started to squirm about a little. I hope I know what to do! I hope I'm not a terrible mother. I wish you could be here, Bea. To meet your namesake.

All my love and kisses and I promise I'll write again soon,

Elizabeth and Beatrice xxx

Chapter 21

Violet's mother had a theory that Violet spent 'several of her past lives in the Bahamas'. Apparently she'd shied away from the cold even when she was in Vera's stomach. If her mother felt even a slight chill during her third trimester, Violet would kick and turn until her mother shrugged on a cardigan or requested an extra blanket for the bed. Violet's father always held that it was actually his wife who had bad circulation, and that it suited her 'down to the ground' to blame it on someone else, but Violet repeated this story about herself at every opportunity. Augustine was musical, Marta was good at sewing, and Violet needed something to define her. What else did she have? Violet was the one who hated the cold. She told the anecdote whenever anyone was talking about the cold winter, or pregnancy, or going abroad… the rest of her family started to leave a pause on purpose when they happened to mention these things and guests were present. Once Charles said that he'd even found himself telling it for her in her absence – his friends were making a joke about their daughter's pregnancy and how the baby seemed to get agitated when the daughter worked on her tax return, and Charles just couldn't resist it.

Her lust for heat grew as she grew. When she was five she started following their cat Treacle around like a shadow. Treacle seemed to have a knack for finding all the warmest places in the house – the section of fluffy carpet next to the radiator in the living room, the pile of clothes in the laundry. Violet would either curl up next to her or unceremoniously shove her out of the way. The best place of all was a spot on the kitchen floor where hot water pipes ran underneath the tiles and kept a small patch perfectly warm all winter. Violet's mother was amused to find her daughter hunched up in the linen cupboard or in a ball under their duvet, but she wasn't sure how hygienic her kitchen floor might be. She dealt with it by keeping a little blanket on a chair which Violet could pull down and lie on if she felt the urge. The hot patch was over in the corner and so she didn't get in the way too much when the kitchen was in use. When she was older she'd revisit the habit when things were going wrong. After Violet had been told off by her teacher one day, her father came home to find his wife and two of his girls making fairy cakes, the air laden with flour and their cheeks smeared with chocolate icing. When he asked where the other one was, her mother pointed at the corner where an eight-year-old Violet was fast asleep on her spot, doing a better impression of a cat than Treacle did.

All through her childhood she remembers a particular kind of sinking feeling when the Autumn half term ended – final proof that Summer had disappeared. On colder mornings she sometimes refused to get out of bed for school, until one morning her mother lost her temper, pulled all the blankets off her and deposited her into the freezing, empty bath. This necessitated a rethink of getting-up-in-the-cold. She hit upon a system of removing her pyjamas and thick pink bed-socks under the safety of the covers and pulling items of clothing one by one into the warm cave so she could get dressed without ever having to leave her bed. After all the strange contortions necessary for getting everything into the right place, this activity also had the happy side-effect of leaving her hot and bothered, and so she was able to leap out of her bed and run downstairs to stand next to the Aga in the kitchen without too much trauma.

She developed a particular dislike of the wind during her first year at University. Her halls of residence weren't too far from the main campus, but the walk was a killer. The long road onto campus bisected a bleak expanse of perfectly flat land – partly football field, partly pointless grass – and the wind was unimpeded as it swept from one end of the world to the other. The row of rangy poplars lining the road only made matters worse, sucking the air between them and transforming the avenue into a wind tunnel. It was really designed to be driven, not trudged along by the never-ending stream of sleepy students. She hated the way the wind pushed against her clothes and found a way inside, through the ends of her sleeves or the gaps between her coat buttons, and she hated the way it dryly scoured her face. Even her skin seemed to revolt against it. She was prone to chapped lips and had small patches of eczema around her eyes, and the wind irritated these parts of her, leaving them red and raw. She discovered Vaseline in the second year, and spent a portion of each day dipping a finger into the oily-smelling goo and smearing it over her lips. This seemed to make a small difference until someone told her that it was possible for your skin to become 'addicted to lip salve', forgetting how to protect itself and becoming completely dependent on external moisture. She stopped applying it for four weeks as an experiment – it didn't make matters any better but her skin didn't seem any worse either, so she thought she'd save her money.

When she looks back on her illness one of her main memories is of the stifling heat. There was a point at which she drifted out of being involved in conversations about what was good for her. The doctor stopped talking to her when he came round (except asking her in a patronising voice how she was coping 'emotionally') and had hushed discussions with her mother out of Violet's earshot. She felt vaguely uncomfortable about this at the time, but it seemed easier to let herself become a child again, complying with all the grown-ups' instructions. There was such a limited amount of energy available to her – even deciding whether she wanted soup or a sandwich was a trial, so to say 'bring me what you think best' was a relief. When she was better her mother explained that it had been one of the doctor's instructions to keep her at a regular temperature, and to make sure that she didn't get cold. Her mother had interpreted this literally and Violet lay in her bed day after day and sweated. She began to crave the feel of a cold draught across her face, or a few raindrops on her forehead, or even a gust of angry wind. Anything but this oppressive, constant, humid heat like a huge grey scratchy blanket that made it difficult to breathe. As time went on, heat became an integral part of her illness, like the smell of the chicken broth her mother made her, and the sight of dust glinting in the morning light from the crack between the curtains.

Her first act of defiance, when she could feel the strength returning shyly to her limbs, her thinking clearing like sediment slowly sinking to the bottom of a bad glass of wine, was to get out of bed and open her window. She remembers lying in ecstasy for a full hour, relishing the kiss of cool air across her face – it felt as if it were revitalising her, fighting the virus, giving her life. A few days followed when Violet opened the window and her mother closed it again, until her mother realised that her time as nursemaid was coming to an end. She immediately started making comments about how Violet should be 'up and about in no time', and how it would 'do her good' to face the world again. With the window open she'd practise being aware of the feeling of cool air as it brushed against her nostrils on the way in, and of the slightly warmer, moister air she breathed out. She could fill whole hours doing this, off and on, letting go of any thoughts that drifted by. It was comforting to know that all she needed to do, all that was required of her, was to lie still and keep breathing.

Violet surprised herself at Abbotsfield by becoming fond of the 'bad weather' she'd previously avoided like the plague. She still seemed to feel the cold more than other people, but for some reason it mattered less. She'd put on an extra pair of socks or the baggy hooded top one of her children had left behind, and get on with what she was doing. It was necessary to become more physical now she lived alone – fetching and stacking firewood, digging her smallish garden without roping Charles in, lugging furniture from room to room. Once, when it was blowing a gale outside, she found herself wrapping herself in layers and layers of clothes and walking along the beach – just to feel the strength of the weather pushing against her body. This is what people mean by exhilarating, she thought, as she watched the sea kicked up into tatters and pushed her shoulders forwards into the wind. On the walk home with the wind against her back she opened her arms as if she were a super-hero and ran – letting out a wild cry that the wind took away from her. 'Waaaaah!' she shouted. 'Waaaaah! Here I am! Come and get me! WAAAAAAAAAAH!'

Chapter 22

The morning after their late night chat, Violet hears Guy traipsing back and forth to the bathroom and realises quite how drunk he must have been. She's always hated hearing other people throw up. She's of the opinion that it's bloody rude of drinkers to inflict their disgusting overindulgence on other people. Except when it's her own overindulgence that's caused the problems, of course. She tuts periodically before returning to her laptop screen. She's not concentrating very well anyway. It's one of those mornings when she keeps catching herself writing a mental shopping list, or admiring the colour of the sky, or pulling the bobbles off her fleece. A year ago, she would have made herself a strong coffee and pulled herself together. Work occupies a very different place in her life now. It's almost become something she fits in when she's got nothing else to do. She suspects she used to treat the rest of life like this, especially by the time the children needed her less. She had a reputation in the department of being a bit of a workaholic, although she wonders if she's ever admitted the full extent of this to herself. Her obsession with work was one of the things Charles had cited in the post mortem of their broken marriage – before her illness he'd started staying out after work and slipping away at weekends and she hadn't even noticed; she'd been too wrapped up in her flowcharts and her calculations. It had been her 'most important thing' for all that time. How had it happened? Why did no-one stop her?

The work that her Head of Department had arranged for her was perfect – it was challenging enough to be interesting, but there wasn't enough of it to eat too much into her days. She could go for a week without looking at it and then sit down to do a solid morning and still keep up. She couldn't quite imagine not having any work at all in her life, like some people she knew. People always seemed to be striving towards doing less work. She wonders how they feel when they actually get there, and what they do with their days instead. People get it wrong – it's not no work that makes for the best kind of life, but the right work. She's started to think about whether she could do a different kind of work on top of her few hours a week. Something completely different – giving tourists guided tours of the Cathedral in the nearest city, or making sandwiches for old folk. They're crazy thoughts, but anything seems possible these days. She could become a milk-woman if she really wanted to, or an amateur photographer, or a volunteer conservationist. She could take up juggling or breed beagles. She could be anyone.

She abandons her work and spends a happy morning in the kitchen, researching various alternative careers on the internet. She loves how you can start at Google with 'pedigree cat breeding' and end up reading about the mating habits of iguanas – skipping from link to link like stepping stones. It's not comfortable working in the kitchen – she misses her little office upstairs. She spent a long time getting the room 'right'. The two framed jazz prints (King Oliver's Creole Jazz Band, and a black and white print of Fleet Street Jazz Club in the 50s) are set off perfectly by the sky-blue walls, and she loves her bucket chair in the corner, complete with fluffy blue cushions. She sometimes takes a cushion onto her lap if Blue is feeling uncooperative, and strokes its pelt while she works as if it's a strange domesticated beastie. She didn't plan on a vomiting son installed on the sofa bed as part of the decor. Things upstairs seem to calm down after midday, and at three o'clock in the afternoon she starts feeling bored with her own company. She thinks she'll take him up a nice cup of tea, like a good mother. She also takes up a glass of water and some alka-seltzer from a half empty packet he left in her medicine drawer after his last visit. She knocks quietly and then pokes her head around the door.

'Morning, my little puker.'

All she can see is a huge tangled heap of duvet and sheets, and the back of a tousled head. She surveys the room – the floor is a mine-field of piles of crumpled clothes, and a pair of boxer shorts is draped over the top edge of a high cupboard where she assumes they were thrown in a moment of abandon.

'Grhhnnnnnnnn.'

She tiptoes round to the upside-down crate he's using as a bedside table and puts down the tea and water, pushing aside two books opened onto their stomachs, his watch, his mobile phone, and three almost-empty glasses of water. She lets out another 'tut' and then smiles – maybe this is how you know when your son has stayed for too long, by counting the calcified rings inside your glasses. She's making an exit when he shifts in the bed, stretching his long arms and writhing around as if he's trying to wring the sleep from his body.

'Roaaaaaaaaaar!'

She perches on the edge of her office chair as he drags himself up into a sitting position. He falls upon the glass of water and alka-seltzer hungrily. He has creases all over his face, and one of his eyes is all gummy. Is she too old now to have the feeling she's having now? It's a warm sweep of 'mother': the urge to fetch a warm damp cloth and wipe his eyes, smooth back his hair with her hands. When he's dispatched the entire pint of water he says, 'Mmmmm, hit the spot,' and turns to the tea, sniffing it and cupping it in both of his hands. He takes a sip and finally turns his glazed, fixed stare on her.

'Mmm, yum.'

'That's OK, darling.'

He realises something. 'Oh dear, did you hear me in the bathroom?' She raises her eyebrows and he pushes the heel of his palm against his forehead. 'Eugh, sorry, I haven't got that drunk for a very long time. It's that George's fault. He kept calling it our last outing, as drinking buddies, before we got down to the… Did I tell you?' He pauses while he searches for his memories from last night, and frowns. 'Did I get all silly on you last night? I can't really remember what… I didn't cry, did I, Mother?'

'You were inconsolable, darling.'

His frown deepens. 'Oh fuck. Did I make a complete tit of myself?'

She lowers her voice a little. 'Well, the dancing on the kitchen table I could just about handle, and that poor chicken you'd found on the way home, but when you insisted on doing that strip on the garden path, when everyone's curtains started twitching, and I couldn't get you inside…'

His eyes, which had been getting wider and wider, suddenly narrowed.

'You, you…' He thinks for a second and settles on

'thing,' seemingly the best insult he can come up with in his current state. He sits quietly for a few minutes and sips his tea, while Violet picks a pile of papers from her desk and shuffles through them, hoping to find a document she needed earlier.

'Did I tell you, Mum, about what George said?'

'You said he's going to take you on for six months, bed and board, so you can work on your writing. Is that right?'

'Yes, it is. It is! I'm absolutely – well, what did you say about it, last night?'

'Not much, darling – you weren't in a very rational mood.' She starts fiddling with her papers again and hesitates. 'I'm not sure that…'

He cuts her off by putting his tea down hard on the desk and covering his ears with his hands.

'La la la la la! Don't want to hear it. Can't bear any of your usual disapproval, Mum, this is too important.'

'What do you mean, usual? I don't disapprove!'

He says 'Ha!' as if this says it all.

Violet peels a Post-it note from the pad on her desk and rips it neatly in half. After a few seconds she tries again.

'I DON'T disapprove. I'm always very encouraging!'

'If you say so, Mother.'

'Well! Of all the things to be accused of…'

'Why do you think Megan's so scared of talking to you?'

'She's not scared of talking to me,' she says dismissively, as if it's a preposterous idea.

'Really? OK, then what about that time I wanted to be a marine biologist.'

'Oh, Guy, don't be ridiculous, that was a silly idea.'

'Point made. And that time Lucy brought her new boyfriend home and you quizzed him for a whole hour, and all you'd say later was "I'm sure he'll grow on me." And when Josie got her 2:1, and she was stoked, and you said average results are better than nothing, or something equally crushing. You can't help yourself, Mum. You don't even know you're doing it.'

Violet puts the pieces of paper down and crosses her arms tightly.

'Well, what a load of... if I'm not allowed to give my opinion, then, well, I'll keep my mouth shut in the future! The cheek of... all the times I've...' she trails off. 'And what about when I let you do that course on mechanics, even though I knew it was doomed from the start?'

Guy sighs, and looks towards the crack in the curtains. When he looks back, Violet is ripping up the Post-it note into confetti. He sighs again.

'Look, I feel far too rough this morning to have an argument with you. What are you cooking me for breakfast?'

She recognises this as her ex-husband's favourite tactic for avoiding any kind of confrontation – change the subject. It works pretty well, as she's usually pleased to swerve away from the conflict too, even though she knows she ought to 'talk things through', or whatever it is that Oprah advises. Surely life is too short for talking everything through? She doesn't reply, pours the dots of paper onto the desk and starts fussing about with her hair, taking a short lock and twirling it around her finger over and over. After a minute the anger has subsided a little.

'Do you want me to open your curtains before I go?'

'Yes please, Mum.'

She realises he's probably only agreeing to this to keep her happy, and so she only opens them a few inches, saying something about the sun streaming straight in at this time of the afternoon. Then she kisses him on the forehead, briefly, and leaves him to his hangover.

The rest of the week passes without anything to mark it out from the others. Violet and Guy's days begin to follow a predictable, comfortable pattern. Violet eats breakfast alone in her beautifully quiet house, reading the papers or getting on with some work on her trusty lap top. When Guy surfaces, she's usually ready for a break, and she makes them proper coffee. Guy always gets excited about filter coffee, calling it 'decadent' – she can't understand why he doesn't make it for himself. The kitchen fills with the earthy, sweet smell of near-boiling water on ground coffee beans and Guy sits on a kitchen stool looking stupefied. It's the same look he wore in his early teens when he had to get up for school, after the biological need to sleep in past ten kicked in. He looks just like an advert for cornflakes, playing the part of 'before'. She enjoys watching him come to life as he sips his coffee and then works his way through two slices of white toast and marmalade, cut so thick (and a little bit wobbly) that they hardly fit into the toaster. For the first ten minutes he only seems capable of saying 'mmm' (meaning 'This tastes good.') 'mmm' (accompanied by a shake of the head and meaning 'Not yet, Mother.') and 'mmm' (accompanied by a nod and meaning 'Go on then, Mother.').

After his engine has warmed up they talk for a while of ordinary things. Guy is developing an interest in the village gossip – Violet has never understood how you get hold of this kind of information, but Guy already knows more about her neighbours than she does. The Bakers' almost-famous actress grandchild has gone into rehab again, apparently, and Winifred from the cottage on the corner has had another stroke. Sometimes Guy talks to her about friends of his that she's known since they were tiny – their various weddings and new jobs. The last time she saw some of them, their voices were just breaking – when did they get so grown-up? Violet talks about the latest goings-on at the Committee meetings, her plans for the day, or any news she has from the girls. They are quite peopled, these mornings chats, which is rather unusual for Violet. When she's had enough she suggests it might be time for him to have a shower, and they go their separate ways. He retires to his room to 'write' or borrows the car to go on a 'research trip', she'll do chores in town or visit Sal for coffee. Sal has been kind to her since what happened with Tom. She doesn't ever mention Tom's name, and hasn't pushed Violet for any information.

Before dinner, Violet and her son sometimes go for a walk along the sea and catch the last of the light. As she watches him looking out towards the horizon she can see the muscles around his eyes and forehead relaxing. It pleases her. It always pleases her when her children take pleasure in the same things she does, things like architecture or numbers or big band jazz. It's as if they're especially clever to like these things. It pleases her even more to see him happy. Did she pay enough attention to her children's potential future happiness when they were young? Is it something she wanted for them? Maybe she approached it a bit obtusely. At the time she'd felt certain of the things that would make them happy later in life – a good education, politeness, looking well-turned out, but she can't summon much faith in them now. Are these the things that really make people happy? Could she have done it all differently? And what about Guy's comment, about her being discouraging? This returns to her now every time she walks along the beach, and although she squashes it quite firmly down again it seems to have a remarkable thirst for the air. It rises up again and again. That's the trouble with walks, and spending time alone. She never used to have to deal with these rogue thoughts; she was far too busy. She knows what Tom would say about that. 'They're meant to come up again, Violet, that's the whole point. They'll keep coming up until you listen to them.' And where would that get her, if she gave credence to every half-formed shadowy doubt? How would anyone have time to get on with their lives?

They eat their evening meal together more often than not, later than Violet would like by the time Guy is ready, and then watch a little television like an old married couple. There are things about their new routine that Violet likes a lot – being able to offer someone a cup of tea when she makes one for herself, and knowing that there's someone else in the house when there are spooky noises at 3am and Blue is where she can see him, curled up on the chair in her bedroom. There are also things that are driving her to distraction. She can't bear the way he turns the kitchen into a bomb-site. Even making a simple sandwich seems to involve three different knives and two mixing bowls and crumbs scattered over a wide enough area to suggest he's actually wandered around sprinkling the bloody stuff like fairy-dust. She hates the Guy-noises in the middle of the night – he's nocturnal really, and will get up most nights to make tea and toast at 1am. It's just not civilised behaviour. And she feels he might be dimming her light, the bluey-violet one that shines from her belly. She isn't sure how or why, but it's definitely started to flicker. She doesn't have long to wait. George has got a plumber in to sort out the shower in the annexe, and once it's finished, Guy is free to move in. He'll be off soon enough, and then she'll miss him. And maybe she'll miss the distraction, too. When he goes, there won't be anyone to take her mind off the Tom-sized hole in her life.

Chapter 23

23rd of November '59

Dearest Bea,

Thank you so much for my parcel! It was such a treat to get it – you should have seen my face when Sister Edith came in at breakfast and told me it had arrived. It was so thoughtful of you to put in some bath salts for me as well as the gorgeous outfit for Beatrice – you're right, I could do with a little pampering of my own. It's lovely to hear your news too – how clever of Janie to get top marks in the whole class, you must be so proud, and your new choir sounds just marvellous. What a shame about old Mrs. Jones at work, making such a nuisance of herself, I wish I was there to join in when you gave her a piece of your mind last week! Hopefully that'll be the end of the whole horrid business. You really ought to speak to Mr. Potts about it, you know. I'm sure he'll be understanding – you're his best worker, really you are, and he wouldn't want you being harassed by that mean old cat. I'm sure you'll handle it perfectly – you were always so good in awkward situations.

Time here is rolling on. I fear I'll have less and less to say to you now – my whole life seems to be taken up with Beatrice. When I'm not with her I'm thinking about her, and when I'm not thinking about her I'm asleep! No wonder new mothers become such bores, mooning about and going on about colic and feeding schedules. I shouldn't think you give a hoot about such things. I do worry that you won't find me interesting any more, but when I talked to Ruby about it she said I was being silly. My little one is getting on just wonderfully. I feel I could gaze at her forever – when she's sleeping, when she's feeding, when she's lying in my arms. Just after her bath the scent of her is like nothing I've smelt before – sweet, earthy, like an exotic flower. I love to kiss her forehead, her belly, her palms, but most of all her tiny perfect feet. Each little toe in turn – mwah mwah mwah mwah mwah! I want to swallow her whole, but she's had her time inside me. I speak to her all the time in a quiet voice so nobody else can hear, telling her how beautiful she is, how clever, and telling her things I hope will be useful to her in her life. I do so want her to be happy. That's the most terrible thing. You'd think if I really wanted her to be happy then I'd let her grow up in a proper household with a mother and a father, and a bit of money, maybe in the country or in a nice smart town flat. That's where she'd be happiest, I'm sure of it – she'd never remember me, and she'd never need to find out. But I can't stop thinking about myself. I can't stop thinking about my own happiness, selfish as I am – I want to be her mother. I don't even know if I'd make a half-decent job of it, because I've never done it before. I can do it at the moment, with the feeding and the cuddling and the nappy-changing, but what about when she gets older and it all gets more complicated? I can hardly write about it, Bea. I don't talk about it with anyone. Nobody does, really – it's as if we're all in a dream here and if we said anything like that out loud we'd have to wake up. We all just want the dream to go on forever. The weeks are passing so quickly – she's already 3 weeks old. That's half of my time gone. I don't know if I can bear it.

I don't mean to go on. I do hope you understand. You don't know how much it helps me to write these things down, to tell someone at least, and I feel safe telling you, Bea. I know you won't judge me. Everybody else does, these days. And who can blame them, really? What a mess I've got us into.

All the girls I'm friendliest with have had their babies now. Everyone is healthy and happy – Trudie has had a terrible time since the birth, but she's back from the hospital now and is starting to get a little colour in her cheeks. All except Doll, that is, who is six days overdue and counting – one of the girls was joking with her last night that she must be crossing her legs, and that if she isn't careful the baby will burst out of her stomach! I'm still worried about her, Bea. She's more like her normal self again now, talking nineteen to the dozen, but the things she says aren't very – well, connected to her. It's difficult to explain. I asked her how she was a few days ago but she wouldn't answer me – I said 'Doll? I'm worried about you' and she just snorted and turned over. Maybe having her baby will perk her up a bit. She'll have someone to love, and someone to tell her secrets to, whatever they are.

Thank you for offering to come and see me again, Bea, but you really mustn't worry about it. Your family might find out, and it's an awfully long way. I would love to see you more than anything, but... oh, I should be more honest with you. I'm scared of you seeing Beatrice. It's a silly idea, but if I don't let anyone in my normal life see her then maybe I can just pretend the whole thing was a dream, afterwards. Maybe my little brain will be able to cope with that. I shouldn't have even told you about her, I suppose. Too late for that. Maybe I'm approaching the whole thing the wrong way. I'm not sure how to do it, Bea, I haven't done it before. None of the other girls will talk about what's going to happen. I asked Trudie, who's done it twice before – all she'd say to me was 'you just do it, sweetheart'. I want to know more than that. Or maybe I don't. Oh Bea, if I let you come and see me I'd only cry on your shoulder, and I don't know if I would ever stop.

I think Beatrice is stirring and so I'd better go. It's harder to squeeze these letters in now, sorry I'm not writing so often. It's hard to squeeze anything in! All my love to you,

Your Elizabeth (and Beatrice) x x x

Chapter 24

Violet was five when she carried her first artistic effort home from school. By this time, her mother already had a hunch that Violet was going to be 'the uncreative one' in the family, based on Violet's inability to appreciate sunsets or 'views' when she was four, but her daughter's painting drove the final nail into the coffin. The class had been asked to paint their families. Violet had been given a huge piece of paper, and so she'd had plenty of space to demonstrate a budding sense of colour, attention to detail, or even a quirky sense of humour. Things started badly when she chose a thick paintbrush that looked like it had been electrocuted. The other children were all clamouring for the bright red, blue and yellow plastic squeezy bottles, and so she decided to rely heavily on the black/brown end of the palette rather than enter the fray. She'd ignored the bottom half of the paper entirely, lining up her parents and sisters as if they were wearing jet-packs, and they were all leaning to the left. Most of their limbs weren't properly attached to their bodies, and their cat Treacle had been relegated to a kind of muddy brown lump on the floor. For some reason Violet had also decided it was snowing, and had covered the whole scene while it was still wet with irregular white blotches. Most of these blotches contained a brown or grey bleeding splodge. When she showed it to her husband Vera couldn't help exclaiming, 'Isn't it the ugliest thing you've ever seen!' Bill ignored her and patted his daughter on her head, saying, 'It's lovely, dear,' but it was already too late, and Violet burst into angry tears. This set Augustine off, which resulted in Vera losing her temper, and Bill quietly retreating to his office. The episode ended with Vera abandoning the half-cooked evening meal and going to her room in a huff, and everyone had to make do with bread and jam.

As the girls grew up, Violet's sisters quickly found their niches. Augustine was always the musician, with her Grade 8s in clarinet and piano, and Marta developed an early flair for making her own clothes, first learning to knit and then rapidly becoming conversant with the finer points of darts, hems, tucks and pleats. From Marta's early adolescence, their old Singer sewing machine would compete with the muted scales from behind Augustine's bedroom door, while Violet would watch old cowboy movies with her parents or read boys' adventure books. For a while she was happy to accept her 'non-creative' designation – it gave her something that neither of her siblings had. Violet would feel a perverse pride at the stories her mother told at dinner parties at her expense – the cake she'd ruined by adding her own creative touch (a tin of peaches, juice and all), and her art teacher's sarcastic comments on her school report. She was satisfied with interpreting her lack of creativity as 'something-special' until a prize ceremony at school to recognise outstanding talent, when all the parents were required to turn up in their best clothes and look smug as their little darlings went up for awards. That year Augusta got 'Musician of the Year' and

Marta got a 'Special Commendation' for her dressmaking skills – Vera was over the moon. Violet got nothing. The icing on the cake, quite literally, was their mother buying a special cream cake for each daughter, and presenting them to Marta and Augustine after dinner with a little speech. When she came round to Violet all she could come up with was '… and well done to Violet for being such a good sport.' Being a teenager, Violet didn't smile and take the cake. Instead she shouted 'Thanks a bloody lot!' and stormed upstairs to her bedroom. Her mother knocked for a few minutes but gave up rather quickly, and when Violet finally ventured out to go to the toilet the house was in darkness and everyone had gone to bed. Her strawberry and custard tart was waiting for her on a tray outside her door. She stepped in it with a bare foot, the custard squeezing between her toes like mud.

Violet took after her mother in preferring to have something other than herself to blame when things went wrong. After the strawberry tart incident, her lack of creativity got the rap for all kinds of catastrophes. If she was better at colour co-ordination, she never would have been teased about the outfit she wore to that school party. If she could sing, she would have got a much better part in the school nativity – maybe even the leading lady to James McCutcheon's rather dashing Joseph. Nobody asked her to dance at family weddings or school discos because of her lack of rhythm, and she even managed to blame her too-few friends on an inability to think up interesting things to say. When things went well they were always attributed to something else – her head for maths, or her hard work, while all of life's small disappointments and challenges were transmogrified into further evidence for her complete absence of imagination. Her lack-of-creativity trait gathered weight and solidified, and in this respect she was no different from anybody else. Being certain about herself was more reassuring than keeping an open mind, even if the certainty was a failing. At least she knew who she was. And if she wasn't uncreative, then who was she?

After several decades of Violet telling people that she didn't have a creative bone in her body, a crack began to appear in her resolve. One of her children brought a book home called 'Drawing on the Artist Within' by Betty Edwards. Violet happened upon it during a rare five minutes with nothing to do after a long boring day at work. It was in their 'music room' – a small room tucked away upstairs and mostly used by Violet when she was desperate for some peace and quiet. It was littered with sheet music and crowded with bent-out-of-shape music stands and the various instruments her children had fallen out of love with over the years. The book was resting up against Josie's guitar, and Violet settled onto a battered leather armchair and opened it up, expecting the usual arty-farty nonsense. As she flicked through, she was pleasantly surprised by the rational writing style – there were sections on the brain, reasonable hypotheses, and clear sensible instructions. Several phrases leapt out at her – 'You will be surprised, I think, to discover how quickly and skilfully you will be able to learn to draw,' and the last sentence in the book: 'The joy of releasing your true potential for creating beauty is right there, right within your grasp, if the mind wills it.' Surely the author couldn't be talking to her? It wasn't a matter of will, was it? Before she could read any further, Megan called to her from the kitchen, wanting to know where the nutmeg was, and she was sucked back into the whirlwind that was her life in those days of teenage children.

Years later, when she was weeks into her long illness, the idea of the book returned to her. She'd asked her mother a few days previously if her bed could be moved closer to the window so she could spend more time gazing out at the sky. That morning it was raining, and she'd noticed the patterns the water was making on her window. She didn't know why she'd never paid proper attention to raindrops before. There was a whole country of individual drops, like citizens, and when a new one splashed down it would either find its own place and sit quietly, or it would merge with a neighbour. If the new raindrop and the neighbour created enough weight they would be smeared across the windowpane by the light wind, and join a whole chain of drops together, gathering speed and fluidity as they streaked down towards the bottom corner of the window-frame. She watched this happen for a whole hour, transfixed by the rhythms and the curves of light, going into a kind of reverie. She started thinking about beauty; Marta's beautiful clothes, the red tulips in their garden, a sculpture park they'd once visited in Yorkshire. Eventually she dared to include herself in the train of thought. Had she ever created anything beautiful, apart from her children? Could she learn? This is when she half-remembered what she'd read in that book, about everyone having the potential to create beauty. She wrote a reminder to herself in the little notepad she kept by the side of her bed, and several months later she managed to track the book down.

Soon afterwards she made her decision about Charles, and then he told her about his affair, and so the book remained unopened until she moved to Abbotsfield. Once her boxes were all unpacked she was finally ready to read it, and to do the exercises. She whipped through the first half in a long weekend, and was astonished at how quickly she was able to create a drawing that actually resembled the object she was looking at. She posted her early efforts to her children, as she didn't know anyone in the village to show them to, and even sent a sketch of Blue she was particularly proud of to her mother. The book was a touchstone for her in her early lonely and rootless days in the house, when her children and parents had gone home again and she was left rattling around and trying to work out what to do with herself. It gave her days a purpose, and a structure. It also prepared her for her mother's suggestion that she sign up for the local drawing class, and of course it was there that she met Tom. Her drawings also gave her hope. If she'd been wrong about not having any artistic talent, something she was so utterly certain about for so long, then maybe she could be wrong about other things as well. Maybe it was possible to change at the age of half a century. Maybe she could adapt to this strange new life.

Chapter 25

Moments after Violet wakes, her dream returns to her. It's the dream which she first had when she was ill, but she hasn't had it since then. She's in a huge, grand hotel, with corridors that go on and on, and occasional ball-rooms full of sinister, dancing strangers. She needs to find a particular room, but she doesn't know where it is or what's inside. She gets more and more frantic; she's running out of time. She wakes up in a sweat, but the dream is always waiting for her when she gets back to sleep. It's kept her awake all night. Eventually, at long past three, she got up and made herself a cup of tea – green tea, which she sipped very slowly in the kitchen whilst concentrating on her breathing and trying to empty her mind. Very Zen – Tom would have been proud of her. Now it's light, and she lies and listens to her quiet house. The heating system is making ga-blurping noises, and a fly is hurling its body at her bedroom window. Her stomach feels unsettled, nauseous from a lack of sleep. She's alone once more. Guy drove back to London yesterday to pick up the rest of his things – the annexe at the big house is painted and plumbed and ready for him to move in. She runs through her tasks for today. First she's going to help Guy move all the flotsam and jetsam he's accumulated here over the past few weeks. She imagines him now, sleeping in his old bed. Or maybe he's lying awake too, brimming with ideas – all that peace and space, all that time for his new writing. In the afternoon there's a Committee meeting at Will's, which she tried and failed to get out of, and then she wants to start thinking about preparing the house for her daughters' invasion on Friday. She can't remember the last time all five of them ate together, and is more nervous about it than she'd care to admit. The light is building strength at the edges of her curtains. Blue is stretched out super-cat style on the duvet, lying against her left leg. He's built a nest of such intense heat that she rises from her prone position and drags him over to a different part of the bed, with him meowling his disgruntlement as he goes. After ten more delicious minutes she takes a deep breath and dives into the day.

She makes her coffee stronger than usual and adds sugar to buck her up. Guy arrives before she's even finished her toast and marmalade – he'd left at 6am to 'beat the rush hour'. She's never known him up this early. He's reluctant to sit down with her while she finishes eating and starts bounding up and down the stairs with carrier bagfuls of his worldly goods. She grumbles about the sudden burst of banging and kafuffle ruining her quiet morning, but secretly she's pleased to see him like this – full of fizz and possibility. A corner of her even dares to hope that he'll make the most of it this time and find a thread to run through his life – something he can hold on to. Everyone needs a thread. She says this out loud to herself as Guy walks back into the kitchen, and he gleefully launches into teasing her about muttering to herself. He describes her slow descent into becoming a mad old woman who talks continually to her twelve cats as they roam the kitchen surfaces and have litter after litter of unwanted kittens under the stairs. She lunges at him and musses up his hair, which used to annoy the hell out of him when he was a teenager and still has the desired effect. When she's called him 'bloody hilarious' a few times they're ready to go.

Guy's energy seems to seep away as they make the short journey to the big house. As Violet turns the car into George's long driveway he sighs a huge sigh.

'What's up, darling?'

'Oh, I don't know really… I just feel a bit odd. I've been high as a kite since yesterday morning and maybe my poor old brain is tired of all this, you know, brave new beginnings and all that, and…'

He glances at her and stops talking abruptly, as if he's caught himself saying more than he intended. Violet is surprised not to get her usual bright 'Nothing, Mother!' but is distracted by a pigeon lingering on the driveway in the path of the car. When they get out of the car the awkward silence between them is broken by the front door bursting open and George spilling out onto the gravel.

'Aha! The final load of possessions, thank heavens! The annex is already full to bursting… how do you put up with him, Violet? Marvellous to see you…' He moves towards her and grasps her on the shoulder as he kisses her cheek. She's taken aback – he's never been this pleased to see her before. He insists on 'a cup of Zhenya's magnificent cocoa' before they bring in the bags, to celebrate the occasion with an 'appropriate ritual'. As they walk towards the cosy room, Violet watches him put a hand on Guy's shoulder. She suddenly understands George's new-found warmth for her – he really seems very fond of Guy. She thinks back to the first time she came to dinner at the big house. The subject of children came up and George said that he didn't feel it was fair to have children 'at his age', as he'd be pushing seventy before they went to University. It looks like he's enjoying this mentoring business. She feels a short flash of jealousy as Guy laughs at something George says, obviously an 'in-joke', but she's interrupted by Yevgeniya coming through, wiping her hands on tea towel.

'Violet.'

When Violet kisses her, Yevgeniya's cheek is smooth and cold and reminds her of a texture she can't quite put her finger on. Is it alabaster? Violet offers to help her with the cocoa and is pleased when Yevgeniya nods and beckons her through. It was Tom who first drew Violet's attention to the jumpy, unsettled feeling she gets in unfamiliar social situations which leads her to raise her voice and pace the room. She protested violently when Tom first pointed it out, as if she were a grumpy child being told that she was tired – why would she get nervous about being around people? She'd never been the type to be bothered by dinner parties – if she got bored she'd just make her excuses and go early, something that used to drive Charles mad in the early days of their marriage. She didn't like realising that she changed into a brasher model of herself when she felt more vulnerable – she'd previously seen this as proof that she didn't care, rather than the opposite. Another legacy of her relationship. Why does Tom keep popping up in her head? She thought these things were meant to get easier as time went on.

Yevgeniya pulls four heavy, pink mugs from the back of a cupboard and rinses them under the tap. She hands them one by one to Violet to dry, and as she can't think of anything else Violet says what's on her mind.

'So how do you feel about all this, then, Yevgeniya? Having your home invaded?'

'Zhenya, please. I don't know this word, invaded?' She pronounces the word with difficulty, and Violet forages about in her mind to think of an equivalent.

'Umm, intruded upon, umm...' Yevgeniya is still looking blank, paused from scooping cocoa from a tin and giving Violet her full attention as if that might help her to find a simpler word. 'When someone comes into your home without permission and lives with you.'

It isn't quite right but Yevgeniya's face clears and she laughs. It isn't a sound Violet has heard very often before. It's a light laugh, without any sarcasm – there's a kind of purity about it. Very pretty, she thinks. And then she thinks something else, or rather feels it, flashing through her body uninvited and making her blush. She desperately looks for something else to say.

'They say that three is company, don't they, I mean, two is a crowd, three is a company, or... bloody hell.'

Yevgeniya laughs again. 'I like this "bloody hell", I will use this. Bloody hell. Bloody hell.'

She plays around with the pronunciation, trying to imitate Violet's accent, and Violet can't help but laugh too. She repeats the phrase again, more slowly, for Yevgeniya to copy, and then Yevgeniya asks if she has any more swear words, and Violet gives her favourite, "bollocks", and, when she's feeling a little bolder, "fucking nora". When Yevgeniya finally replies Violet has forgotten her original question.

'I am looking forward to it; Guy is making George very happy. I have been worried, his writing is slow, and he moves around the house like this,' she drops her shoulders and chin and makes her arms long and dangly and moves back and forth across the kitchen. 'The house is a little empty, sometimes. For only two people.'

Violet nods, and wonders how Yevgeniya feels about not having any children. There is a note of sadness in her voice. As if reading her mind Yevgeniya continues.

'But I will not be playing mother, Violet, you must not worry about that. I will not be cleaning up any clothes on the floor or doing ironing. We already talk about this — it is very clear. My brother is a teenager when I still live at home, I know about the boys. You need not to worry.'

'Good.'

She does feel reassured. She doesn't imagine Yevgeniya is easily swayed once she's set her mind on something. She can't be many months older than Guy, but she seems to have made it very clear that she's one of the 'adults'. Violet also feels better about a concern she hadn't even completely admitted to herself — that Guy might fall in love with her and steal her away from George. She doesn't want George, or Guy, to get hurt. Yevgeniya speaks about George with such fondness — whatever they have, however unconventional, it seems to work.

After the hot chocolate, which is delicious, George takes Violet aside and has a private word with her about the new arrangements. From what he says, Violet guesses that he sees Guy as a bit of a mummy's boy, and imagines that Violet is going to miss him terribly. George stresses several times that the big house is usually 'a house of work', and that dinner parties or drinks only happen on special occasions. She interrupts him as soon as he gives her the chance and says she's very happy for Guy to move out, honestly, and that he's a big boy and can look after himself. She says it so emphatically that, reflecting on it later, she wonders if she might have been trying to convince herself. She helps Yevgeniya take the cups back to the kitchen and looks out at their garden. Yevgeniya offers to show her around, and they spend a pleasant half hour sharing their knowledge of plants. When they come back in, Guy is in his new room. She finds him sitting on his new bed with piles of his possessions surrounding him, staring blankly at the wall. She kisses him on the top of his head and leaves him to it.

She feels jittery when she gets home, and decides to walk the half hour to Will's house to give herself a bit of breathing space. When she gets there Helen opens the door, halfway into her coat and struggling with one of the sleeves. Violet has only met her once before and had forgotten how glamorous she is – she has a kind of willowy look that she's always envied in other women, more fluidly elegant than her own rangy body. Her face could be seen as quite unattractive in isolation – she has a rather hooked nose and quite small eyes – but with the glossy feathered hair, immaculately done make-up and accompanying halo of confidence, she could pass for an actress or a successful entrepreneur. She manages to push her arm through the sleeve and turns a dazzling smile on Violet. She was wearing the same smile the last time Violet saw her. It reminds her of something Will has said, about how she has to display 'ability to cope' at all times. Violet can see how it might tire you out after a while.

'Hello Violet! You've just caught me – I'm just popping out to my girlfriend's so William can have the house to himself. Do come in, do come in. There, let me take your coat.' She lowers her voice. 'William gets a touch stressed about people coming around.'

A dog is barking from somewhere upstairs – Will's badly behaved terrier. Helen ushers Violet through to the kitchen where Will is putting mugs out onto the counter. Helen rubs his hair between her fingers as if rubbing butter into flour, a concerned look on her face.

'Have you got that ghastly wax concoction in your hair again?'

Will ignores her question and flaps his hands around her as if trying to drive away a fly.

'Go on with you, woman.'

Helen sighs, a large theatrical sigh, and gives Will's hair a last tweak.

'Bye then, darling, make sure you don't…'

She hesitates and decides not to carry on. Instead she looks at Violet and rolls her eyes, as if they are complicit in something, but Violet isn't quite sure what. Helen kisses Will perfunctorily on the cheek and picks up her handbag and a tin that looks like it might have a cake inside it. She leaves the room in a bit of a whirlwind. After the loud slam of the front door the room is quiet except for the clink of china on china.

'Can I help at all?'

'No, no, I'm alright.'

She sits on a stool at the breakfast bar. It's too high for her to put her feet on the ground and so she dangles her legs, feeling like a small child. She looks around the room and then examines her nails. Will still isn't saying anything.

'What are you so het up about? It's only them.'

Maybe she should have said 'Are you OK?' instead. She doesn't usually have time to think before the words leave her mouth. Maybe Charles did have a point when he once said in the middle of a raging argument that Violet had 'the social skills of a tortoise'. Violet wasn't sure how sociable tortoises actually were, but she imagines that it wasn't a compliment.

Will makes a noise under his breath, a kind of 'uh-huh', and carries on moving around the kitchen. His movements are faster and jerkier than usual. It's as if he's putting together a petrol bomb, or making cucumber sandwiches for the Queen.

'Will.'

He glances round at her, and turns back to what he's doing. She tries again.

'Will, oi!'

He frowns and puts the packet of coffee down. He still isn't looking at her, as if he's done something naughty and is afraid of catching her eye. Violet isn't sure what to do next – Megan would know, what would Megan do? Or Tom? Other people know what to do in situations like this, she thinks to herself. Shouldn't I have learnt by now? What did I miss? She gives it her best shot.

'Look – just sit down for a minute and I'll do that. You're going to put it in that plungy thing, are you? And I can fill the kettle up and put the sugar in that bowl – just sit down and take some deep breaths or whatever it is that you do.'

He does as he's told and after a few minutes he says 'sorry.'

'Why?'

'Oh, I don't know, I get myself into a bit of a tizzy.'

She hasn't heard anyone use the word 'tizzy' for years, not since an old friend of her father's, and it tickles her.

'It's not funny, Violet!'

'No, I was laughing at you saying "tizzy" – tizzy, tizzy, what a tizzy! Are you better now?'

'Not really. But I'll be alright. I'll feel better once the others all arrive. Don't worry, I'm not going to have another breakdown or anything. Or at least if I do then I'll give you three minutes warning.'

'Oh, that's alright then.'

She's reassured to hear him attempt a joke. As she's opening a packet of digestives, the door-bell rings. Will looks panicked, and she puts her hand on his arm.

'I'll get it. We're sitting in the living room, aren't we?' She holds out the half-opened packet of biscuits for him to finish, pulling one from the end and cramming it into her mouth on the way to the door. Dark chocolate ones, her favourite. She always forgets to buy them for herself, so always makes the most of getting them at someone else's house by eating at least three.

As she expected, it's Margaret. Violet makes her best attempt at polite conversation so Will can concentrate on making drinks until the others start arriving – first Sue, then Peggy, then Rob. Just as they're about to start without her, Angie rushes in with a red face, emitting a stream of apologies. As they gather around the table the tension quickly becomes evident. Sue is sitting with a stiff back and not catching anyone's eye, just taking short sharp sips of her coffee, and Angie keeps taking her hair out of a pony-tail and putting it back up again. Rob has cornered Will and is rabbiting on about the recent levels of rainfall. Violet finds herself sighing a lot, as if she can't quite get enough air into her lungs. She looks at Will – he was so good at the last meeting, taking charge of everything, but he still looks a little manic to her. They'll have to rely on Margaret to hold it all together today. Or maybe it'll be every man for himself. Margaret shuffles her papers and the room grows quiet.

'Thank you all for coming today, and thank you to Will for hosting this… er, unusual… meeting.'

Violet tries to catch Will's eye but he's bending forwards to look for something under the table. She catches Rob's eye instead and they both raise their eyebrows. Margaret continues.

'I make a proposal that our usual format is put on hold for today, bar a quick check of the Minutes, so we can deal properly with the matter that has arisen. All in favour?'

Everyone except Angie puts up their hands. Violet wonders if she hasn't understood the proposal, and is about to explain it to her when Margaret barks 'carried'. She shuffles through her pile of papers as if she's trying to find something, and Violet notices that her hand is trembling. Margaret finds what she's looking for and looks up, almost a glare, and meets everyone's eyes in the circle in turn. Before she starts speaking she strokes her chin a few times and then straightens her hand out to bounce against her mouth with the tips of her fingers. Violet's chest feels tight and she glances over at Will – he gives her a little wink, and she smiles back. Margaret takes a deep breath.

'As you all know, at our last meeting Angie made an allegation that we needed to investigate.' She nods at Angie as she speaks her name, as if the others might have forgotten who she is. 'With William's assistance, I have made a full investigation of the allegations. I have given both Angie and Sue the opportunity to come forward and submit further pertinent information, and I have now come to a conclusion about how we need to resolve this matter. I would like to announce that the allegations have no basis in fact, and that from forthwith Angie will be required to take a three month sabbatical from the Committee, upon which time we will ascertain whether she is fit to stand again.'

Margaret lowers her eyes, and everybody else looks at Angie. She has a strange smile on her face – a sort of smirk, as if she's hardly able to stop bursting into laughter. She doesn't say anything, and neither does Margaret. It's as if someone has pressed the pause button and they're all waiting for someone to press play. Eventually something does happen. Angie's face starts to change. It's imperceptible at first, like watching an icicle shrinking drip by drip, but as they watch something new starts to surface, through the layers of smiles, the layers of subservience, the layers of needing to please. Violet recognises it at once – fury. Angie takes a precise sip of her tea, as if she's enjoying making them wait, taking her time. She looks directly at Sue. Her voice is cold, calm.

'She deserved it, you all know that. Such a chilly old trout. You know what she thought about me, don't you? "Silly little Angie, ooooh, don't give her anything too complicated, her poor little brain might burst. The poor little thing, how we must pity her." And you, Will – she thinks you're a nut-case, but she'd never say it to your face. A raving loony. She thinks you're a cold-hearted, bitter old maid, Violet, and the things she's said about you and your, well – you know. She could hardly contain herself. What a prize – what an opportunity. And Margaret. You get the best treatment of all. Oh yes.'

Sue has turned her head to one side, as if trying to avoid her words. She looks over at Margaret, beseeching her.

'Angela,' Margaret says. Angie ignores her.

'She goes on about you for hours. I'd listen to her, like an idiot. I'd invite her round to poison me, poison my own home. She's tainted my house, with her evil. It pours out of her.'

Violet flinches at the word evil and glances over at Will. Sue makes as if to stand up, but loses her balance a little as she's rising and slips back into her chair. She opens her mouth again as if she's going to say something but then screws her eyes shut, puts her hands over her ears.

'I say,' says Rob.

'I think that's enough,' says Margaret. But Angie hasn't finished. A stream of accusations pour out of her. Most of them sound well-rehearsed. Her voice gets louder, in an attempt to get through Sue's hands and into her ears. What can be done? thinks Violet. How it will end? She feels glued to her seat, her mouth sealed, like one of those nightmares when the air becomes thicker than treacle and you can't move away from the terrible thing. When Sue lets out a yell it takes everyone by surprise.

'STOP!'

Angie is finally silenced. Sue crumples forward again, her eyes still tightly screwed shut. Margaret is the first to recover her senses and stands up. She looks around at everyone and holds her hands out towards Angie, keeping her at bay.

'This isn't helpful, Angela. Tempers are frayed, and people are saying things that they'll regret. I hereby conclude this meeting, forthwith. Full details of the investigation will be available to all members. Any Committee member wishing to discuss this matter further must do so in writing, with myself as the addressee. Is that clear? Is that clear?'

The Committee nods – all of them except Angie, who started gathering her things together when Margaret started talking. In the silence after Margaret's words she stands up and points at Sue. 'Fuck you,' she spits. She looks wildly around the room. 'Fuck the lot of you.' And she's gone.

Chapter 26

26th of November '59

Bea – something terrible has happened. I was very close to calling you this morning. I so want to hear your voice. But I couldn't bring myself to do it. I think I'm afraid that if I talked to you now I wouldn't be able to hold myself together anymore. I need to hold myself together, for Beatrice. It's not fair for her to have a mother who's in pieces – there's no time for that, we don't have any time. Why don't we have more time?

I'm writing from Marjory's house. She picked us up from the mother and baby home last night, once I was back from the police station. She's been so wonderful, Bea, I don't know what I would have done without her. She's been remarkably calm – she made me a cup of tea when we got in, and sorted out some bedding for us both, and then she just chattered about her day and told me some stories about her grandmother who used to work as a nurse. Silly little stories, but it was exactly what I needed to hear – ordinary things, about ordinary people. I must have looked like a ghost when she picked me up. At breakfast she said it was lovely to see me with a little colour back, and I thought I looked an absolute sight when I was brushing my hair this morning. I looked sort of vacant, as if I wasn't quite all there. That's how I feel, anyway. Beatrice has been a tonic – she's been as good as gold, as if she knows I can't cope with much today. She's already had her feed and is fast asleep, she's usually gone for forty minutes or so, so I've got lots of time to write to you. Marjory had an appointment this morning – she asked and asked me if I was sure it would be all right, but I managed to reassure her in the end that I could survive a few hours without her. Although now she's gone I'm feeling awfully alone. She almost called mum last night, I had to beg her not to, and she said we'd talk about it today, so I'm sure I haven't heard the last of it. I'm terribly scared about that, Bea, about mum finding out – not after I've come so far. I've done so much of this on my own. Anyway, I have to tell you what happened. I feel quite cold about everything still and so I think I can write it all down without getting agitated. I hope it doesn't upset you too much. I did think about not telling you, but you're my best friend – I can't bear not to tell you. Maybe that's selfish of me, but there it is.

Doll finally had her baby girl, three days ago. Ruby heard one of the Sisters saying that Doll cried all the way through the labour, hardly making a sound, just tears streaming and streaming. I went to see her as soon as I could, and she seemed all right – she was quieter than usual, but she seemed rather hopeful. We talked a little bit about what she might do afterwards, when her baby was with its family, and she kept saying she'd always wanted to be in a choir. A choir, of all things! I didn't get to see her the day before yesterday at all – I'm back on laundry duties again now, and Beatrice just wouldn't settle later on, and Sister Edith said Doll was asleep for most of the day anyway.

Yesterday morning, quite early, I thought I'd go and visit Doll . They said they'd moved her to a new room, she was eager for some privacy. But I bumped into Ruby on my way to see her, and then got caught up with something else, and in the end I didn't get round to visiting her until lunchtime. Bea, I knocked, but there was no answer, and so I opened the door, and I saw something on the bed. Doll wasn't there, and my first thought was – she's left her toiletries bag on the bed, she must have gone to have a bath, she must have forgotten it. I almost shut the door again. But a different part of me already knew, and wouldn't let me. I stood there at the door, staring, staring, and I couldn't take it in. I just couldn't take it in. It was all crumpled, all out of shape, and it was still. She was so still, Bea, I'd never thought... I can't remember what happened next, it's as if my mind has just crossed it out, put a black line through it. The next thing I can remember is looking into the toilet bowl – I was bent over it, I hadn't been sick, I didn't even feel sick. I can remember noticing the water shivering a little when I breathed on it, tiny ripples... in and out, in and out. I felt safe, I felt like I wanted to stay in there for ever. And then a sound started up. The sound was there already, but it was as if my brain was fading it up, like the end of a record in reverse. I got up, my knees hurt, and I didn't know how long I'd been there, I wasn't really there at all. I walked back out into the hallway and Ruby was standing at the open door of Doll's room, holding onto the door-frame with one hand, facing into the room, and screaming. She'd scream until she ran out of breath and then she'd start up again, it was a horrible sound, she was meant to be sensible, she was meant to be in charge, and suddenly I saw her as young – younger than me – and afraid. People started running towards her then, they suddenly appeared from all over the place, all converging, all with the same kind of look on their faces, fear, a fear of what they might find. Running towards Ruby, and also wanting to run away.

I stood in the hallway, quiet, my head racing, and it wasn't until I saw Sister Agatha approaching that I came to my senses. I knew what I had to do. I knew where she'd be, you see, she'd told me about this place, you can get to it on the bus from here, it's near the sea – nothing special, she'd said, but there was a little abandoned beach hut – she'd told me she'd put an old chair in there, some rugs in a plastic bag, and she could see the sea from the door. She'd go there on her own. I knew I had to act fast – that before long there would be police swarming all over the place like flies. Like maggots. I went to find Ruby first, asked her to make sure Beatrice would be looked after, told her I had to go somewhere. I grabbed my handbag and coat and some money for the bus and left the building as quickly as I could.

I didn't think about what I was going to say to her until I was on the bus, looking out of the window at everyone walking along the pavements with their shopping bags as if everything was normal. I knew it hadn't been an accident. I'd seen the anger in her, I'd felt the coldness. Why was I even going? I only knew that I cared about her, it might even be a kind of love. You might think me terrible for saying that, that I could have any feelings for anyone who'd done what she'd done. Is there something wrong with me, that means I could feel tender towards her, affectionate, after she's shown such violence? But she was only a little girl, Bea, she was so little and afraid and someone had been so wrong to her, had killed a part of her off, and I was guessing how that little girl would be feeling – so lost, so frightened. So utterly alone. I was the only one who would understand that. I want you to understand, it's important to me that you can see it too. When we care about people, it shouldn't be dependent on what they do, should it? We should be able to hold on tight to our caring, and use it to see behind the bad things people do, understand them. Nobody really wants to be bad, do they? Surely they're only doing what they need to do to survive?

It took me half an hour to find the hut. When I saw it I knew it straight away, remembering Doll describing it to me late one night when we both still had our bumps. She told me about the fading blue paint, 'the same blue as the sky in the morning', she'd said, and it was. She told me about the odd little chimney at the top, which wasn't connected inside and must have been put on for show. She told me about the piece of crate she'd pulled over to cover up one of the gaping holes in the side, and the pieces of stone and driftwood she'd tied to pieces of string and hung at the front above the door. I approached it from the side, and I could see a pair of feet sticking out at the front – as I moved round I could see ankles, shins, knees, lap, hands. The white and blue striped deckchair she was sitting on. And then her face. I was almost beside her before she saw me, and she smiled – the most spontaneous, relaxed smile – as if we were bumping into each other on a pleasant day out at the beach. 'Elizabeth!' she said, 'Elizabeth, you're here!' And then something happened to her face. The smile cracked in half suddenly, her eyes lost their purpose, her whole body tensed. I was afraid she might run, and put my hands up in front of me, as if to show her I wasn't carrying any weapons, and backed away from her a little. She wasn't even looking at me any more, she was looking out at the sea, with a look of complete bewilderment on her face – Bea, it was the saddest thing I've ever seen. And then it changed again, she looked hopefully at me, and said 'have you brought my baby?' I felt a wave of grief rise up in me, and I couldn't stop it showing on my face, and I just shook my head, tears starting to squeeze their way out of my eyes, my stomach cramping like I was having a contraction. She looked blankly out to the sea again, and said, absentmindedly, 'I did it, didn't I? I did it. I didn't want her to die.' I was crying properly now, hiccupping tears, and I sat down next to her, on the cracked and broken wooden floor out the front of the hut, and I put my head onto her lap. She stroked my hair, she said 'there there', she kissed the top of my head. We stayed like that for a long time. Listening to the sea. The sea carried on breathing – in and out. In and out. We stayed like that for a long time. And then I knew it was time for us to go, and I took her back to the home, leading her by the hand. And then they took her away.

The rest of the day was hellish, question after question after question – most of them the same ones over and over. I think they maybe thought I was some kind of accomplice to start with, because I'd shared a room with her, because I'd known where Doll was, but it was straightforward enough for them to work it all out, once they knew what her father had done to her. There was a lovely policewoman, Bea, she looked after me – maybe she imagined me as her daughter, or maybe she was just a good person. She fetched me a sandwich for my lunch, and she hardly left my side. If it wasn't for her I don't know what I would have done. And then I was picked up from the station by Marjory, who'd already fetched Beatrice from the mother and baby home – they said they could look after her perfectly well while I was gone but I made such a fuss, they gave in eventually. I'm not missing a single one of my days with her. I can't go back to the home, it would be too horrible. I haven't got my things yet, or said goodbye to anyone, or anything – I'm in one of Marjory's jumpers today, and a pair of jeans that don't fit me very well. It's good to wear the jumper – it smells of Marjory and I feel like I'm safe here, in a different place, a different world. It almost feels as if we could stay here forever, Beatrice and me, and I could get a job as time goes on, Marjory would watch her for me, and I could pay my way, and be a good mother. I'm going to allow myself to dream today, Bea, I'm going to allow myself that at least.

That isn't everything yet. There's one final thing I haven't told you – not about Doll, nothing to do with her. I just want to warn you about it today, so you can prepare yourself. I don't think you're going to want to be my friend when I've told you, not any more. I don't want to tell you today. I need to think of you missing me today, I need to think of you wanting to see me again. I've put Marjorie's address on the back of the envelope, maybe if you get a chance you could write to me here. Beatrice loves your letters. I read them out loud to her over and over and her eye-lids get heavy and she drifts off into the loveliest, sweetest dreams.

With all our love,

Elizabeth and Beatrice.

Chapter 27

Violet first met Theresa, her first proper friend in the village, at Babette's life-drawing class. Six weeks after moving into Jacquet House, Violet had returned to her parents' for Christmas. She'd taken the local paper with her, and her mother had picked it up and spotted an advertisement for art classes starting in Amberly in January. She launched a determined campaign to get Violet to sign up, with her main reasons being 'getting her out of the house' and giving her a way to 'mix with the local colour'. She even went so far as to suggest that there might be some hope for Violet 'artistically' now she was divorced, and that the sketch she'd sent her of Blue was almost passable. By the time of the first class, Violet was roundly cursing her mother. The college was huge and industrial-looking – she couldn't find a parking space, and then she had to walk across dew-soaked grass and ruined her suede boots. Surely once a person reaches fifty, they should be old enough to stop listening to their mother's advice? She certainly felt old enough here, where students half Lucy's age fussed with their mobile phones and pushed into each other as they roamed the endless corridors. There it was – room 313. She clutched her handbag under her elbow, hoping she wasn't crushing the brand new sticks of charcoal inside, and knocked.

A smiling woman opened the door and held out a perfectly-manicured hand, introducing herself as Babette. Babette was something of a legend amongst the local men. They particularly approved of her generous cleavage and long eye-lashes, both of which were fake. She had long since lost her bloom of youth, but took such care over her appearance that Violet could see her wowing the gentlemen well into her sixties. She belonged to that group of women who seem willing to put up with extreme discomfort to look a certain way – not quite heavy corsets and powdered wigs, but high heels, an hour's worth of make-up, and skirts that restrict you to a silly totter. She welcomed Violet to the class by saying something reassuring about them being 'a friendly bunch', maybe spotting Violet's nerves under her carefully prepared nonchalance. Most of the class were already sitting at easels surrounding an empty chair. Babette sat Violet next to a jovial elderly gentleman called Stan, who put her at ease immediately by telling her quite matter-of-factly that he could never quite get boobs right, no matter how hard he tried. Babette then introduced them all to their model, 'Storm', a girl in her mid-thirties with sausages of flesh around her middle and a beautiful elegant neck. The class quickly settled into a concentrated silence while Babette circled, praising an ankle here and commenting on the angle of a nose there.

After thirty minutes of charcoal scratching on paper, Babette gave the sign and Storm stretched with obvious pleasure. The group filtered through to a nondescript room set aside for mature students and descended upon the tea and coffee machine. As Violet stirred sugar into her coffee Stan introduced her to a few of the other 'girls', for the class was mostly middle-aged women. They pounced on her and started asking her what she thought of Babette and whether she'd been to classes before anywhere else. It was like being the new girl at school with everyone fighting to be 'best friends' with her, before the novelty wore off and she became just another classmate. Over their shoulders Violet could see a woman on the other side of the room engaged in an intense conversation with a frail man in his seventies. The woman was dressed in a palette of dark browns, with a fitted V-neck over a darker T-shirt, and a long pair of wide trousers. A dark brown leather strap hung around her neck, resting a large glossy violet disc on her collar-bone. Her black, tightly-coiled hair was shorn close to her scalp, and her skin was a mid-shade of mahogany – Violet couldn't decide from looking at her features whether she had roots in Africa or somewhere in the South Pacific. There was a certain glamour about her that Violet envied – she wasn't wearing any make-up as far as she could tell, and her clothes were quite ordinary, but she carried her body in a way that suggested that she liked it, and that she liked herself. She caught Violet looking at her and smiled, and Violet turned quickly back to her questioners.

At the next class Violet was invited to supper with 'a few of the girls' by Sal, who seemed to have taken Violet under her wing. She was an aromatherapist who wore long smocks over swishy skirts with tiers like a wedding cake, strings of beads, and assorted velvet caps that made her head look like a mushroom. She always had a faint whiff of joss-stick about her; later Violet joked with her children about whether she used joss-stick-scented shampoo or dabbed a little 'eau de joss-stick' behind her ears before she went out. Maybe she still actually burnt the horrible things. They slid easily into conversation at the classes, usually about their gardens or their cats, and so it was with a relatively calm heart that she knocked on Sal's door later that week. Her porch was crowded with overgrown pot plants, and wind-chimes clustered around the eaves like a flock of strange birds. The woman with the violet pendant opened the door, and Violet felt a warm fluttering in her stomach that she put down to nerves. The woman smiled an empty smile and lingered for a second too long.

'I'm sorry, I'm racking my brain and I think I'm almost there, but I can't remember your.... Violet! It's Violet, isn't it? I haven't met you officially yet, I'm Theresa. I was going through all the colours I could think of, I almost went with Scarlett. But you're not really a Scarlett kind of woman, are you?'

As she spoke, she moved backwards and opened the door wide, gesturing her in. Violet wasn't sure how to respond, and when Sal appeared she was glad to greet her rather than try and think of something to say to this woman. She was taken through to sit in Sal's conservatory, which looked out over a small but perfectly formed garden. Violet was introduced to the other two women present – she'd met them briefly at the class already – and shown to a wicker seat which reclined too far back for her taste. She felt like a beetle on its back. When Sal came back with a gin and tonic for her Violet struggled up and walked over to the window.

The sun had long since gone to bed, but an exterior light threw illumination towards the back fence and made the garden look like a stage. It was a small space, but somehow Sal had managed to squeeze in a greenhouse, a tiny garden shed, and a vegetable patch with cane rows waiting for runner beans or raspberries. If she squinted she could just make out a neat row of blood-red chard. Closer to the house were clumps of ornamental grass; bronze, black, dark red.

It reminded Violet of a prairie garden she'd seen in a glossy magazine at the dentist the week before. She was standing with her back to the rest of the women, and their conversations clattered away in the background, quite separate from her. She wondered how long she would get away with looking at the garden before she had to turn back and enter the furore. It was usually at this point in the evening, when she hadn't enough alcohol in her system and she didn't know anyone very well, when she asked herself why the hell she'd come out in the first place when she could have been sitting in her own front room in her pyjamas, watching Morse.

Something brushed against her naked elbow, and she was just about to swat it when she saw that it was actually Theresa, who'd come up to stand beside her. It was the diaphanous cloth from her sleeve – she was wearing a long tunic over a pair of trousers, both in the same beautiful bluey-green colour, embroidered with gold stitching. She was quite stout, 'chunky' as the girls would say, but Violet couldn't tell if she was carrying fat or if it was bone and muscle. The style suited her better than it did Sal somehow – maybe it was her darker skin. She managed to look authentically ethnic, as if she belonged in her clothes. Violet looked behind her and saw Sal disappearing into the house. Theresa nodded and stood beside her for a while, looking out, and Violet did the same. The grasses twitched in the breeze, the stars flickered. A black cat balanced his way along the fence at the bottom of the garden, his tail straight up like a brush. Something settled between them in those moments, as if a chemical reaction had taken place in the air between them. Violet's nose now put Theresa's slightly musky aroma into a different category – 'familiar'. Theresa used her sleeve to rub a smudge from the glass.

'I help Sal out quite a bit with her garden. It's a fair deal

– my own garden's little more than a square of gravel, so I have my own key to the gate out the front and let myself in whenever I fancy a bit of proper gardening. We share out the spoils, not a lot at this time of year. I'm pretty nifty with a spade. Shall I show you around? You wouldn't be too cold?' She raised her voice. 'Sal, how long until dinner's ready?'

Sal shouted back from somewhere inside the house. 'Oh, the bloody pork will be another twenty minutes or so, I reckon. Bloody! Ha ha!'

'Shall we?'

Theresa slid the glass door across and held it open for Violet to step outside. As she walked through she felt temporarily smaller, even though Theresa was a good three inches shorter than she was. They wandered around the garden at a leisurely pace, their arms crossed to keep their hands warm. Theresa pointed out any specimens she was particularly proud of, and looked pleased when Violet spotted a pretty Hellebore. There was a carpet of small pale pink cyclamen under an apple tree near the back, and they glowed supernaturally in the artificial light. As Violet said, it was as if they might suddenly take wing and flap their pink petals, rising up into the branches. She felt quite disappointed when Sal opened the doors again and called them in, as if she was suddenly six and in the middle of an important game, and the grown-ups were dragging her away to homework or to a boring dinner of chops and boiled potatoes. They both squinted when they re-entered the bright house.

It was chops, but with buttery garlic mash and early green cabbage from the garden – good, simple food. Gardeners, especially ones with vegetable patches, often seemed to be better cooks. Over pudding, a magnificent raspberry Pavlova decorated with sprigs of mint, someone looked at Theresa and commented on how much 'Barb would love this pavlova'. Violet found herself blurting 'Who's Barb?' and there was a strange silence at the table. Sal and another woman exchanged a quick glance and hesitated, looking over at Theresa and waiting for her to speak.

'She was my partner. She died just over a year ago.'

'Oh, I didn't know. What business were you in?'

This seemed to have an even worse effect on the atmosphere around the table, and Violet wondered what she'd said now. Sal looked quite wretched, and wrung her napkin in her hands. Theresa spoke again, smiling gently.

'She wasn't my business partner, she was my lover.'

The word hung in the air like a bruise. Nobody knew where to look. After a few seconds Sal couldn't bear it any longer and sprung up from her seat.

'Would anyone like any more pavlova?' she offered, aware that most people were still tucking into their first portion. She scanned the table. 'Can I get anyone anything else?'

Theresa spoke to Violet again. 'She had breast cancer – it was a pretty long haul in the end. We were together for twenty years. I'm not just going to brush over it and move swiftly on to the coffee.' She spoke this last sentence to the general audience, and there was anger in her voice.

Sal stood with her arms hanging awkwardly by her sides and spoke to Violet as if Theresa weren't in the room.

'It's been a terrible time for her. She's coped marvellously, really, quite marvellously.'

Sal's extreme discomfort seemed to shift something in Theresa, and she softened and held out a hand, grabbing Sal by her wrist as if stopping her from saying anything more. Sal looked at her blankly, and Violet wondered if any losses of Sal's own were flashing behind her eyes. One of the women, who'd been talking to Violet all evening about the finer points of arranging humanistic funerals, raised her glass.

'A toast to Barb. Because she can't be here to eat this wonderful pavlova.'

Everyone around the table raised their glasses, relieved. Nothing more was said, and Violet shook off her curiosity by working her way towards a second portion of sweet, gooey meringue and tart, juicy raspberries.

Violet must have passed a secret test, as from then on she was included in all the women's get-togethers. The five of them, with the occasional addition or subtraction, often met up for early evening tea and cake, or for sketching sessions in front of bowls of fruit or reluctant husbands. They seemed to ask little of Violet except that she was there, and she began to form acquaintances with all of the women individually, moving from one to the next when she ran out of things to talk about. She wasn't quite sure what to do with the knowledge that Theresa was a lesbian. She'd had gay colleagues and students over the years, and her mother often invited a local couple, George and Reggie, round for tea, but she'd never had a lesbian in her immediate circle of friends before. She felt out of touch with the etiquette and found herself making broad pronouncements about 'what men are like' at the dinner table, and kept saying 'bugger' by mistake. Was that OK? Where could she find out what the rules were? Maybe her daughters would know.

These matters felt entirely separate from her friendship with Theresa, which bloomed. Theresa had always had an interest in buildings and once she found out that Violet was a structural engineer she pumped her for information whenever they met. Violet spoke to her about calculating loads and stresses, flawed foundations, and the behaviour of beams and columns in steel and concrete. She talked to her about the

Eden Project, a series of structures she'd had involvement with as a consultant, and how she'd visited it every year since it was built. She also recommended various books to her, and Theresa plucked out concepts to explore in her sculptures. She spoke to Violet about the principle of equilibrium and bending moments as if they were phrases from a newly discovered ancient language, and asked her strange questions like 'What does it feel like to know the mathematics of a material so well?' Violet enjoyed being listened to, and even though Theresa was only a beginner it was good to be appreciated for her professional knowledge again – she hadn't realised how much she'd missed her students. In return Theresa helped her out with her drawings, offering praise and advice at their various gatherings. They became a twosome within the five, helping each other out when it was their turn to make the coffees, and exchanging amused glances when Sal used her 'I surrender!' catchphrase.

It was Violet who asked Theresa if she fancied joining her for one of her morning walks along the coast. As soon as the words were out of her mouth she'd started regretting them – after only a few months in Abbotsfield she had already come to appreciate her time alone on these walks. She didn't have to 'do anything' or 'be anybody', she could just look out at the waves and put one foot in front of the other. She would have cancelled, but had lost the telephone number Theresa had scribbled onto a scrap of paper for her. She met Theresa in the car-park and they greeted awkwardly, Violet going in for a single kiss and Theresa for one on each cheek. It was the first time they'd met alone without the back-up of the other women, and Violet wondered whether they'd have anything to say to each other. She can't have been dong a very good job at hiding her feelings, as Theresa asked her before they'd even stepped down onto the pebbles if she was always this grumpy in the mornings. Violet admitted that she didn't feel up to saying much this early in the morning. They came to an arrangement that they wouldn't say anything to each other on the way down the beach, and in the silence Violet immediately remembered that she'd wanted to tell Theresa about the new novel she was reading. Theresa wouldn't let her speak, laughing and putting her finger to her lips, and so Violet had to hold on to the thought (and the others that joined it) and wait. She looked around her instead, at the tangled line of flotsam and jetsam further up the beach, at the short cliffs rising up to scrubland. Her next-door-but-one neighbour Sylvia had given her a list of the flowers she could expect to see later in the year, and Violet imagined them as she walked, repeating them in her head like a poem: Sea Kale, Mallow, Campion, Thrift.

After that first walk, Theresa joined Violet a couple of times a week and they settled into a routine -- walking along the beach in silence, and talking on the walk back to their cars. Theresa was a good listener, and Violet talked about her disappointment in her marriage break-up, her concerns about Guy, and her strained relationship with her mother. Violet listened to Theresa too -- and she spoke about her four-day-a-week job with the regional arts council, studying applications and doling out money, but mostly about being on her own. She often enjoyed it -- being able to cook herself curries as hot as she liked, leaving her sculptures in the middle of the living room as she worked on them, and growing out her armpit hair now there was nobody to see it. Now that she had so much space around her she was rediscovering things about herself too -- that she didn't really enjoy listening to Radio 4 after all, and that she got nervous before her brother came round, especially when he brought his wife. Whenever she talked, Violet was conscious of all the things she wasn't saying – how she lived her life before, with Barbara. She was quite happy to put Charles behind her, and look at him with occasional affection but always with relief that they weren't still together. Despite this he still popped up in her thoughts frequently. He played a central role in so many of her memories – here he is letting go of the back of Lucy's bike as she rides without stabilisers for the first time, and here he is holding her hand in Kenya as they stood in front of the most amazing sunset she'd ever seen. What was it like for Theresa? Does every memory stab her with grief as it rises up?

Sometimes they had nothing to say to each other, and almost the entire hour passed without them exchanging a word. Violet had never spent so much time in silence with anyone outside her family. She had imagined that you had to say things to get to know people – swap information, stack up nuggets of knowledge – but there was something about these silent walks that seemed to be giving her a different kind of knowledge about Theresa. It was as if they had a chance to tune in to each other, and that words would only have got in the way like gnats whispering around their faces. It was as if they were skipping the usual ingredients of close friendships – shared experiences, time, and cutting straight to the chase. Their walks continued, and then Violet invited Theresa to dinner when Guy and Josie were visiting. She bought lobster and champagne, and the evening was full of laughter and easy silences. They became more and more entwined in each other's lives without any conscious effort – Violet joined Theresa's second art group, which met once a month, Theresa looked after Blue when Violet was away, Violet bought Theresa's clay from a specialist art shop when she visited the nearest city.

A couple of months into their hot-house friendship,

their relationship got more complicated. Violet had always felt little bursts of anger when Theresa said or did certain things – she experienced these when she was with most people – but she started feeling small bloomings of sadness as well. She wasn't used to feeling sad, and she didn't like it. It happened when Theresa cancelled at the last minute, which happened with increasing frequency, or in the middle of long silences when they were walking. She also experienced something which almost felt like jealousy. When they were out together and Theresa got deep into conversation with another woman, Violet found it difficult to concentrate her own conversation and kept one ear open to what Theresa was saying instead. Theresa had a way of talking that encouraged intimacy – you felt like you were the most important person in the universe when she was talking to you. She would touch people lightly on the back of their hands when she was making a point, and Violet found herself wanting to go over and tell Theresa to stop… to stop what? She didn't know. She didn't say anything to Theresa –maybe this always happened when you became good friends with someone – she didn't have a great deal of experience. She remembered her perplexity at Megan throwing herself onto her bed as a teenager and weeping profusely at something this or that friend had or hadn't done. The sense of unease grew and got more troublesome, interrupting her when she was at art classes or getting on with her work. She started thinking that there might be something about Theresa that she'd missed – maybe she was being manipulated, or strung along. She didn't share these feelings with anyone.

Violet's growing annoyance with Theresa's unreliability was first aired when Theresa was due to come round for a fish and chip supper. They'd done it twice before – getting mushy peas and buttered bread rolls with their meal and stuffing themselves silly before watching a BBC drama or a nature documentary. Violet had had a terrible day, including a run-in with Margaret, clearing up cat sick, and a plaintive phone-call from Guy, and had been looking forward to a relaxing evening with Theresa. She'd bought a good bottle of Shiraz, and had spent an hour tidying the piles of magazines and arranging three bunches of daffodils in the front room when the phone rang. It was Theresa cancelling with an hour's notice – she'd been asked to a private showing by a friend and had double booked by mistake. Violet felt a surge of fury and before she could stop herself she'd shouted down the phone, 'Typical, stand me up again like you always do!' She hung up and stormed upstairs with her bottle of wine, and when she poured herself a glass she noticed that her hand was shaking. She vowed to break off the friendship – it was more trouble than it was worth – and wondered how one did such a thing – could she just ignore Theresa's phone calls until they stopped? Would she demand an explanation? What exactly was it that was bothering her so much?

Two glasses of wine later she was bored of sulking, and went downstairs to clean out her kitchen cupboards, a chore which was long overdue. She ignored the phone ringing, and when the door bell went she was kneeling on the kitchen floor with most of her torso shoved into the back of her saucepan cupboard. She made an attempt to brush the dust from her clothes and opened the door to Theresa, who was holding a bulging carrier bag from 'The Right Plaice'. Violet had already forgiven her, but didn't refuse the bottle of Glenlivet whisky she'd brought. Later in the evening Violet offered her terrible day to Theresa as a kind of apology for losing her temper, and said brusquely that she wasn't very good at this 'friendship stuff'. Theresa admitted in return that she often got herself into tangles by accepting more invitations than she should because she didn't want to let people down, and she'd guessed that Violet would have been less upset than her other friends. She said she was usually good at reading people but Violet's outburst had been a complete surprise. That felt like enough 'talking things through' for Violet and so she changed the subject to the floods in Cornwall, but later she was pleased that she'd let Theresa know how she felt, even if it might have been better not to shout.

Later that week Theresa called Violet to say that she'd been given a couple of free tickets for a concert in the Cardiff Millennium Centre. The programme included Rodrigo's Concierto de Aranjuez, a record Guy had played to death when he was a wan sixteen years old, and Violet still thought of it fondly. Theresa said she'd already booked a twin room in her usual hotel near Cardiff Bay – would Violet fancy coming along? Violet hadn't been to Cardiff since a conference there fifteen years ago, and welcomed the thought of a weekend away from the DIY jobs stacking up in Jacquet House. Violet drove them both in her battered Astra, and recognised the journey as a fine opportunity to continue Theresa's education in big band music, although Theresa wasn't quite so enthusiastic. Tension arose over the number of times that Violet stopped for petrol – Theresa wanted to stop every hour to have a cup of coffee or stretch her legs, but Violet was of the 'get there fast' school of driving and she even made Theresa cross her legs for the last half an hour of the trip as they were 'almost there'. Theresa threatened to wee on the passenger seat to teach her a lesson, and passed the time by making various faces of relief, asking Violet to judge the most convincing. By the time they arrived they'd moved on to swapping stories about other bodily functions. Violet had the upper hand by being a mother, and won easily with her story of Charles lying on his back and holding baby Lucy above him, playing aeroplanes, and Lucy getting airsick and a long string of vomit dripping down into Charles' mouth. They laughed so much that Violet missed a turning twice and then circled a roundabout as if it were a merry-go-round.

After checking in and smartening themselves up a bit (Violet borrowing Theresa's plum-coloured lipstick and then wiping it off again as it looked far to dark on her) they hoicked their handbags over their shoulders and set off for the bay. The golden light was beginning to fade, and pooled into bright patches on the water. The gulls circled and cried, competing with each other. Theresa put her arm through Violet's (Violet could smell her jasmine perfume) and they promenaded. On the drive Theresa had told Violet about an old Norwegian church converted into a tea-house, right on the bay and facing the open sea. Violet could see why Theresa loved it – it was just her thing. It had an effortless beauty – plain lines, nothing unnecessary, all faded black and white. It looked as if it had been built by decent people, who did honest work and who were kind to each other, unlike the modern shiny buildings surrounding it. As they headed towards it Theresa quizzed Violet on its engineering secrets – which part would they have built first? How would they know how many beams to use? It was busy inside and they took the last free table. The pretty Scandinavian girl behind the counter said she'd be right with them before returning to the shrieking coffee machine. They had an impressive array of cakes in a tall spinning glass cabinet, and Theresa took a full five minutes to decide what she wanted, ordering her cup of tea first and then returning when she'd thought it through. Her carrot cake was much nicer than Violet's slightly dry coffee sponge, and so Violet ordered a carrot cake for herself too, throwing caution to the wind.

They sat across from each other and looked out at the bay. Children were running around outside like horses on a windy day, copying the cries of the gulls. The edge of land was marked with shiny black railings, and on the water white triangles of sailboats cut across each other like skaters on an ice-rink. Higher still was more land; a line of crenellations against the sky (was it Cardiff castle?), a steep cliff giving way to grass. Behind them was the meandering music of conversation and the clinking of cutlery, underlined by the low insistent hum of a fridge. After they looked and listened without speaking for many minutes, Theresa said that the last time she'd been here was with Barbara. As she started to describe her, Violet realised how little she knew about Theresa. Theresa's words accumulated and clotted, building a picture of a quiet but determined woman who was always ready to fiercely defend her beliefs. Violet could see her walking her beloved cocker spaniels through the village, and fussing with her blouse before a night out and asking Theresa if she'd put on any more weight. She could hear her gravelly voice reading fairy tales to Theresa late at night, and imagine the sudden fits of weeping that continued for a full year after her father died. She could feel her outrage when she marched against Clause 28, and her grief at the end of her third attempt at IVF and at her decision to give up hope of a baby of her own. Most of all Violet could sense the angry currents running beneath her measured surface, giving her the energy to fight for her rights as a woman, a lesbian, an artist, a Jew, and later on to fight for her life, as the cancer took hold of more and more of her body.

As Theresa continued to talk their table became separated from the rest of the busy, bustling café. They were cocooned away from the elderly couple talking about bunions, and the squawking three year old straining to get away from his mother. Theresa's voice got softer and she looked down at her fork, playing with the remains of her cake. Violet leaned in so she could hear her better. And then Theresa said 'I loved all of her, Violet, even the darkest parts,' and had nothing more to say. Finally she looked up through her short dark lashes and her eyes caught on Violet's gaze, like a key turning in a lock. There was a sudden heat, pushing Violet's blood around her body. She felt stuck, like looking at road-kill – desperate to flick her eyes away but pulled to examine the mess of fur and blood. And when she did look down she felt her face redden, and her body suddenly belonged to her again. She mumbled 'back in a minute' and tripped over the chair leg as she went to find the toilet, feeling Theresa's eyes still on her. She sat on the toilet seat and waited for her heart to get back its usual rhythm. She tried to make sense of it. She decided she must have felt strange because they'd talked about Barbara. It had brought up difficult feelings for Theresa, and she'd transferred them into Violet like a pass the parcel. She checked her mobile, and after she'd replied to a text from Josie she felt herself again. When she got back to the table Theresa had already paid, and Violet didn't catch her eye until they were safely walking along the bay again, looking up at the stars that had sneaked out while they were talking. By the time they stood outside the Millennium Centre it was if nothing had happened. They stood and looked up at the poem written onto the face of the building, and Theresa translated the Welsh half for Violet.

> *'In these stones horizons sing,*
> *creating truth like glass from inspiration's furnace.'*

When Violet woke up the next morning the slice of window underneath the blind was still black. She squinted at her clock – 5am – and felt dismayed. It had been a terrible night; as soon as she'd shut her eyes she'd been assaulted by all kinds of irritating thoughts. They were like a swarm of bees – one of them would dive-bomb her, and when she'd flicked that one away there'd be a whole bunch of them queued up and ready to take their turn. She'd worried about Guy turning to drink, she'd worried about one of her daughters taking mortal offence at something she'd said and never speaking to her again. She'd even worried about Charles, because he'd sounded down when she last spoke to him on the phone, which was ridiculous – it was nothing to do with her any more. She lay flat on her back and tried not to move, as if she might have had a better chance of finding sleep if she kept perfectly still. She could feel sleep floating in and out of the room like puffs of smoke. It felt delicious when the smoke got closer, brushing against her cheeks or creeping up her wrists, but however hard she tried she couldn't sink into it entirely. The frustration was almost painful, like not being able to orgasm.

She lay there waiting for dawn to colour the sky, listening to the loud 'tick tick' of the hotel clock and trying to calm her breathing. She managed to relax a notch, and then she noticed another feeling creeping over her. She couldn't quite identify it to start with – fury? grief? Once it had started lapping at her toes it got stronger and stronger until great waves of it crashed over her as she lay in her single bed. She turned over onto her side, trying to escape it, telling herself to stop being such an idiot, but it followed her and rubbed sandpaper on her insides. She doubled up, hugging her knees to her chest, but this just seemed to squeeze something out of her like toothpaste and she let out a small sob, a kind of gasping noise, as the air fought to get inside her and the feeling fought to get out. She couldn't stop it then, and tried to cry as quietly as she could, the tears at high pressure and running down her cheeks in rivulets. She thought about going to the bathroom, but she didn't want to wake Theresa. Maybe it will end in a minute, she thought, maybe if I just let this water out then I'll feel better again, like having an upset stomach. It was no good though, she needed tissues – she was going to drip snot onto the pillow like a child. When she returned from the bathroom Theresa was propped up on her elbow in bed, one cheek lined with creases, waiting for her to return. When she saw the tears she pushed herself into a seated position and raised her eye-brows in a gesture of concern.

'What's up?'

Violet turned away from Theresa and got back under her covers. She shrugged, and made a small noise in her throat which could have meant anything. She sat up in her bed, hugging her knees, and felt like she'd been caught wetting the bed by her mother. This made her feel even more miserable and un-loveable, and the tears started again, despite herself. She sat in her bed and felt desperate to be alone, desperate to be held. She wanted to scream, and instead she turned it inside out and kept it close to her, just like always. But it hurt, it hurt. From where she sat in the bottom of her pit she became aware of Theresa standing over her. Violet shuffled aside, and it was cold in the room, and so without thinking she lifted up her covers and Theresa got inside with her. Theresa held open her arm and Violet ducked under it and put her head onto Theresa's chest, and suddenly she moved into a different space inside herself. It was a dark place, like a cave, and there were people standing at the entrance, looking out for trouble. There was still a hurt, but instead of being capable of eating her up it became smaller than her, a hurt she knew would heal. She felt a huge relief, sweet relief, and she lay there and let her tears subside, feeling soothed, her rough edges being smoothed out. She became aware of Theresa stroking her hair. How long had she been doing that? It felt wonderful, as if every hair had a nerve ending in its tip, like a fibre optic lamp, and every touch sent another spume of relaxation shooting down towards her scalp and throughout her body to the tips of her toes. She let out an involuntary 'mmm', and Theresa laughed. Violet squinted up at her.

'I don't want to come up ever again,' she said, her voice thick and sleepy. 'You won't go away, will you?'

Theresa didn't say anything, just kept stroking, slowly, tenderly, with all her concentration. Violet closed her eyes again and focussed on the feelings of pressure on her scalp. She couldn't be sure of the exact point at which things changed. Theresa's hand slowed down a little, started lingering. And then she moved it a little to the side and brushed her thumb over Violet's forehead, letting it rest there for just a second, but for that second the small place where their skin met became Violet's whole universe. The air around them took on a charge, an expectation – Violet could imagine mini-whirlwinds of electricity appearing from nowhere and floating on the air. She felt a tingling in her breasts, between her legs. Her whole body became something-that-was-waiting, helpless to turn a single cell away. She listened to Theresa's breathing and heard it speed up, get deeper. When she couldn't bear it any longer she turned her face towards Theresa's hand and nudged it a little with her nose. She wanted to touch it with her lips. She manoeuvred a little more and could see Theresa's fingers – they were trembling. She moved towards the tip of Theresa's little finger and took it into her mouth. She sucked the skin slippery – Theresa tasted of comfort and of warmth. Theresa let out a little sigh, and shifted her legs so they were in contact with the length of Violet's under the covers. Violet kept her eyes shut as she moved her head up towards Theresa's. She stayed there for a few moments, hoping Theresa's eyes were open, hoping she knew what she wanted. And eventually she felt a tickling on her cheek, and then again, Theresa's cheek brushing against hers, the velvet of a moth's wings, her nose touching Violet's nose. When their lips arrived at the same place they sipped at each other as if tasting wine.

As they kissed Violet felt Theresa's hand settling on her hip, on top of the covers, and shifted towards it to increase the pressure. It had been so long. She felt like a teenager. She kept her eyes closed, not wanting to break the spell. She put her hand on the back of Theresa's head, pressing gently against her springy hair, feeling the texture with her fingertips. Her lips were so full, so soft. She kept her eyes shut and concentrated on what she was doing, her hand finding Theresa's and linking fingers, the tip of her tongue finding the cool silk of her teeth. When Theresa pulled away, Violet was forced to open her eyes. She opened one at first, as if afraid of what she might see.

'I'm still a woman,' said Theresa, not smiling but with a twinkle in her eyes.

'I'm just going to call you Tom. That'll make everything OK.'

Violet tried to snuggle back down into Theresa's chest, where everything was dark and wonderful, but Theresa pulled away again and took Violet's hand from around her waist. She held it and squeezed it tight, angling her face so she could catch Violet's eye.

'I want you to be sure you know what you're doing.'

Violet was distracted by the feel of Theresa's hand in hers, and started to play with her thumb.

'Um, kissing you?'

'Violet.'

Her tone snapped Violet out of her warm haze and she looked at Theresa and saw her friend again. She waited as Theresa took a deep breath as if she were about to give Violet some important information, but her serious look faded into resignation.

'I just want you to… oh, fuck it. I don't know. I like you, we've… I've enjoyed the time we've spent together. I just don't want to do this again.'

'Do what again?'

'Satisfy some straight woman's curiosity. Be the one who gives bored housewives their little kicks for the year.'

'Ouch.'

Violet pulled away from her, and they sat for a few minutes with their hands on their knees, looking ahead like two old ladies on a bus.

Eventually Theresa sighed. 'Look, I'm sorry. I just don't know if I want to risk it.'

'What – giving this bored housewife her little kicks?'

Violet listened to the violent ticking of the clock. She wondered what time it was.

'I don't… After… I haven't…' She faltered and tried again. 'I don't want to get…'

Violet looked over and when she saw the pain on Theresa's face she was overwhelmed with tenderness. She said 'hey', looped her arm through Theresa's and took her hand, squeezing it between both of hers. They hugged like sisters and the sex in the air disappeared altogether. After a few seconds Theresa sighed.

'Can we talk about this another time? My head is all fuzzy.'

Violet nodded, and Theresa got out of bed. She held Violet's face in her hands and kissed her on the forehead – the gesture had a finality to it.

'Right, you. I'm going to have a bath. Are you feeling OK now? Tears stopped?'

Violet nodded again.

'As far as I know.'

They both smiled easy smiles. When Theresa had gathered her clothes in her arms and shut the door of the bathroom behind her Violet flicked on the TV and put the volume down low. She could hear Theresa sloshing and plashing, and after a plastic farting noise the clean scent of her mint shampoo filled the hotel room. She licked her lips – she could still taste her. Tom's taste. What would she do with this? It didn't matter right now – she just felt tired and happy. She burrowed down into her pillows and drifted back off to sleep.

Violet had a house full of an assortment of children for the next few days, and work to catch up on, but whenever she had a spare moment she'd close her eyes and remember and grin to herself. She re-ran the feeling of Theresa's thumb on her forehead, the soft give of her lips, the honey smell of her. She found herself fantasising about her as well – at night, in bed – wondering what colour her nipples were, and what it would be like to press her cheek into her bare breasts. She imagined placing Theresa's hand between her legs and making Theresa hold onto her like a fruit. She masturbated and saw Theresa's face in her mind, relishing the unexpectedness of finding sexual pleasure here, where she'd least expect it. There was no communication between them – no phone-calls, no texts, no visit had been arranged. On the third night after they came back, Violet's house empty again, she lay in her bed after eleven and burned. Fuck it, she thought – and sent Theresa a text in capitals – 'I WANT YOU.' Almost immediately a text came back – she could hardly bring herself to look at it. It said 'I'm coming.'

Twenty minutes later Violet let Theresa in. She almost pulled her inside the house and they started kissing – hungry kisses, as if each of them were trying to pull the other inside themselves, suck off their tongues. Violet's whole body was aching, her cunt was aching, it was almost unbearable. Violet tried to manoeuvre her towards the staircase, and Theresa tripped up on the edge of the rug, falling on her bottom. She looked up at Violet and laughed. Violet spent a moment comparing her recent fantasies with this real live woman sitting on the floor in front of her – did she still desire her? Now that she was here in the flesh, in her fluffy sheep-patterned pyjamas with a wax jacket over the top? The feelings swirled and pulsed in her – affection, fear, curiosity.

'Have you got a glass of water?'

Violet went to the kitchen to fetch her a glass, running the tap for thirty seconds until the cold kicked in. By the time she'd returned Theresa had taken off her coat. Violet handed her the water, and they both smiled and raised their eye-brows. What now? Theresa knew what to say.

'Shall we go to bed then?'

Violet bounded up the stairs, leaving Theresa to follow. She'd never even shown Theresa her bedroom before. She got back under her duvet, ridiculously glad that Blue was there to distract them both. Theresa put her glass on the other bedside table and paused at the side of the bed by the motionless cat to give him a bit of fuss. She'd learnt the trick of rubbing around his ears from Violet, and he stretched out, opened his eyes a sliver, and moved his head towards her to get the maximum benefit. She coo-ed to him – 'There's a blue boy, who's my bluey... yes! Yes!' Eventually he got tired of the fuss and started twitching the tip of his tail, eager to return to the more serious business of sleeping. Theresa turned to Violet.

'Here I am, then.'

'Hello Tom.'

Violet dragged Blue to the bottom of the bed and lifted up the duvet for Theresa to climb in. They cuddled, and Violet was relieved, because all the heat had gone out of her. Where had it gone? Maybe the sexual attraction was all in her mind? She felt comfortable, though, sliding her finger up and down Theresa's arm, smoothing the dark hairs one way and then the other. She felt comforted by Theresa's hand resting on her thigh. Theresa talked about what she'd thought of Violet when she'd first met her. She'd been watching her at that first class when Babette shook her hand and sat her next to Stan, and she listened to her responding to the other women's questions during the break. She thought she sounded confident to the point of arrogance, and rather lacking in social skills. It was only later that Violet had intimated that there might be something different underneath. Theresa described a moment when the women started to talk amongst themselves about a class last term, and all at once Violet looked lost and frightened. Violet was hungry for these details about herself, as if Theresa had discovered truths about her that no-one else had ever seen. What was it about her voice that made her sound arrogant? What did her clothes say about her? How did Theresa know that she was bored last week when Sal had gone on about her rising damp?

An hour later they'd talked themselves out, and Violet clicked off the lamp so they could settle down to sleep. Violet pushed her feet against Blue and he plopped down onto the carpet and padded out, heading towards the landing, where he knew he wouldn't be disturbed. Theresa turned onto her side and Violet fitted in behind her like a spoon, draping an arm over her waist. As soon as they stopped wiggling their bodies into a comfortable position and silence settled, Violet started to feel turned on again. She shifted towards Theresa as if she was moving in her sleep, and the increased pressure stoked her desire even further. She started to imagine Theresa's naked skin against hers – smooth, creamy, slippery with sweat. She moved her head in closer towards the nape of Theresa's neck and, like a baby moving towards a nipple, nuzzled her lips against her the skin underneath her hairline and sucked. Theresa breathed out a 'mmm', low in her throat, and turned towards her.

They made love then, taking their time. Violet rolled Theresa's ear-lobe around in her mouth as if it were a butterscotch. They pushed their cheeks up against each other and listened to each other's breath becoming ragged. Theresa lifted Violet's nightgown over her head and ran a finger lightly from her neck down to her belly button and back again. Violet unbuttoned Theresa's shirt and pulled her pyjamas trousers off, pausing to playfully slap the cheek of her arse before pulling the covers right back so she could take her body in all at once. She couldn't help compare her own body to Theresa's, which was darker skinned and plumper, as if she had more juice inside her, as if she'd been left out longer in the sun. Her own felt straight and boring in comparison, and she wondered if she was womanly enough for Theresa. Theresa's breasts were lower than they would have been twenty years ago but they looked full, the skin taught with the soft flesh they contained. Since her illness Violet's had felt half empty, but Theresa didn't seem to mind, and took a breast into her mouth as she walked her fingers down her side and into the tangle of hair at the base of the flat expanse of her pelvis. And then an exploring finger found its way inside, to silky skin that was already swollen and wet.

Violet wasn't ready for Theresa to go down on her, and was afraid to move her own lips past Theresa's belly button, but there were a thousand other things for their bodies to do. Violet was amazed at how easily she climaxed, four or five times during the night. It had become a bit of an effort with Charles, requiring sustained concentration and careful instruction – 'left a bit', 'not so hard'. These orgasms slipped out of her as if she were singing them. Each time she lay back and basked in the afterglow, thinking she was finished, but Theresa would start to draw shapes on her thighs with her fingernails, or nibble her neck, and despite herself she set off up the hill again. She gave Theresa pleasure too, discovering that she couldn't get enough of having her palms kissed, and that she was turned on by watching Violet touch herself. They failed to fall into sleep, and when the sun finally came up they were pulled into the kitchen by a sudden ravenous hunger for bacon and eggs.

It was over their bacon and eggs that they decided to 'give it a shot'. Their first week was perfect, heady, unsullied by reality. Theresa called in sick and they'd spend long afternoons in Violet's bed, taking up their meals on a tray and littering the floor with chocolate wrappers, magazines and empty mugs like teenagers. Blue couldn't believe his luck either – not one but two warm bodies to lie against in the middle of the day! They spent time at Theresa's house too, and Violet would read while Theresa worked on one of her sculptures. Violet would wander around her house and try to memorise everything – what books she had on her shelves (Wharton/Woolf/Walker, travel books on Morocco, political tomes, and a complete collection of Wodehouse), the colour paint she'd chosen for her bedroom (sage), what she had in her kitchen cupboards (twenty different spices, coconut cream, and an impressive stash of Cadbury cream eggs). She nagged Theresa to let her look at her photo albums going right back to when she was small, and pored over the faces of her adoptive parents, both dead now, wondering what kind of people they'd been. Had she wanted to know everything about Charles when they first got together? She supposed she must have, but she couldn't remember it being this important, this urgent. She had so much catching up to do – her best friend Tanya had known Theresa for more than thirty years – how could she compete with that?

For a while, nobody knew. It suited Violet to keep things quiet, and they conducted their relationship cosseted away in the warm. Their first major disagreement took place under Theresa's duvet at three o'clock one afternoon in the middle of 'Doctor At Large'. Theresa announced out of nowhere that she'd had a lifetime of hiding and being ashamed. She said she'd only continue to see Violet if they became open about their relationship. Violet said 'it's alright for you' and Theresa said 'no, actually it's not – that's the point.' Their first experiment was holding hands when they went on a long weekend to Brighton, but it was hardly a challenge considering the people walking along the front – it might have been more controversial to not hold hands, or to wear a conservative pin-stripe suit. Violet was quite content – proud even – to show Theresa off in public – it was her family that she really worried about. She first introduced the idea of a new lover to her children by calling her Tom, and trying to avoid personal pronouns to kid herself that she wasn't actually lying. They all seemed to like the idea of Violet having a new boyfriend, especially Megan, and they started hassling her about meeting 'him'. Violet always came off the phone with a sick, unsettled feeling in her stomach.

As time went on Theresa told her that people in the village were gossiping about them. Violet decided to tackle the people she didn't really care about first, and chose a day when they could 'do everyone at once'. They turned up at a local bingo night together, and then made sure that Angie was amongst the people who saw them kissing each other goodbye. The news reached Bristol by the next morning. The family phone calls were more difficult. Violet had asked Theresa for some suggestions about how to break the news – after her years of practise, surely she had an approach that was less likely to cause upset? Theresa just said, 'Welcome to the world, darling,' and kissed her on her forehead. Eventually she came up with 'Tom is actually a woman,' and used this on Charles, her father, her mother, Guy, Lucy, Josie and finally Megan, with wildly differing results. Her father surprised her by sounding quite shocked and upset, whereas her mother, after an initial silence, rallied quickly and started planning a 'homosexual civil wedding' for them, and professing that she'd secretly always wanted a 'gay child'. Guy's reaction was the most measured: 'OK, Mother, cool, it'll take me a bit of time to get used to that – give me a call tomorrow, yeah?' Her daughters were the most difficult, as she'd suspected. Josie was a little upset, and kept Violet on the phone quizzing her about the link between her sexuality and her divorce from Charles. Lucy couldn't help making a cutting comment about the importance of honesty in families. And Megan was quite openly angry. Even though Violet had taken five deep breaths before the phone-call and vowed to herself that she wouldn't lose her temper, she'd been so upset by what Megan had said that she retaliated despite herself. ('I wanted Tom to come to my party next month – I don't want him to be a woman! How could you do this to me?' 'It's none of your fucking business how I live my private life!' etc. etc.) Before she'd regained her senses Megan had hung up on her. After her anger faded she asked herself whether it was really worth it.

Theresa had made a comment about there being something not quite believable about their relationship, and she was probably right. They both had their own agendas for needing to make it work. Theresa was desperate to find something as lasting and nourishing as her partnership with Barbara, and Violet was caught up in the novelty of being in love with a woman. A woman, who had a luscious woman's body and a sensible woman's mind. No need to remind her to take her empty mug into the kitchen, or to explain why she didn't fancy going out to dinner but would rather stay in and watch a trashy film. No need to flatter and pander to her, to minimise her own intellect, or to make sure she looked good on Theresa's arm. Why she hadn't thought of having a relationship with a woman before? Violet often wondered whether their relationship would have lasted through the early teething problems if the beginnings hadn't tasted so sweet. They drank each other up like nectar. Slowly, the haze cleared, and after the first few months of honeymoon their rough edges began to rub up against each other.

Their slight disagreements started to grow in strength, and clustered around themes. Violet became increasingly annoyed by Theresa's interminable phone calls to her best friend Tanya in Australia, and Theresa wondered why Violet found it so hard to remember how she liked her toast. More difficult to resolve were the 'Violet doesn't share her feelings' theme, and the 'Theresa always wants to be reassured' theme. Their first really vicious argument started over a cup of tea. They were both at Theresa's house – Theresa was working from home, and Violet had brought her laptop with her. Despite a slight, unnameable background tension that had been with them for days, things were going well. Mid-morning Violet made herself a cup and Theresa, who'd been sitting in her office and listening to the noises in the kitchen, thundered into the room Violet had appropriated as an office.

'I thought so!' she said, triumphantly.

'What now?' asked Violet, in a tired voice, and accompanied by a long, weary sigh.

'It probably didn't even occur to you that I might have wanted a cup of tea, did it?'

'Do you want a cup of tea?'

'Well, no, I don't, but I might have done.'

'So you didn't want a cup of tea?'

'That's not the point, Violet, the point is that...'

It didn't help that Violet's daughters, especially Megan, were still finding the whole thing difficult to understand. Violet only occasionally mentioned Theresa, always referring to her as Tom, and was usually met with silence. Her mother also handled the situation without grace, and made such a big deal of it every time they spoke that Violet became more and more embarrassed for her. 'My daughter is a lesbian now, you know,' became her favourite phrase, and she was increasingly prone to drop the information into polite conversation without prompting.

Their arguments seemed to circle like aeroplanes stuck in a holding pattern, but gaining in altitude as Theresa grew shriller and Violet moved towards a furious silence. They took short-cuts to exactly how they'd felt at the peak of their previous argument at the smallest provocation – Theresa not liking the way Violet left her out of her conversations with her daughters, or a difference in opinion about how to make the best omelettes. Violet started to feel suffocated and tried to pull back, but she found that as she pulled back, Theresa moved forwards. She thought of Theresa as too sticky, tacky, like PVA glue. Theresa was different to Charles – she wouldn't just leave it and roll over, she'd bite back – and sometimes their arguments escalated into those fights you'd be embarrassed to hear coming from your neighbours house. Occasionally they even spilled out onto the pavement as one of them tumbled out of the front door with their stuff gathered in their arms, shouting a last insult through an open window. The arguments would often be concluded with a text message from Theresa in the middle of the night – 'I miss you', or 'I'm sorry'. They'd prise Violet open like a clam and she'd turn up on Theresa's doorstep twenty minutes later. Their make-up sex was always enthusiastic, passionate, and tender, but they'd speak sadly afterwards about how these fights wounded them, as if they were gouging huge holes in each other, and they wondered how many times they could manage to heal.

The general consensus in the village was that they were good for each other. The women from the art class discussed how Theresa had got her sparkle back, and Sal nudged Violet in the ribs. One day Violet helped her to get rid of the last of Barbara's clothes. Theresa encouraged Violet to be more sociable, and she felt she might even get the hang of being a part of the community. She even got roped into the annual ten mile walk for breast cancer, she and Theresa getting into a competitive frenzy about who could get the most sponsorship money. Something about being with Theresa started to seep through to Violet's core. It was as if Theresa was soft, persistent rain, and Violet's stone wall began to soften, to weaken. Strange, unfamiliar feelings started sprouting and catching her unawares – tenderness, trust, a sense of letting go. She'd come upon Theresa doing the washing up and want to lift her hands from the soapy water, remove her marigolds and kiss the tip of each of her fingertips. She'd worry about her in the middle of the night – how will she get on with her presentation tomorrow? Will she be careful on the icy roads? Sometimes when chopping carrots or watching TV in bed she'd turn her head and catch

Theresa looking at her in a certain way. When this happened she thought her lungs might burst.

The final argument, which caused Violet to run out of Theresa's house and into the rain, had come from nowhere. It had been a bad week – Theresa's brother had been in hospital with suspected liver disease, and Josie had split up with her boyfriend. Violet couldn't even remember how it started or why it escalated so violently. Maybe Theresa was hormonal, or maybe they were both just tired of the endless repetition of pain and reconciliation. She could remember the last phrase Theresa flung at her – 'You're as cold as fucking ice,' and also the last thing she screamed at Theresa – 'How could Barbara bear you, you're such a NEEDY fucking PARASITE!' She remembered the look on Theresa's face as it landed, before she turned and left her – it was like grief. She remembered thinking at the time 'I can't go back from this.' 'I can't carry on wounding this person, who I love.' She didn't believe she could learn how to do things differently – she was too old, too much a novice at the impossible art of relationships. Most of all she couldn't risk Theresa kicking her out, before she had the chance to leave her first. She couldn't even bear the thought of that.

Chapter 28

The tins of condensed milk chatter away in the pan of boiling water, rising and falling with clinks or clacks. Violet gives them a wide berth as she slices the soft bananas with a sharp knife – it's never happened before but the tins warn that 'boiling can cause bursting'. The racket competes with a woman's voice, floating above the piano and guitar like a kite. Not Violet's kind of thing at all – something Will has leant her. She's determined to give it a chance, but the singer's voice is high-pitched and whiny. Making banoffee pie for her daughters when they come to stay has become compulsory. They never make it for themselves, saying they're 'so in love with it' that they'd eat the whole thing at once and make themselves sick. This theory has several cracks – the largest of which is that they usually polish the whole thing off at Violet's anyway, each having a heaped bowl of the stuff for breakfast if there's any left the next morning. Guy likes to parody the noises they make as they eat it – sex grunts and satisfied moans – it's really quite obscene. Violet has always found it too sickly sweet, but she enjoys watching her daughters eat. As she finishes the bananas she hears Guy's distinctive knock on the door: knock, knock-knock-knock. She looks at her watch – she still has at least an hour before the girls are due. She opens the door, still holding the knife in her hand, and pecks him quickly on the cheek before letting him pass by her into the house.

'Hello, darling. I'm right in the middle of cooking.'

'Hello, Mother.'

He follows her back into the kitchen and sits on a stool, looking forlorn. As she gets out the butter, her mind flicks back to when he was half the height he is now. He used to love helping her out in the kitchen – peeling hard-boiled eggs for kedgeree or shucking the skins from broad beans, always wearing a look of intense concentration. She often looked at his face back then and thought of the word 'beatific'. She thinks about her own face at that time – how many of her frown lines had appeared by then? What did she spend her days thinking about? Was she happy? She thought she was at the time. She tears open a packet of plain digestives and starts emptying them into a big plastic bag. She's never been one for weighing, unlike Charles, who used to feel it was important to follow recipes to the milligram. He was always a big fan of Delia. So was Tom. So is Tom. Violet can't bear her – she's far too pernickety – half a teaspoon of water, stir this four hundred and twelve times... life's too short. Although she liked her more after she saw her going mad about the football club she supports – or does she own the team? Violet was always more into Jamie's style of food – a dollop of this and a handful of that and chuck it all in the oven for a while until it looks ready.

She takes a whole digestive from the packet to munch on. Just to keep her energy up as she cooks. She offers the packet to Guy, and he nods. She stands for a few seconds with the packet outstretched, but he seems unable to move and so she sighs and walks around the counter, rolling her eyes at him. He grins, looking a little sheepish. She busies herself with the rolling pin, trying to ignore him, but relents as she's running her fingers through the crumbs.

'Is there something the matter with you?'

'No, why do you say?'

'I haven't got any patience today, Guy, I've still got lots to do before they all get here. Spit it out.'

'Well, it's just that… it's nothing, really. Just that I don't think I'm a writer after all.'

She stops what she's doing, holding her crumb-covered hands in mid-air. She wants to go over and slap him on the cheek, hard, as she did once in the middle of a supermarket when he was seven years old. She fixes her eyes on her hands and tries to stay absolutely still – maybe if she can do that then the rage will subside a little and she'll be able to keep control of herself.

'So what are you cooking for us tonight?'

His voice is already lighter, his confession confessed. She says nothing. The butter is starting to simmer on the stove, she can hear it. The whole thing will be ruined if the butter burns, and she's damned if he's going to spoil that as well as everything else. Now that she's started things off by saying nothing, she isn't sure how to proceed. Her usual reaction would have been to shout at him, and then to take things from there, but this silence… Maybe she has learnt something from the terrible arguments with Tom after all. Maybe she's developed a greater capacity for holding things inside herself, maybe she's become a stronger container. The feelings she's had, no, the feelings she has about Tom are stronger, more insistent, and just plain bigger than anything else she's experienced before in her life. Except maybe when she was a baby – feelings she can't remember

– the raw desperate need for milk or mother, the piercing disappointment of being let down, the animal fear of being left alone. How do babies contain it? Their soft little bodies… How could any mother not do damage to their children, with such high stakes? Such tiny bundles of complete helplessness, who don't know at any moment whether they'll be fed or abandoned, whether they'll be given life or left to die. In which ways has she wounded her own children? In which subtle and not-so-subtle ways has she damaged this man sitting here in her kitchen? She pours the crumbs of biscuit into the molten butter, like a child's dumper truck in a sand-pit. She stirs them together with a wooden spoon. She is alone with her thoughts, and is suddenly amazed that anyone manages to hold their lives together from day to day. With these deep wounds inside us all, isn't it a miracle that we can bear to get up every morning, go to work, kiss our partners when we get home? As if everything is normal. Isn't it a miracle that we don't pour our rage and grief out onto the people around us, driving everyone away? How can we ever bear the terrible risk of being in relationships? How can we ever bear to be alone?

She adds a little sugar and a pinch of cinnamon to the mixture. She can never really taste the cinnamon but it's something her mother always does. Putting it in is more important than whether or not it makes any difference to the taste. We add cinnamon to our biscuit bases in this family, and that's that. It's what makes us different from the others. It helps us belong to each other. She finishes patting the biscuit crumbs down, and looks round at Guy. He's looking at his nails, fiddling with them. What is the word for his face? Crestfallen. She wonders what that means – crestfallen. What is a crest? He's one of us, she thinks – he belongs with me, and his sisters, and she even adds Charles to the mix in a sudden burst of generosity. Family. Where we can be as bloody infuriating as we need to be, and we don't get chucked out. Where we can fuck things up as much as we need to and still be forgiven. Oh, he was fucking it up all right. He'd been screwing up since he left school. But if he couldn't come back here and tell her what he'd done, where would he go?

She walks over to her son and takes his face in her hands. He looks up at her, surprised, a little afraid.

'You…' she says, drawing the vowel sound out, as if sharing a joke with someone else in the room. Look at this person, whom we love. Look at the ways in which he's making a mess of his life.

She kisses him on the forehead, and studies him for a few seconds, and sees the water come to his eyes. And then it's too much for him, and for her as well, too much tenderness, and he takes one of her hands and holds it away from her and turns it into a play-fight. He makes his other hand into a loose fist and pushes gently at her shoulder, and after a little grappling she pulls away and goes to put the banoffee base in the oven. He brushes the crumbs from his sleeve. Nothing more needs to be said.

Just after six, Violet is looking out at the pale clouds and worrying about Elizabeth. Her last letter keeps running through her mind. She kept thinking she ought to do something when she got it, but what? She lost sleep over it last night. Maybe she could search the internet and find a record of what happened? What should she do? It was too late now, anyway. She's thinking about telling Will about it when Lucy's bright red Micra pulls up outside the house. She parks inexpertly on next-door's grass verge and they all pile out – Lucy has brought her own pillows, and Josie seems to have enough luggage for several weeks. It's the first thing Violet says to her, 'How long are you staying for?' – half as a joke, but also because she's wondering if Guy might want to move back in with her. She kisses her three daughters as they come towards her. Here's Lucy with her narrow eyes, her lashes always clogged with mascara, and her long sheet of dark hair, straightened every morning with those exorbitantly expensive ceramic straighteners. Here's Josie with her bouncing layers of newly henna-ed hair, and a high brow which she hated when she was younger but has grown into, telling Violet it gives her an 'air of mystery'. Megan is last to climb out, and look! – her hair is all gone! It's cropped almost down to the scalp, and Violet stares at her over Josie's shoulder, trying to decide whether it suits her or not. It's so dramatic. She's wondering how Megan will greet her – things have been strained since their late night phone call. If anything Megan seems overly glad to see her, and when they hug she holds on too long. She looks a little anxiously at her mother and asks what she thinks of her hair, and Violet has reached her decision, yes, it's a little severe but she definitely pulls it off. On that conciliatory note they go into the house, Violet waving at Wendy Peters from next door who's peering out of her window to see what all the commotion is about.

Once they're inside Violet feels outnumbered. The girls take over, noisily greeting Guy, taking their stuff up to the office, milling about in the kitchen and opening and closing cupboards. Violet wants to hold her hands up in the air and say 'Whoa!', although if they all stopped and looked at her she wouldn't know what to say next. She feels like a spare part, and that's what she is. So difficult to work out her purpose as a parent, now they don't need her to wipe their snotty noses or fetch them a drink from the high cupboard. Josie sniffs the air and says, 'Mmmmm, cheese! Tell me you've made one of your amazing pies, mother!' and that does make her feel better, but before she can frame an answer Josie has disappeared out the back door to 'check out the garden' (smoke a cigarette). Her youngest daughter is the only one in the family who's picked up the filthy habit, and Violet can't make any sense of it. Her other children are so anti-smoking that she's surprised Josie feels it's worth all the ribbing. Guy did tell her late one night that he was partial to the odd 'doobie', which she assumed at the time was marijuana, but she Googled it the next morning just to make sure it wasn't the new word for crack cocaine.

When they've settled down, Lucy announces that she and Megan are going to have a stroll before dinner. Her oldest two daughters have always had a close relationship. Josie used to idolise her sisters and made frequent frustrated attempts to join in. It angered Violet to see her fail time after time, and for a while she tried to intervene, sending Josie into Lucy's bedroom with chocolate biscuits or messages. Eventually Josie found her own way through it. She started taking pride in being the one who could do things 'on her own', and basked in the praise that her grandmother gave her for being her 'special girl' who was 'smallest and bravest'. It was only years later that she formed an alliance with Guy. He'd always preferred the company of boys. He had a knack for seeking them out wherever they went – in restaurants or on holiday, Violet would turn her back for a few minutes and when she looked around there'd be three small boys running around like tiny missiles. Guy first caught on to the advantages of being Josie's little brother when she was nearing the end of secondary school. She'd developed an impressive line in sarcastic wit, and wore black eye-liner and a shaggy, layered haircut that made her the envy of all the goths and alternatives in her class (Vera liked to call them 'the misfits'). She even had a little notoriety in the rest of the school by virtue of her 'experiment' in the chemistry lab which resulted in the need to re-surface a whole bank of lab desks. Guy started saying hello to her in the halls when he passed her and her pack of noisy friends, and eventually they discovered a common love of alternative music. They shared a room and so could listen to John Peel in bed in the dark, and recorded tape after tape of songs that were never played more than once. Josie even took Guy to his first gig when he was only fourteen – Cornershop – Guy sang 'Brimful of Asha' around the house for weeks and drove the rest of the household to distraction. The pair of them still shared a penchant for obscure bands, even now that Guy was mostly into 'that dance rubbish' as Josie called it, and Violet enjoyed listening to them comparing notes about 'The Ribs' and whether they were all hype or if there might be something uniquely brilliant about their riffs after all.

When Megan and Lucy return from their walk, they have a strange atmosphere hanging around them. As Megan brushes past her into the living room, where they are going to eat on their laps, Violet notices that her eyes looked red-rimmed. The two of them exchange surreptitious glances over the crab cakes, and Lucy seems to be urging Megan on. When Violet brings in the pie, a thick steaming wedge on each bright blue plate, Lucy sighs sharply and looks at Megan.

'Are you going to get this over and done with, then, Gannie?'

Megan glares at her and picks up her knife and fork. Violet hasn't heard Lucy call her Gannie for years. She notices Guy and Josie tucking into their food without interest – they are obviously in on it, whatever 'it' is. She puts her plate down on the glass coffee table with a clank and crosses her arms.

'Would anyone like to tell me what's going on?' she asks, surveying the room, and Megan promptly puts her cutlery down again and starts crying.

Lucy puts her dinner down too and goes over to squeeze in next to Megan on her armchair in solidarity. Violet has gone to such trouble with that bloody pie, and now it's getting cold. It's not fair; she wanted the evening to be successful.

'Well?' she asks, not able to keep the annoyance from her voice. Megan always makes such a big fuss of things. She continues to stare at Megan, but it's Guy who speaks, his mouth half full.

'She's building up to tell you about this ashram thing, Mother. It really isn't a big deal.'

Megan flares up with anger and makes a sudden gesture with her hands as if she's throwing something up into the air.

'Thanks, Guy! You couldn't have… you're so…' She finishes her sentence with a harrumphing-horse noise. She bows her head and starts eating her dinner again, angrily. Violet looks at Josie with a question, and she puts out her bottom lip and shakes her head. Megan catches her and flicks a fierce glance sideways at her, and Josie turns back to her dinner as if she's been caught cheating.

Violet looks around the room in disbelief.

'So what's this about a bloody ashram? Why am I always the last to know anything in this family?'

After an uncomfortable pause Lucy speaks to her as if she's a child.

'It's just your reaction to things like this, Mum – we're all terrified of telling you anything. You go right off at the deep end, and then after the first huge explosion there's the chilly silence, or the little digs…' She pauses, searching for an example. 'Do you remember how long it took you to let

Guy forget that maths exam he failed? You were mentioning it at parties YEARS later! Gannie just wants to...' she falters, looks at Megan and thinks better of speaking for her. 'It's just difficult for us to, well – you can see what I mean, can't you?'

Violet sits with her eye-brows raised.

'Is it true, Josie? Is that how you feel?'

She's tried Josie first because she's the most likely daughter to stick up for her, but Josie just looks up sheepishly and shrugs.

'Guy? What do you think about all this nonsense?'

'Well, you do make it completely impossible for people to be, well, you know, to be who they are.'

His words hang in the air and then swoop towards her, wanting to get inside her. She half turns her head in an attempt to avoid them, but they keep repeating themselves. There's a real affection in his voice after their moment earlier, and this makes what he's said even harder to hear. Thoughts flash up like lightening and fade quickly. She thinks about who Guy 'is', and how much she's resisting it, and what that might feel like for him. What about the others? She does faintly disapprove of Lucy and Josie's partners, and she's always thought Megan deserved a better job. She can't abide Lucy's political views, and Josie's friends have always rubbed her up the wrong way... She's still adding to this list when Megan speaks.

'I'm going away. To a place I've found, in Nepal. I'll be gone for at least six months – maybe a year or two, I don't know.' She takes a deep breath. 'I'm going to be a Buddhist nun.'

There's a defensive note in her voice, as if she's aware of how ridiculous it sounds.

A guffaw explodes in Violet – 'Pah!' And now she's started, she can't help it, she dissolves into hysterical laughter. She can't get a hold of herself. She looks at her children's faces. Guy looks bored by the whole situation and is examining his fingernails for dirt. Josie looks incredulous. Lucy looks like she could murder her – a violent disapproval. But Megan's face is the worst. Her anger melts before Violet's eyes and a softness appears, the raw yolk inside the egg. She imagines her laughter coming into contact with Megan's soft spot and burning it like a hot poker on a bare stomach. Megan puts her hand over her mouth and lets her eyes crinkle up and her forehead move downwards in furrows. When Lucy tries to put an arm around her back she shakes her off as if she's given her an electric shock. She sits forward, shaking in dry, silent tears, and Violet finally gets hold of herself and is quiet. Everyone is quiet. No-one is moving. Violet can't take her eyes off Megan. Everyone is looking at her. And eventually she stops shaking and the skin on her forehead relaxes and she lets out a sigh, a quiet sigh meant only to comfort herself and not for anyone else's benefit, and she gets up without looking at anyone and goes upstairs.

Lucy looks daggers at Violet and then follows Megan. Josie says, 'Well done, Mum,' and takes her half-finished pie into the kitchen. Guy regards her curiously for a second or two and just carries on eating, as if nothing in particular has happened. But she knows him, and she knows that he disapproves too. It's too deep down for him to show her, too hidden, swallowed up. What has she done to him, that he can't call her a stupid bitch and stomp out of the room like he should do? Look at how she has ruined her children. Ruined them. She looks down at her plate – the cheese sauce is congealing, taking on the look of plastic. The pastry looks pale and doughy. It sickens her. She sickens herself. She can't bear to be in the house with them any more, they don't deserve it. They don't deserve to be infected by her disapproval any more. They are shining and perfect without her. How can she not have seen it before? She lets out a whimper and leaves Guy with his eyes wide. She lurches to the hall, pulls open her front door and bursts out into the night.

The stars are the first things she becomes aware of. There are so many of them. They are so sharp and bright here, away from all the leaking city lights. The air is cool, and runs its fingers across her hot cheeks and forehead. It soothes her like a balm. She becomes aware of the bare patch of skin across her breastbone – it's cold. She hasn't worn a coat. Her soles slap the tarmac, one after the other. She's wearing her slip-on shoes, and she can feel the jagged shapes of stones pushing up into the flesh of her feet. Her bent arms move in a steady rhythm. She looks up at the stars again. Her nose is running, she's nothing to wipe it with. Where is she running to? She couldn't bear to go to the usual place, not tonight. There is too much loss there, pocking the landscape. Where can she go? She's slowing, desperate, when the realisation hits her – the last time she was running like this, she was running away from Tom, towards her home. There's nowhere to run to this time – she's running away from her family. What is she going to do – disown them? Bundle them all back into Lucy's car and send them away? She's heading towards the beach despite herself. Her side is starting to cramp. Here is the sea. Here she is – slowed to a walking pace now – moving down towards the water in her unsuitable shoes, with her hands thrust deep into her cardigan pockets. Here is the faint horizon, and a thin sliver of moon. Here are the stars, the stars, the stars. And here she is – alone. She is all alone. Is this how she likes it? Is this how she'll live out the rest of her days? She feels desperate, she feels like crying, but if she lets out a tear, even a drop, then her body would erupt into sobs, and she'd fall onto the sand and cry until all of her bodies' water was outside of her. She'd be all shrivelled, like a cherry left in the fruit bowl too long. Her children would find her here in the morning, and they'd be glad.

She half-smiles at this over-dramatic thought, and the tears start rising in her anyway. They are held back only by what looks like a figure in the distance. It's just a black shape, and she can't work out if it's moving or not. Her heart beats faster and she considers turning back, considers running again, but instead she stands still and waits. Eventually she sees a smaller black shape at the base of the other one, moving quickly from the shape to the shore and back again. A dog. Do axe murderers take their dogs out with them when they're looking for a victim? Probably not, she decides, and starts walking again, but holding in her tears – she may have to say 'good evening'. As they draw closer she sees it is a man, and then she sees it is a man she knows. They raise their hands to each other before they are in audio range. She'd planned on starting by apologising for her appearance, but he seems to be in even worse shape than her – his hair is all over the place, and his eyes look wild.

'Will. Are you alright?'

'Not really, Violet. Not really, no.' He stands with his head bowed, shaking it from side to side. There's an awkward silence as his dog circles her and yaps excitedly, and Violet realises that he wanted to bump into her even less than she wanted to bump into him. She could just leave him here, leave him to his own troubles, but she's had enough of being on her own.

'I'm feeling like shit too. Shitty evening. How about we just,' she looks around her, 'how about we just go over there and sit down and, oh, I don't know, do that bloody thing they're always telling us to do.'

'I'm not sure I'm up to it, to be quite honest, Violet.'

'Even more bloody reason to talk to me then. Come on, you.'

She links her arm through his and leads him to a washed-up wooden crate. He almost collapses against her, and has already started crying by the time they sit down. It's a forlorn kind of crying – his eyes shut and his head held still as his diaphragm contracts in a slow rhythm. He leans his head on to her shoulder and cries quietly for a little while, and she just looks at the sea and feels sad. Such a deep sadness, as deep as the sea. She's not sure how much of the sadness is his and how much is hers, but after a while it seems to start draining away. Will sniffs a few times, finds a handkerchief in his little rucksack and blows noisily. He doesn't look at her, but after a few moments pulls out a flask and pours steaming tea into the red plastic cup. He offers it to her, and flicks his eyes up towards her as they take turns taking sips. His eyelashes are clotted with tears and there are red tide-marks across his cheekbones. He manages a smile, and she smiles back. He takes a deep breath and blows the air out noisily.

'Aaah, tea.'

'Are you going to tell me what's going on, then?'

'No, I think that's all I can manage for today, Violet. Thank you.' He calls his dog over and starts to fuss him. 'So what brings you here at this ungodly hour?'

And so Violet talks to him. She tells him what her children had said about her, and how right they are. She tells him about each of her daughters and her son in turn – the weak points in their characters, their many sadnesses, and how all of it is her fault. She talks about Tom too, and how desperately she still misses her. How deserted she feels, how abandoned. She doesn't feel anything as she talks, but it feels good to say it all out loud, and Will doesn't dismiss her like her mother would have done, he doesn't say 'Don't be an idiot,' and she appreciates that. She still feels an idiot, but he doesn't say it. She says everything, and by the time she's run out of words something has shifted inside her. She thinks about Guy, and how tears came to his eyes. Maybe she can carry all this after all, hold on to it without it bursting and blowing her life apart. Maybe they will survive it.

They've drunk the whole flask of tea between them, and Violet starts to badly need the toilet. She realises when she watches Will's dog cocking his leg. Her knees feel stiff, and her chest is covered in goose-pimples. It's time to go home. She makes Will promise that he'll go back to his own home now, back to Helen. 'Talk to her!' she says, 'Just fucking talk to her.' She realises she's also talking to herself. They walk back to the car park gingerly, like convalescents. They don't say anything else to each other, just hug before Will gets into his car. He feels warm beneath his layers of clothes. She refuses his offer of a lift and strides off into the darkness.

When she gets home Megan is still upstairs in Violet's bedroom, where the girls will be sleeping. Violet ignores Lucy's 'I don't think she wants to see you, Mum,' and goes up the stairs two at a time. The word is bursting out of her, distracting her from her full bladder. She knocks and then opens the door immediately.

'Sorry!'

Megan is lying on the bed with her head turned away from the door. She turns her head and her body rolls after it, and Violet can see her tear-stained face. So many tears tonight. Her shaved head makes her look so vulnerable, as if Violet can see right into the centre of her. So tender, so raw; this is what you get behind abrasiveness, behind brusqueness. Behind cruelty, the cruelty of a mother laughing at her own daughter, laughing at her most important ambition.

'I'm so sorry. I'm so sorry, darling. I'm a complete idiot. Not just tonight. I've screwed up so much of this… I'm so late with… darling? Can I come in?'

Megan doesn't say no, and Violet goes to sit on the side of the bed.

'I'm really sorry.'

Megan lets out a little sigh. Violet sighs back, and starts to stroke her daughter's forehead, gently, with the tips of her fingers. From the left to the right, skimming her eye-brows, rubbing against the prickly hair on her forehead. She used to do this when the girls where very small – it was the only way she could get Josie to settle down. She stopped when they got older and started wriggling about. Megan doesn't protest now, just closes her eyes and gets more comfortable on the bed. Violet sits there for a very long time and watches her daughter's face. She tracks her muscles in her forehead making tiny twitches, and sees the thin blond hairs on her upper lip shiver as she breathes. Her eyes roll under the delicate skin of her eye-lids. The whorls of her ears, the faint lines around the corners of her mouth – everything is perfect. Sounds drift upstairs from the living room, Guy's voice rumbling underneath the others. After ten minutes Blue butts open the door and jumps up to see what's going on. He finds the warmth of Megan's stomach and leans up against it, curling into a tight ball. Megan moves her hand to his neck and fiddles lazily with his fur for a few minutes until her hand relaxes. Violet stays and rains love over her daughter until she's sure from Megan's breathing that she's fast asleep.

Chapter 29

The next morning Violet comes downstairs to find her children scattered around the living room amongst half-empty cups of coffee and the detritus of a Saturday paper. Radio 2 is drifting in from the kitchen, and she can smell fresh toast. Her head feels muzzy, but the girls look as fresh as daisies, damn them. Josie has already had a shower and her damp hair is combed neatly back from her face like cornrows. Even Guy looks wide awake. Blue is on his back in raptures, being ministered to by Lucy and Josie alternatively. Violet smiles shyly at Megan, and she smiles back. She bumps into the table like a moth and groans a little, and they laugh at her.

'Could one of my lovely children make me a cup of coffee?'

'It's just brewed, Mum.'

She stumbles into the kitchen, looking at the clock as she goes. Ten past ten! Outrageous — she must have slept right through. She doesn't usually sleep much at all when she's not in her own bed. A fragment of a dream floats back, something about riding a roller-coaster, but were they under the sea? She sees a pile of mail that one of the girls has put onto the kitchen table, and picks it up on the way back through to the living room. Guy moves to sit cross-legged on the floor so she can have an armchair, and she sinks into it gratefully. When she's taken a few sips of coffee she feels ready to flick through the stack of letters. Bill, bill, junk mail... and there it is, the familiar envelope, the familiar handwriting. Her body goes still and she takes a sudden mouthful of air. Josie says, 'What is it, Mum?' but she doesn't hear her. She opens the letter and starts to read.

14th of December '59

Bea –

I told you there was another secret I had to tell you.

The baby isn't Mick's. I lied to you about that as well. I couldn't bear to tell you the truth. It belongs to a man that... a man I was seeing, only a few times, behind Mick's back. We'd only done it twice, I didn't think that... His name is Errol. He's black, Bea. Beatrice is black. That's why Marjorie doesn't want to keep us both here. That's why I can't tell Mick where I am, or anyone. She's proof of what I am. She's so pretty, Bea, so pretty. She's beautiful. Just like he was. I think I might have even loved him. But I can't ever see him again. I can't see him, and once I've handed her over I can't see her. I need to give her a better chance at life. I need to get on with my own life as if she doesn't exist. I can't look back.

I only have another four days with her now.

I wouldn't be surprised if you didn't want to speak to me any more, Bea – I've lied to you again, I've been lying all along. I was so frightened that you wouldn't want to know me. I've needed you, in here – your letters have kept me going. I just can't think how awful it would have been if you'd left me here alone. I know I should have told you, I should have let you make your own mind up. But I've heard the things your family have said about the black family down the street. I've heard the words they've used, Bobo, black boy, nigger.

Maybe if I could bring Beatrice home and show them, then everything would be different. I would defy them not to fall in love with her, to look at her soft creamy skin and her little tufts of hair and think her completely perfect. I still think about running away, late at night when she's just settled back to sleep after a feed. Making a run for it and going, oh, I don't know, somewhere anonymous and open-minded – the seaside, or a big city somewhere. I can see our whole lives ahead of us – the things I'd teach her, the hopes I have for her, the love I'd pour into her. It seems possible, in the middle of the night. It seems like the only sensible thing to do – because without her I know I'm only going to be half a person for the rest of my life. But don't worry, I'm not going to do anything stupid. When the morning comes all the facts come crashing back, through the window with the sun. It would be a selfish act, to take her to save myself. I need to give her up to save her life.

Just like I needed to lie to keep our friendship, while I was in St. Mary's at least. I'm not sure what kind of shape I'm going to be in when I get back. I had no idea it would do this to me, my insides are going to be completely ripped away, I'm not even sure I'll be able to stand up straight. But

I'll know that Beatrice will be in the world, getting the best of everything, growing up to be a happy little girl, a happy woman. I made her! I can hold on to that.

Thank you, Bea, for being there. I'll be home before too long, as if nothing has happened. None of it – my new friends, Beatrice, poor, poor Doll. I'll be back to face my mum and dad. I'm going to pretend that the job was a disaster, that I was unhappy, that I don't want to talk about it.

I think she's stirring. I feel so glad to have told you everything, like a huge weight is gone. I'll wait for you to come to me, once I'm home, I won't presume anything. I just want you to know – more than anything – that I love you so much. So much.

I'll go now. Your Elizabeth.

Violet reads the letter silently, and when she finishes everyone is looking at her.

'Mum, what is it? Is everything OK?'

She's thinking about the letter. The baby was mixed race. The girl baby. Something is nagging at her. She grapples desperately with the numbers – the letters were written in 1959. It's a simple sum, but she can't get it right, she needs to be sure before she lets the knowledge sink in.

'Mother?'

The baby would be forty-six now, or thereabouts. When is her birthday? She should know this, why has this piece of information suddenly disappeared from her memory? Her birthday was just before Violet met her, it was November. The baby – the baby that Elizabeth gave away…

'Mum!'

She's suddenly aware of Lucy in front of her, looking down at her, her face scared. Violet gazes at her hand – the letter is no longer there. She looks around wildly and sees it on the table. How did it get there?

'Mum, you're scaring us.'

Megan is getting up from the sofa, coming towards her.

The letters are from Tom's mother.

The little baby, Beatrice – the baby that was given away. It's Tom. It's Theresa.

She puts her hand over her mouth.

Guy is there too, where did he come from? He's sitting beside her on the armchair. He's put his hand on her back and is saying something to his sisters. Something that is calming them down. The feeling of his hand on her brings her back into the room.

She looks at him and says, 'What do I do now?'

'What do you do about what?'

'The baby, it's Tom.'

'Look, Mum, you're making as much sense as a bag full of frogs. Just take a deep breath and then tell us what's in the letter.'

She starts at the beginning. She pauses when Lucy brings her another cup of coffee, and some toast and honey to 'put some colour back into your cheeks'. They listen intently, and when she's finished, she tells them about Tom too, although she can't really explain what was so terrible about their arguments, or why she hasn't tried any harder to get her back. Josie asks to see the other letters and Violet brings them all out, and her children sit and pass them back and forth between themselves, all of them talking at once. Megan slips away and comes over to sit next to Violet. Violet says it again – 'What do I do now?'

'You have to call her, Mum.'

And so Violet gets up and shuts the noise of the living room behind her. She goes to the phone and dials Tom's number. Her knees feel weak. Tom answers.

'Hello?'

'Tom?'

There's a silence. Violet tries again.

'Theresa! Please!'

'What do you want, Violet?'

'I know. I know about the letters.'

There's another silence. And before she hangs up, Theresa spits out the words she's been waiting to say for weeks, the words that have been growing inside her like a cancer.

'Now you know what it's like to be abandoned too.'

Chapter 30

That Christmas, Bill drinks too much sherry and falls asleep into Violet's home-made trifle. The cherry trees in Violet's garden froth with blossom, and then fade. Megan leaves for Nepal, and makes several expensive long distance phone calls to her mother to try and explain Buddhism. Violet holds her breath and tries hard to listen, and occasionally she succeeds. Lucy finds out she's pregnant, and a summer birth begins to take shape like a mirage on the road ahead. Josie's partner gets a job in Bristol, and they begin planning a move which will bring them closer to Violet. Guy changes his mind three times about what he wants to do with his life, and pings back and forth from London to Abbotsfield. His friendship with George continues to strengthen. One weekend he begins to talk, tentatively, about a strange fog of confusion that follows him everywhere. Will has another breakdown, and Violet visits him in hospital twice a week, taking him fresh infusions of Big Band music which is, he says, the only thing he can bear to listen to. And in late October everyone, even Megan, even Will, even Sue and Angie, gather together in a barn lit with hundreds of flickering candles to celebrate

Violet's wedding.

It took Violet months to persuade Theresa to marry her, even once they were firmly settled back into their relationship. Violet tried to explain to her that when she'd made that phone call to her, to tell her she knew about the letters, that even after Theresa had hung up, she'd felt less abandoned than she ever had before. Theresa had gone to such effort to share her history with her, to share the most secret and important part of her. She couldn't believe that Theresa really intended revenge. With the letters, Theresa was communicating her fierce love for Violet – the love they couldn't kill off, however hard they tried. Violet knew right then that she was ready to throw in her lot with Theresa, to stop the ridiculous dance of stepping outside the relationship whenever things got difficult. It was like a new religion – she was heady with the idea, evangelical – and eventually Theresa started to understand that she was serious, and started to believe that she might be able to trust her.

Theresa had applied for her original birth records from the Office for National Statistics when her adoptive father died. She didn't tell anyone she was doing it. By then Elizabeth was already dead. She was knocked off her bicycle on the route she took through the village every day to fetch her newspaper and a pint of milk. She was only sixty-five – Theresa missed out on meeting her by less than a year. Theresa did manage to track down an old cousin of hers, who put her in touch with a family friend, who put her in touch with Bea. Bea had been waiting for her. Theresa described her for Violet – a small, neat woman with her hair in an old-fashioned bun, all dressed in pale green – really rather elegant. She squeezed Theresa into a bear hug when she met her at the door, and dabbed at her eyes with a handkerchief for the duration of her visit. Bea said that she'd been waiting for most of her life to talk to Theresa about her mother. She had easily forgiven Elizabeth for her deceits. They'd remained close for the rest of Elizabeth's life. Elizabeth had never married, had never had any more children. She was in love with a married man for most of her life. He probably loved her back, but he never had the courage to claim her. Elizabeth told Bea that she felt it was a kind of retribution for what she'd done. The relationship was a great sadness to her, but she drew comfort from her many dogs, mostly red setters, and she looked after them better than most people treated their children. She mostly enjoyed her job, running the reception at the local vet practice, and spent a lot of time at Bea and her husband's house. She took a big part in raising Bea's own two children, especially her daughter, doting on them and having them for long weekends. They called her 'Secama', as Bea would say, 'Your second mum is coming round today,' or, 'Show your second mum how you can tie your shoe-laces.' Bea said that Elizabeth only spoke of Theresa once, after the birth of Bea's daughter. She said she never stopped regretting her decision to hand her baby over, but at the same time she never doubted that it was the right thing to do. Bea's whole family were devastated when she died. As she described the funeral, Bea had to stop and blow her nose. When she recovered she leaned forward in her chair and took Theresa's hand in both of hers. Her skin was cold and her grip was firm. 'Your mother always did her best, Theresa. She always did what she thought was best.' She nodded to herself and looked past Theresa and out of her bay window, across the grass tipped in icing sugar, towards the frozen pond. Theresa had passed it on the way to the front door and had paused to watch the smears of orange circling under the ice. Bea looked and looked, and Theresa wished she could share the memories she was conjuring, just for a second. She so wanted to see her mother's face. It was then that Bea pulled herself up from her chair and fetched Theresa the small bundle of letters, tied together with a pale blue ribbon. She handed them over as if they were finely hammered leaves of gold. Violet tied the blue ribbon around Theresa's wrist, the day they were married. She tied it tight and then covered it over with her hand, her thumb and forefinger meeting, making a circle.

Acknowledgements

Thanks to Anna Torborg, Emma Barnes and all at Snowbooks for looking after my books.

Thanks to Heather Butler for you-know-what.

Thanks to Claire Arnold-Baker, Sarah Lindon, Grant James, Barbara Lee, Nicola Weller and Jon Berry for important details.

Thanks to Sage Cohen for being my writing-sister-across-the-water.

Thanks to Charlie Mounter and Joanna Quinn for being so clever and generous.

Thanks to Catherine Perry, Patrick Andrews, Ann Rapstoff, Kate Burton, Caroline Smailes and my blogging colleagues for all your support.

Thanks to Duncan Hall, Lauren Peile and Meatball for a lovely weekend.

Thanks to Steve, for feeding me.

About the Author

Fiona Robyn was born in 1974 in Surrey and grew up in Sarawak. Her website is at www.fionarobyn.com. She currently lives in rural Hampshire with her partner and her vegetable patch.

The Letters is her first novel.

Next from Fiona Robyn...

The Blue Handbag

Coming Summer 2009

Chapter 1: A Posy of Painted Ladies

Leonard is feeding the dusty, battered suitcase into the mouth of the wheelie-bin when he catches a flash of azure blue shining from inside. He judders to a complete stop and holds himself perfectly still to give his eyes a chance to focus. There's something in there. His heart speeds up. He pulls the suitcase back out and opens the jaws of the zips wide, letting in light. It's a handbag. It must have been one of Rose's. Rose, his dear, dear wife. His body softly crumples in on itself. He presses his forehead with his left palm. It's been nearly three years now. Three years since that last migraine that wasn't a migraine at all, but a clot of blood that had detached itself from one of her arteries and travelled up to her brain. Setting off an explosion of pain, filling her with a beating, rising fear. His Rose. Three years. It seems like yesterday. It seems like a lifetime ago.

He hunkers down on the pavement, his sixty-two-year-old knees reminding him to move carefully. He lifts the handbag out, brushing away cobwebs from the material as if he were stroking his daughter's cheek. He places it on the step beside him, wiping dust from the cold bricks before he sets it down, and checks the inside of the suitcase, sliding a flat hand inside the pockets. A biro lid, a sweetie wrapper, nothing else. He pushes the suitcase back into the wheelie-bin - it just fits and the sides of it scrape the plastic. He looks around nervously to see if anyone has seen him, not knowing why it matters if they have. His heart is slowing down. He sucks in two lungfuls of late October air and turns away from the road and towards his house. He carries the handbag as if it were a baby. As if it were alive.

He's on his way to the kitchen when the phone rings and forces him back into the hall. He rests the handbag up against a green glass vase full of pink-spattered lilies on the telephone table. As he picks up the receiver, all thoughts of his wife leave him as if he's flicked a switch.

"Hello?"

All he can hear is a faint squealing noise. His daughter comes onto the line just before his second hello.

"Hi, Dad, is that you?"

"No, it's the Viscount of Prussia. How may I be of assistance to you?" he says, disguising his usual Berkshire accent with his best aristocratic voice, which despite his efforts comes out a little Welsh.

Raine makes a harrumphing noise. Leonard feels a little sad for the giggling girl in pigtails who got lost – when? When did he lose her? He used to love making her laugh. He seems to have lost the knack.

"Dad, for goodness sakes. How are you?" He can hear the familiar edge of brusqueness in her voice and guesses she's only asking from a sense of duty.

"Tickety-boo, darling. How are the twins?"

"Oh, fine, fine. Rory has a bit of a temperature. He's playing up something rotten; I can't get him to eat anything, the bugger." She breathes a quick sharp sigh. "I'm sure he'll survive. He's annoyed with me right now – I tried to force some bread and marmite down him just before I called you."

Leonard already feels a rising impatience with the conversation.

"Mh hmm," he says, to encourage her to carry on. She pauses, waiting. There's a small fluttering in his stomach.

"Is everything OK, darling?"

"Oh, yes, all fine." She pauses again. "Yes, everything's fine. I'm just tired, I suppose. Are you still coming down this weekend?"

"Yes, of course."

"Great." The squealing noise starts up in the background again – it sounds as if it's coming from a trapped animal. They both listen.

"Look, Dad, I'm sorry but Rory is making a fuss. I better go and check on him. You'd think I'd been starving him, the way he carries on. I don't know what to… well – anyway – I'll call you in a couple of days to arrange things."

"Yes darling, talk to you then. I'll let you know what train I'll be on."

"Bye Dad."

"Bye."

Just as he's pulling the phone away from his ear he hears her say "Oh – wait! Dad?"

"I'm still here."

"I forgot – the whole reason I rang was to ask you if you liked turkey. Rory, wait a minute! I can't remember if you said something about... last time I... RORY! We're... Dad? Turkey?"

She rushes him into answering. He wonders how she ended up like this, never stopping for long enough to catch her breath. So unlike him, so unlike Rose. He slows his voice down, willing some of his calm to infuse into her, to infect her.

"Yes, that'll be lovely, darling. You're sure you're OK now? Is Ed helping you with the boys?"

"Yes, Dad. Speak soon. Bye! Oh, Ed's fine! Bye!"

By the time he gets his goodbye out she's already hung up.

He stands with the empty phone against his ear for a few seconds until his eyes catch on something blue. The handbag! The colour reminds him of Rose's wedding dress. They were so young - she was seventeen, still a child. He pictures her now, grinning at her friends from work in the congregation, her arm linked through his. The dress was plain, full-skirted and the colour of cornflowers. She told him it was a tradition in their family to wear blue rather than white. She looked so pretty with her painted lips and her dark hair cropped close to her scalp. He'd loved to run his flat fingers against the grain of her softly prickly hair. He gave it a quick skim most days, while teasing her about her temper, or when coming into a room and finding her there. She wanted sweet peas for her wedding bouquet - they'd always been her favourites. They got married in May so he grew her 'Painted Ladies', pale pink with a deep pink nose. She held them in a fat posy at her waist and ticked him off for crushing the petals when he kissed her with too much enthusiasm. He'd whispered into her ear that now they were married he'd grow her bucketfuls and bucketfuls until she was sick of them. And he had - year after year, until she really did get fed up of the sight of them. She finally spat it out one night during an argument, and it had pierced him in his chest. He didn't blame her, really. He always did go a bit over the top with things.

He leaves the handbag on his chair and goes into the kitchen to click on his shiny silver kettle. He can take his time - nothing is going anywhere. One of the advantages of living on your own – nobody will be bursting in to ask him if he can fix the Hoover or get a child a drink. He unhooks his favourite mug from the mug tree, winter-berry red on the outside and glossy green on the inside. Raine bought it for him a few Christmas ago. He readies it with a Yorkshire teabag and turns the lid off the milk. He's been drinking Yorkshire tea for twenty-five years, since a trip to a National Trust property up North. He doesn't enjoy tea at other people's houses; it always tastes insipid. He flicks his eyes around his tiny kitchen as he waits for the water to boil. There are bright crayon scribbles from the twins taped up on the fridge. According to Raine the blocks in the middle are tanks – 'They're utterly obsessed with the bloody things,' but they have bright yellow suns above them and sit on solid green grass spotted with purple flowers. There's a single glass, plate, knife and fork on the washing up drainer. He can see his face reflected, ghost-like, in the white kitchen tiles above the work surface. He notices a smear of something greasy and gets out a cloth to disappear it. He's kept the place clean since Rose died; he prides himself on that. Rose would be impressed. She always kept things neat and tidy.

As the kettle gathers steam and clicks itself off, Pickles jerks his head up and looks at Leonard, startled. He lets out a small wake-up growl. His eyes are button black and shiny, perfect rounds. He's looking scruffy again, his fur choppy as a rough sea, old mud clinging to tufts of hair on his belly. Leonard makes a mental note to tackle bathing him at the weekend. It's always a messy affair. As soon as Pickles sees there's nothing to worry about he drops his chin back onto the well-worn fur of his basket and goes back to his doggy dreams. He's always liked to sleep in the kitchen, even at their old house. Maybe he likes to stay close to his food bowl at all times just in case there are any ad-hoc doggy snacks. Leonard fills his mug and gives the bag a good squeeze, encouraging it to release its dark flavour. Rose used to say it looked like he was milking a cow in there. Finally he jolts in a small splash of milk to stop the horrible floating film that comes with black tea. 'I like it dark and sweet, just how I like my women,' he used to tease Rose – she'd always come back with, 'And I like mine weak and lukewarm, just like you, darling.' He holds the spoon under the tap to help wash away this memory so he can return to the job at hand.

He sets down his tea on the small table next to his chair, resting it on top of a rickety pile of crossword books, and lifts the handbag into his hands. It feels silky against his fingertips and reminds him of the silvery leaves of the canary clover, *Dorycnium hirsutum*. He laughs at the memory of sneaking away from his digging in the middle of the afternoon so he could crouch beside a new batch of them and stroke them. They'd have him carted off if they knew. Leonard lets his mind rest on what he's holding. One of Rose's handbags. What was it doing in their old suitcase? He can't remember ever seeing it before. Is it definitely hers? He lifts it to his face and sniffs, tentatively at first, then great, sucking-in breaths. It's only an echo now, but he remembers the original scent so well - a hint of jasmine, sandalwood, and then something underneath… what is that Indian spice called? Cardamom? The handbag was hers alright. He'll never forget that perfume until the day he dies. She must have kept one of her little bottles in here, where it spilt a golden drop or three. This scent is as familiar to him as her face is – no – more familiar. It's more of an effort now to remember exactly what she looked like, and this worries him. But that smell. Mmm. He feels his eyes prickling and allows a single tear to escape from each one, warming his cheeks, before taking a sharp breath and blowing his nose. He's done his crying.

He studies the material close-up for a moment. It's woven, and has lots of tiny hairs like the hide of a strange blue animal. Maybe one with six legs and purple eyes and a huge mane like a lion. He places a flat palm on one side and moves it across and back, across and back. He's aware of taking his time with it, as if he's choosing the perfect chocolate from the box. The clasp is one of those old-fashioned metal ones where the metal prongs push hard against each other before finally snapping free. He un-clicks it, and then clicks it shut and un-clicks it absentmindedly a few times more before pulling it open and peering inside.

Nothing. Empty. His heart sinks – and then he laughs at himself – what exactly was he expecting to find? A new photograph of her? A bright burst of her laugh? The things she left behind are all souvenirs now – her wedding ring, the favourite cardigan he keeps in his top drawer in the bedroom. He puts his hand inside to feel the silk lining, already thinking about putting it back into the bin outside, and as he slips a thumb under the piece of silk-covered cardboard at the bottom he encounters something sharp. It's the edge of something. A small piece of paper. He checks first to make sure there's nothing else there, and then pulls it out and holds it in front of him so he can see it properly. It's a return train ticket from Pangbourne, where Rose worked as a nurse for many years, to Didcot. It's dated the 15th of December 1998. Nearly seven years ago. On the back she's written *'decide about next Tues??? L's on hol'* in blue felt tip. She'd never been to Didcot. He never went to Didcot with her. He pauses to search his memories more carefully. Did they ever go shopping there? No. To see the railway centre, or friends? No. Had she cried off when he'd suggested it, saying something about not liking the town, something about a bad memory? He can't remember. Why would she go there? What is it she needed to think about next Tuesday? Why would it make a difference that he was on holiday?

These busy thoughts fade away and he sits and points his eyes in the general direction of the window for five whole minutes, not thinking of anything in particular. He's noticed that he 'phases out' like this sometimes – if someone else were in the room they might ask him what he was thinking about. No-one asks him. He rouses himself with a shake. He used to growl like Pickles when he did this, to make Rose, and then later Raine, laugh. He does it now anyway – grrreeowwwwWWW-HUH! – and makes himself laugh instead. He puts the ticket back where he found it and goes outside to throw the handbag in the wheelie-bin. He comes back into the sitting room and considers rolling a cigarette. Instead he turns on a programme about ancient Rome and picks up his hot cup of tea and a crossword book. He flicks the pages, gulps his tea, and tries to ignore the ichneumon wasps who have laid their eggs inside him.